My Little Pony

Friends Forever

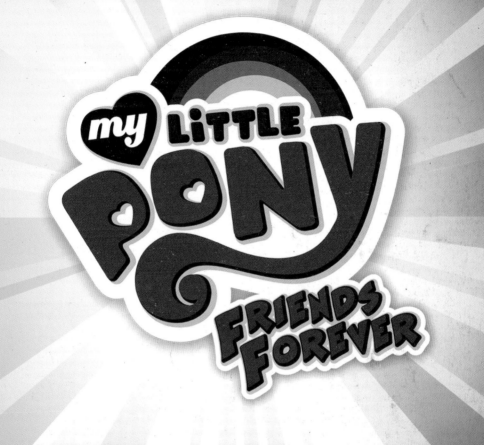

MY LITTLE PONY
FRIENDS FOREVER

RAINBOW DASH & TWILIGHT SPARKLE

Written by
Barbara Randall Kesel

Art by
Brenda Hickey

Colors by
Heather Breckel

SHINING ARMOR & PRINCE BLUEBLOOD

Written by
Jeremy Whitley

Art by
Tony Fleecs

Colors by
Heather Breckel

Special thanks to Meghan McCarthy, Eliza Hart, Ed Lane, Beth Artale, and Michael Kelly.

For international rights, please contact licensing@idwpublishing.com

ISBN: 978-1-63140-707-9

19 18 17 16   1 2 3 4

www.IDWPUBLISHING.com

Ted Adams, CEO & Publisher
Greg Goldstein, President & COO
Robbie Robbins, EVP/Sr. Graphic Artist
Chris Ryall, Chief Creative Officer/Editor-in-Chief
Matthew Ruzicka, CPA, Chief Financial Officer
Dirk Wood, VP of Marketing
Lorelei Bunjes, VP of Digital Services
Jeff Webber, VP of Licensing, Digital and Subsidiary Rights
Jerry Bennington, VP of New Product Development

Facebook: facebook.com/idwpublishing
Twitter: @idwpublishing
YouTube: youtube.com/idwpublishing
Tumblr: tumblr.idwpublishing.com
Instagram: instagram.com/idwpublishing

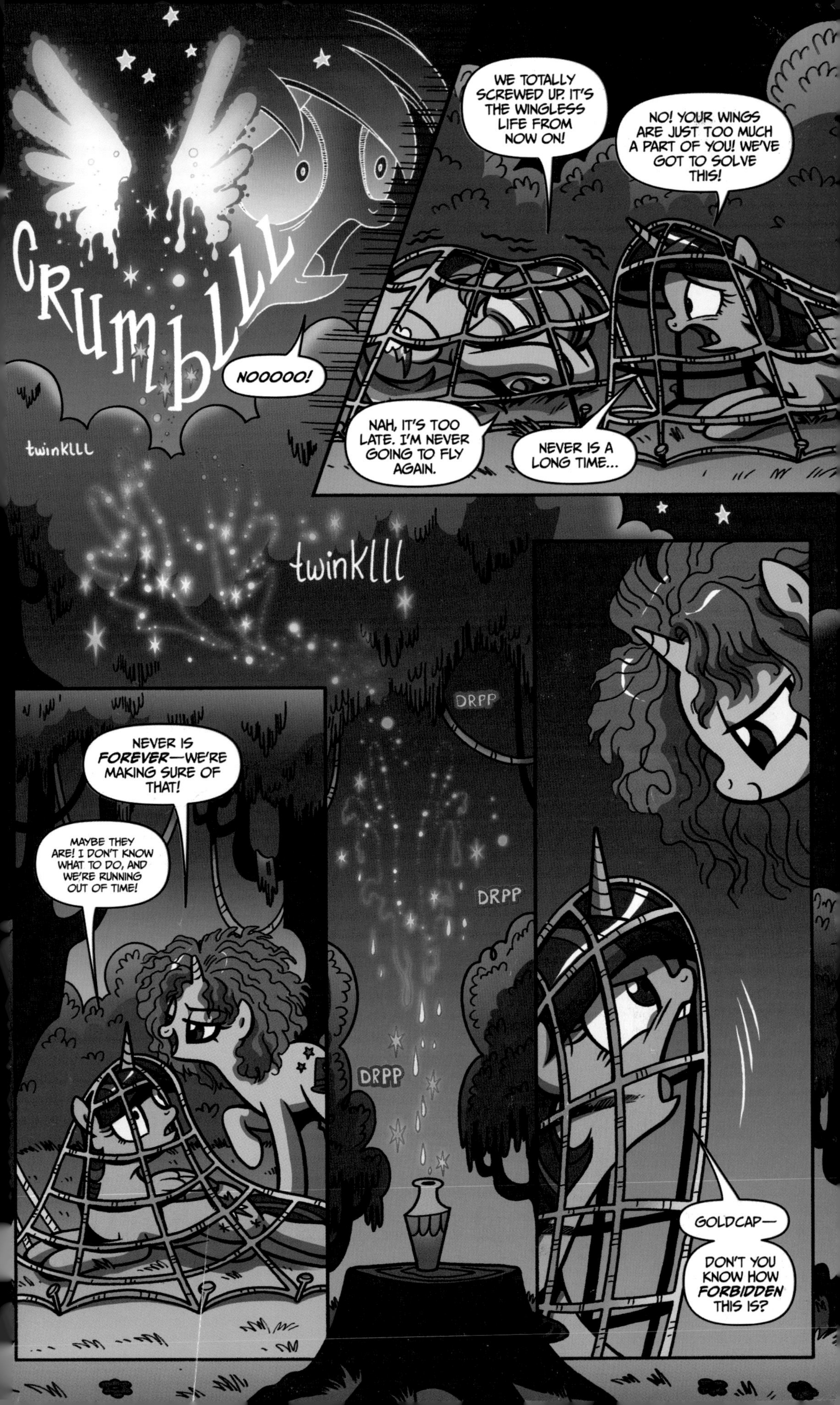

CRUMBLLL
NOOOOO!
twinkLLL
WE TOTALLY SCREWED UP. IT'S THE WINGLESS LIFE FROM NOW ON!
NO! YOUR WINGS ARE JUST TOO MUCH A PART OF YOU! WE'VE GOT TO SOLVE THIS!
NAH, IT'S TOO LATE. I'M NEVER GOING TO FLY AGAIN.
NEVER IS A LONG TIME...
twinklll
NEVER IS FOREVER—WE'RE MAKING SURE OF THAT!
MAYBE THEY ARE! I DON'T KNOW WHAT TO DO, AND WE'RE RUNNING OUT OF TIME!
DRPP
DRPP
DRPP
GOLDCAP—
DON'T YOU KNOW HOW FORBIDDEN THIS IS?

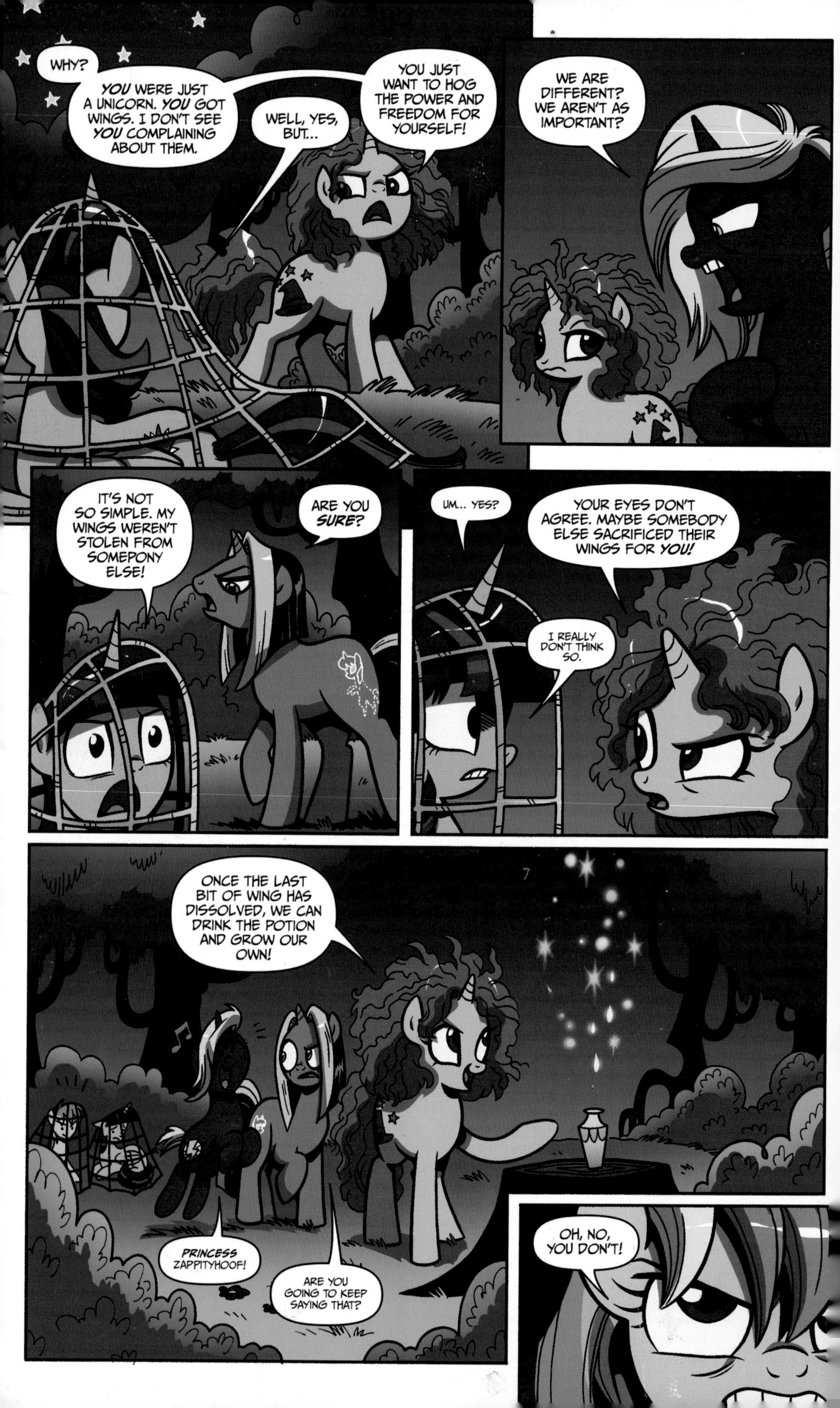

WHY?
YOU WERE JUST A UNICORN. YOU GOT WINGS. I DON'T SEE YOU COMPLAINING ABOUT THEM.
WELL, YES, BUT...
YOU JUST WANT TO HOG THE POWER AND FREEDOM FOR YOURSELF!
WE ARE DIFFERENT? WE AREN'T AS IMPORTANT?
IT'S NOT SO SIMPLE. MY WINGS WEREN'T STOLEN FROM SOMEPONY ELSE!
ARE YOU SURE?
UM... YES?
YOUR EYES DON'T AGREE. MAYBE SOMEBODY ELSE SACRIFICED THEIR WINGS FOR YOU!
I REALLY DON'T THINK SO.
ONCE THE LAST BIT OF WING HAS DISSOLVED, WE CAN DRINK THE POTION AND GROW OUR OWN!
PRINCESS ZAPPITYHOOF!
ARE YOU GOING TO KEEP SAYING THAT?
OH, NO, YOU DON'T!

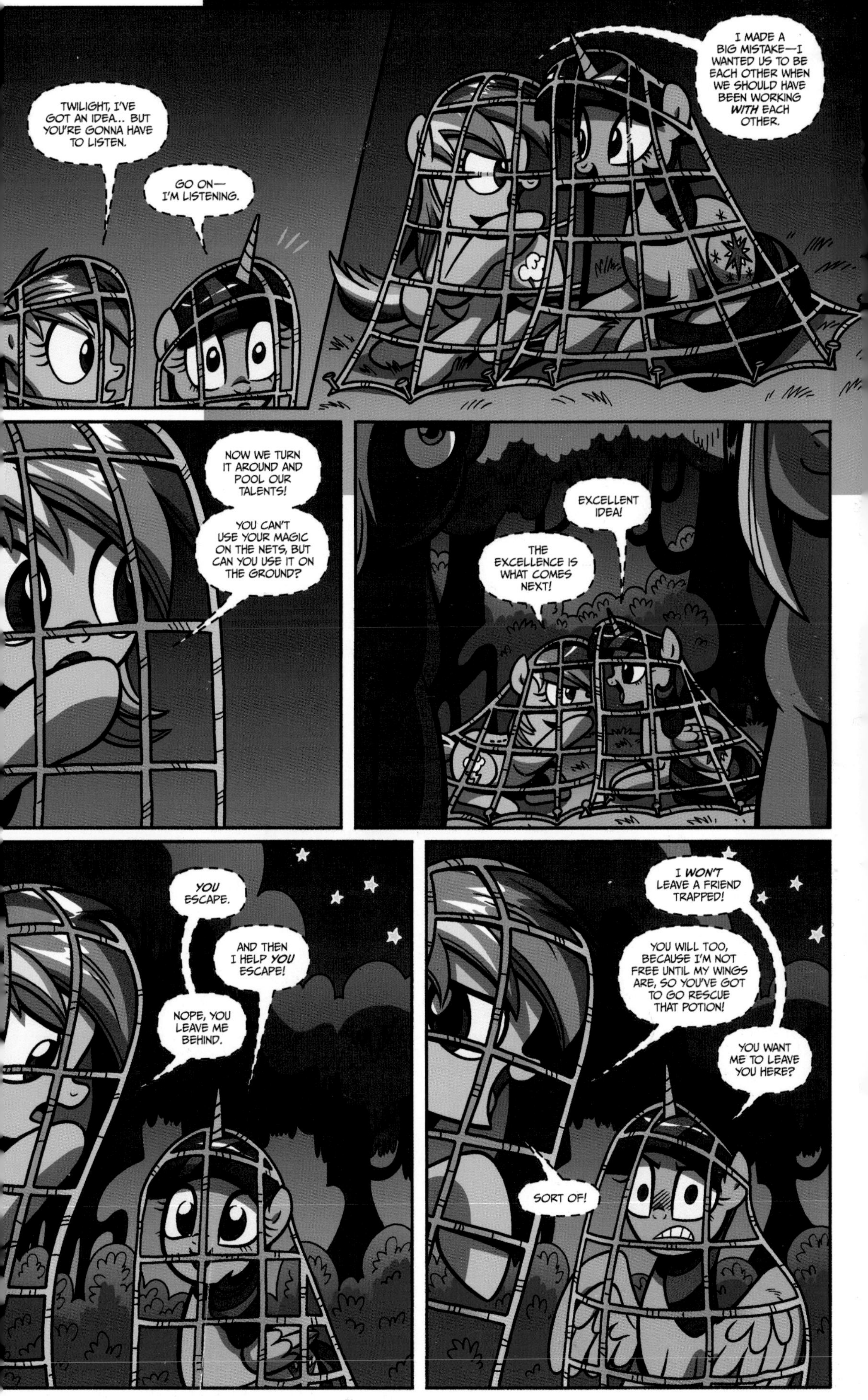
TWILIGHT, I'VE GOT AN IDEA... BUT YOU'RE GONNA HAVE TO LISTEN.
GO ON— I'M LISTENING.
I MADE A BIG MISTAKE—I WANTED US TO BE EACH OTHER WHEN WE SHOULD HAVE BEEN WORKING *WITH* EACH OTHER.
NOW WE TURN IT AROUND AND POOL OUR TALENTS!
YOU CAN'T USE YOUR MAGIC ON THE NETS, BUT CAN YOU USE IT ON THE GROUND?
EXCELLENT IDEA!
THE EXCELLENCE IS WHAT COMES NEXT!
YOU ESCAPE.
AND THEN I HELP *YOU* ESCAPE!
NOPE, YOU LEAVE ME BEHIND.
I *WON'T* LEAVE A FRIEND TRAPPED!
YOU WILL TOO, BECAUSE I'M NOT FREE UNTIL MY WINGS ARE, SO YOU'VE GOT TO GO RESCUE THAT POTION!
YOU WANT ME TO LEAVE YOU HERE?
SORT OF!

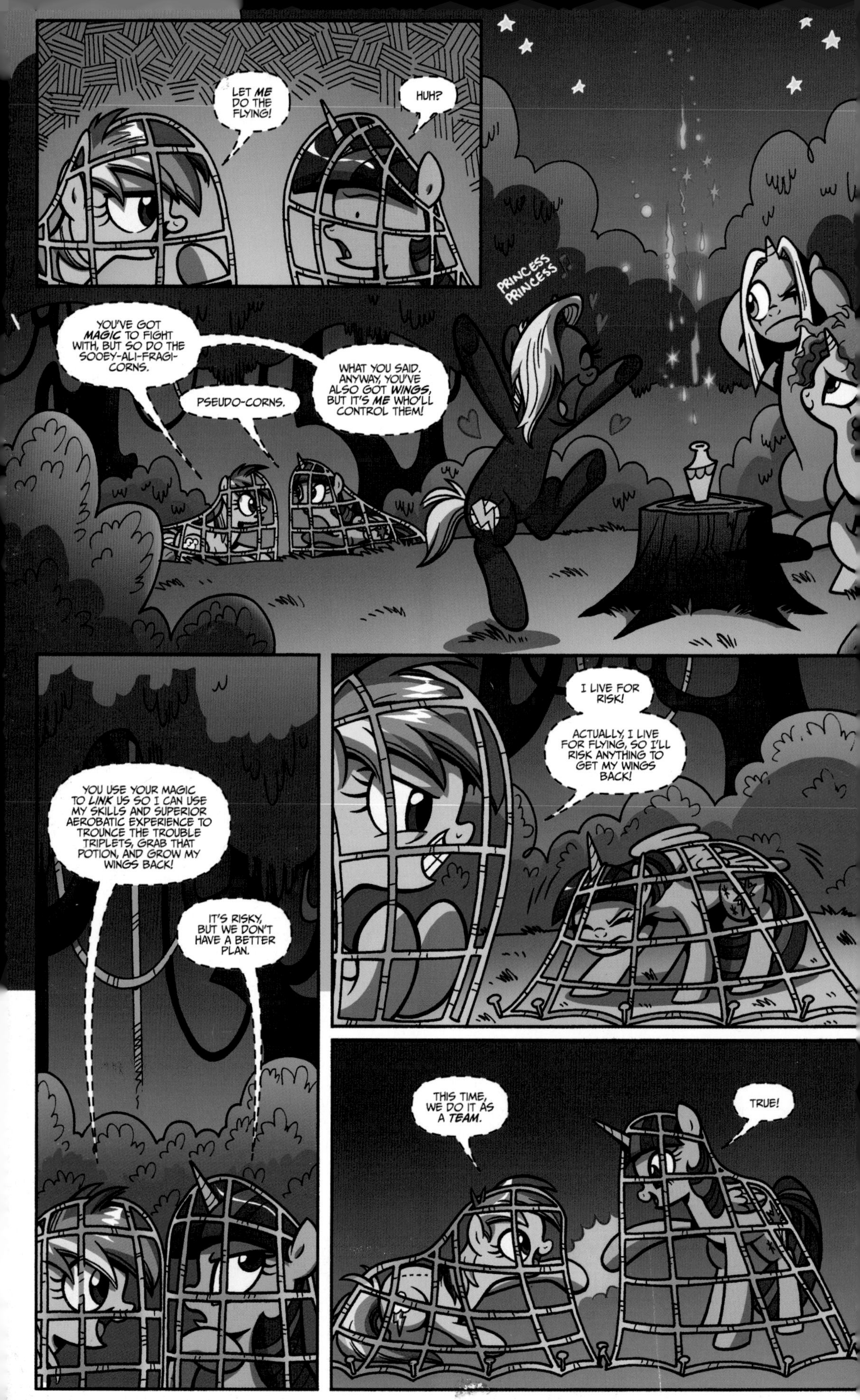
LET ME DO THE FLYING!
HUH?
PRINCESS PRINCESS
YOU'VE GOT MAGIC TO FIGHT WITH, BUT SO DO THE SOOEY-ALI-FRAGI-CORNS.
PSEUDO-CORNS.
WHAT YOU SAID. ANYWAY, YOU'VE ALSO GOT WINGS, BUT IT'S ME WHO'LL CONTROL THEM!
YOU USE YOUR MAGIC TO LINK US SO I CAN USE MY SKILLS AND SUPERIOR AEROBATIC EXPERIENCE TO TROUNCE THE TROUBLE TRIPLETS, GRAB THAT POTION, AND GROW MY WINGS BACK!
IT'S RISKY, BUT WE DON'T HAVE A BETTER PLAN.
I LIVE FOR RISK!
ACTUALLY, I LIVE FOR FLYING, SO I'LL RISK ANYTHING TO GET MY WINGS BACK!
THIS TIME, WE DO IT AS A TEAM.
TRUE!

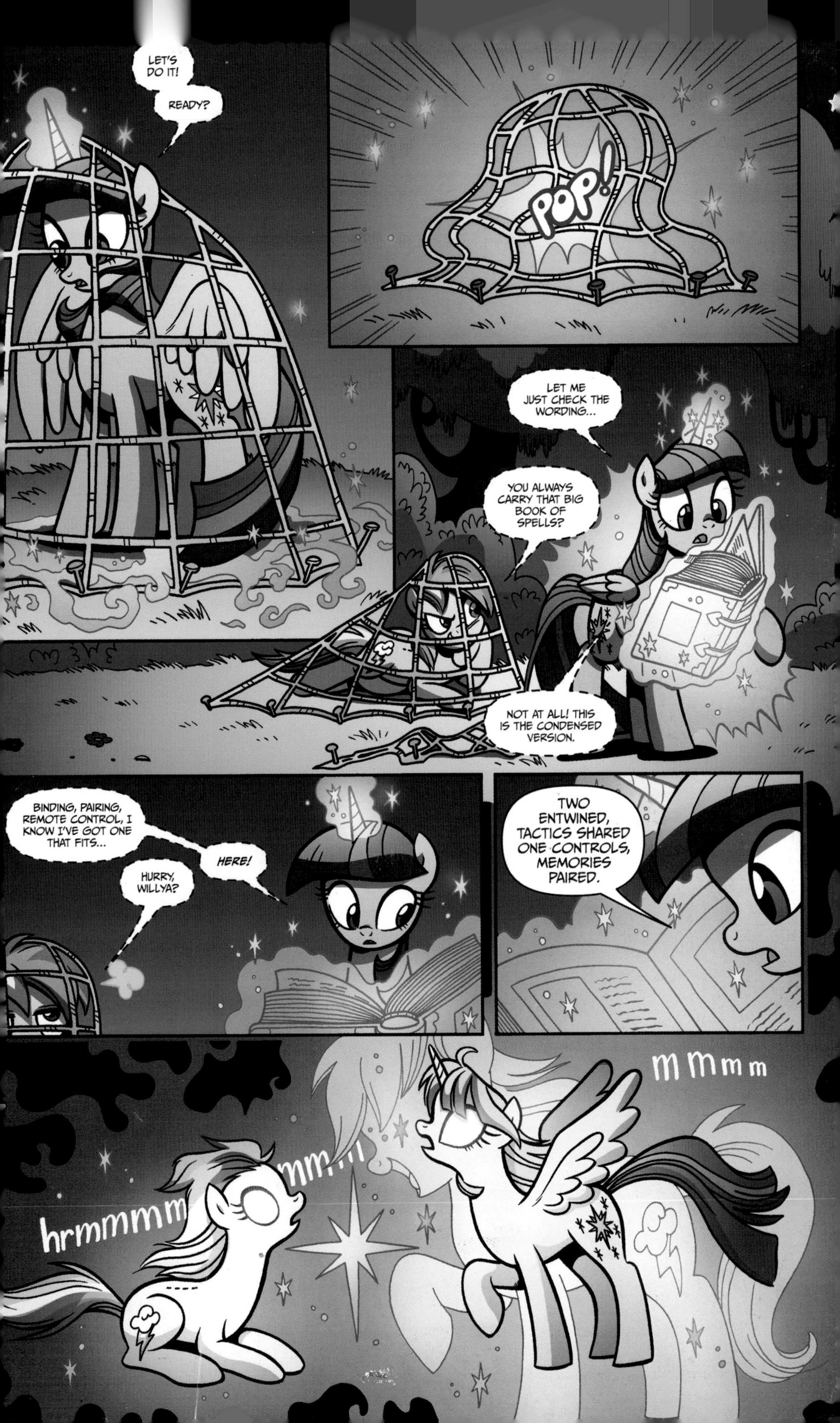
LET'S DO IT!
READY?
POP!
LET ME JUST CHECK THE WORDING...
YOU ALWAYS CARRY THAT BIG BOOK OF SPELLS?
NOT AT ALL! THIS IS THE CONDENSED VERSION.
BINDING, PAIRING, REMOTE CONTROL, I KNOW I'VE GOT ONE THAT FITS...
HERE!
HURRY, WILLYA?
TWO ENTWINED, TACTICS SHARED ONE CONTROLS, MEMORIES PAIRED.
mmmm
hrmmmmmmm

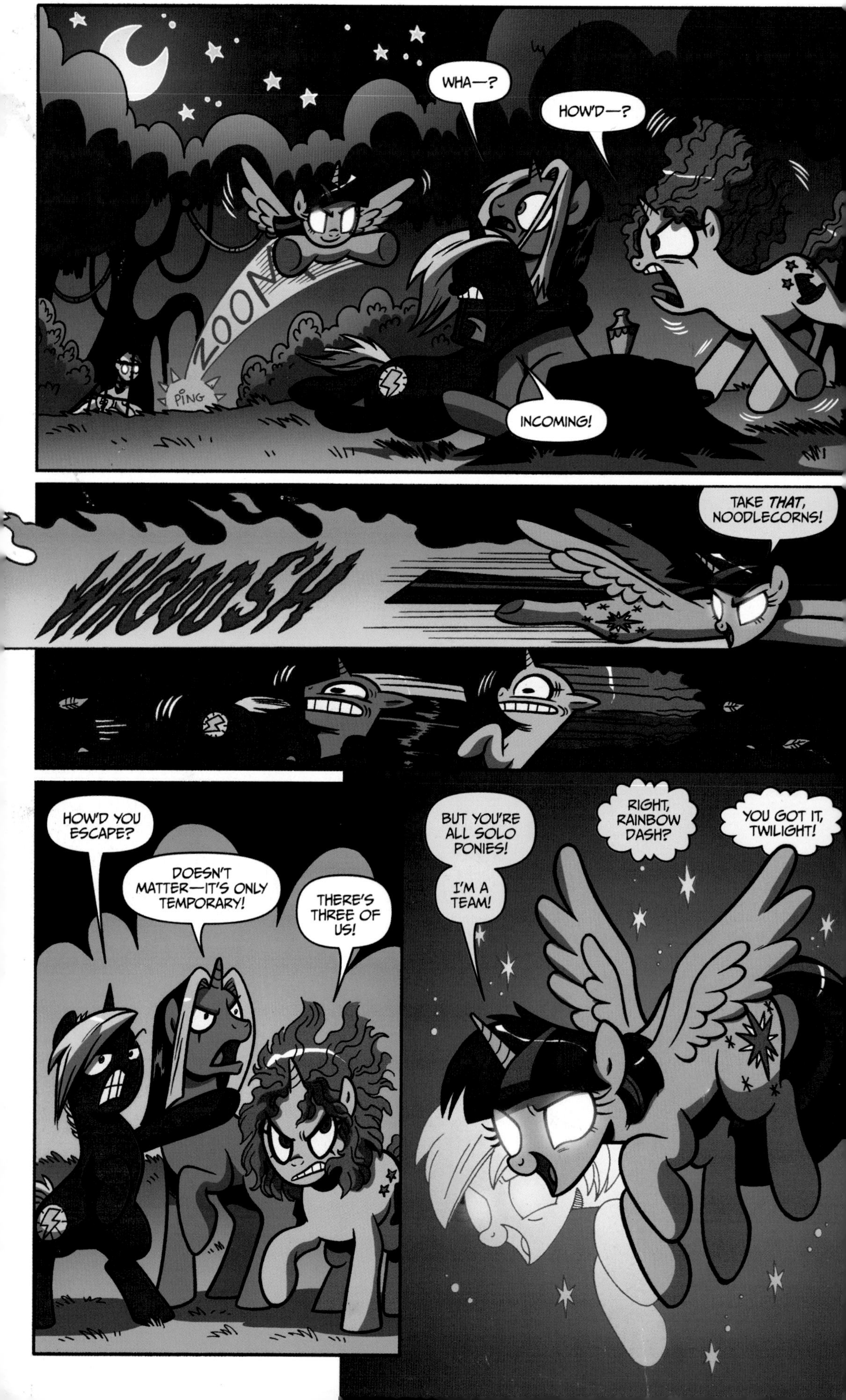
WHA—?
HOW'D—?
ZOOM
PING
INCOMING!
TAKE *THAT*, NOODLECORNS!
WHOOOSH
HOW'D YOU ESCAPE?
DOESN'T MATTER—IT'S ONLY TEMPORARY!
THERE'S THREE OF US!
BUT YOU'RE ALL SOLO PONIES!
I'M A TEAM!
RIGHT, RAINBOW DASH?
YOU GOT IT, TWILIGHT!

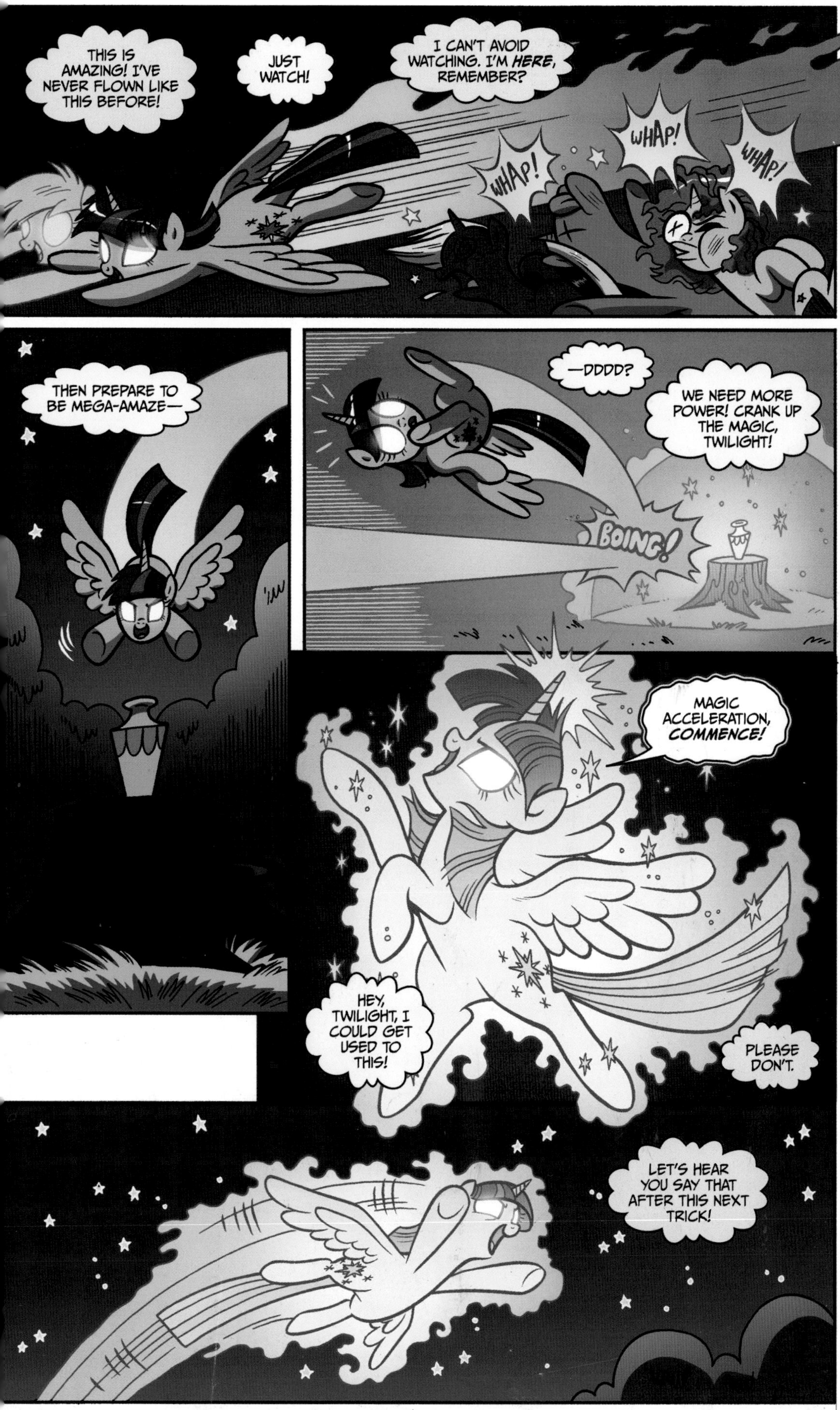
THIS IS AMAZING! I'VE NEVER FLOWN LIKE THIS BEFORE!
JUST WATCH!
I CAN'T AVOID WATCHING. I'M *HERE*, REMEMBER?
WHAP!
WHAP!
WHAP!
THEN PREPARE TO BE MEGA-AMAZE—
—DDDD?
WE NEED MORE POWER! CRANK UP THE MAGIC, TWILIGHT!
BOING!
MAGIC ACCELERATION, **COMMENCE!**
HEY, TWILIGHT, I COULD GET USED TO THIS!
PLEASE DON'T.
LET'S HEAR YOU SAY THAT AFTER THIS NEXT TRICK!

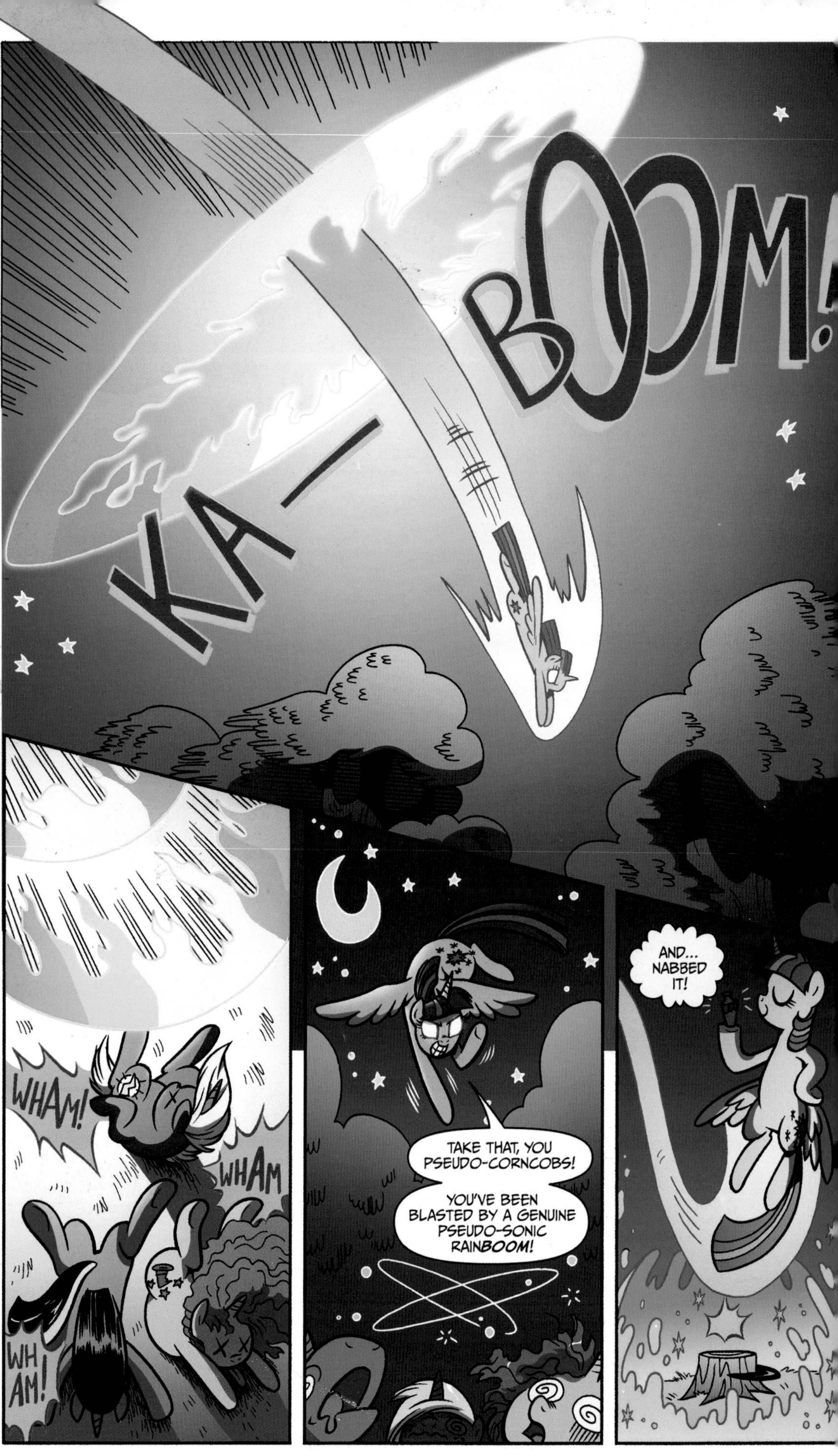
KA—BOOM!
WHAM!
WHAM
WHAM!
TAKE THAT, YOU PSEUDO-CORNCOBS!
YOU'VE BEEN BLASTED BY A GENUINE PSEUDO-SONIC RAINBOOM!
AND... NABBED IT!

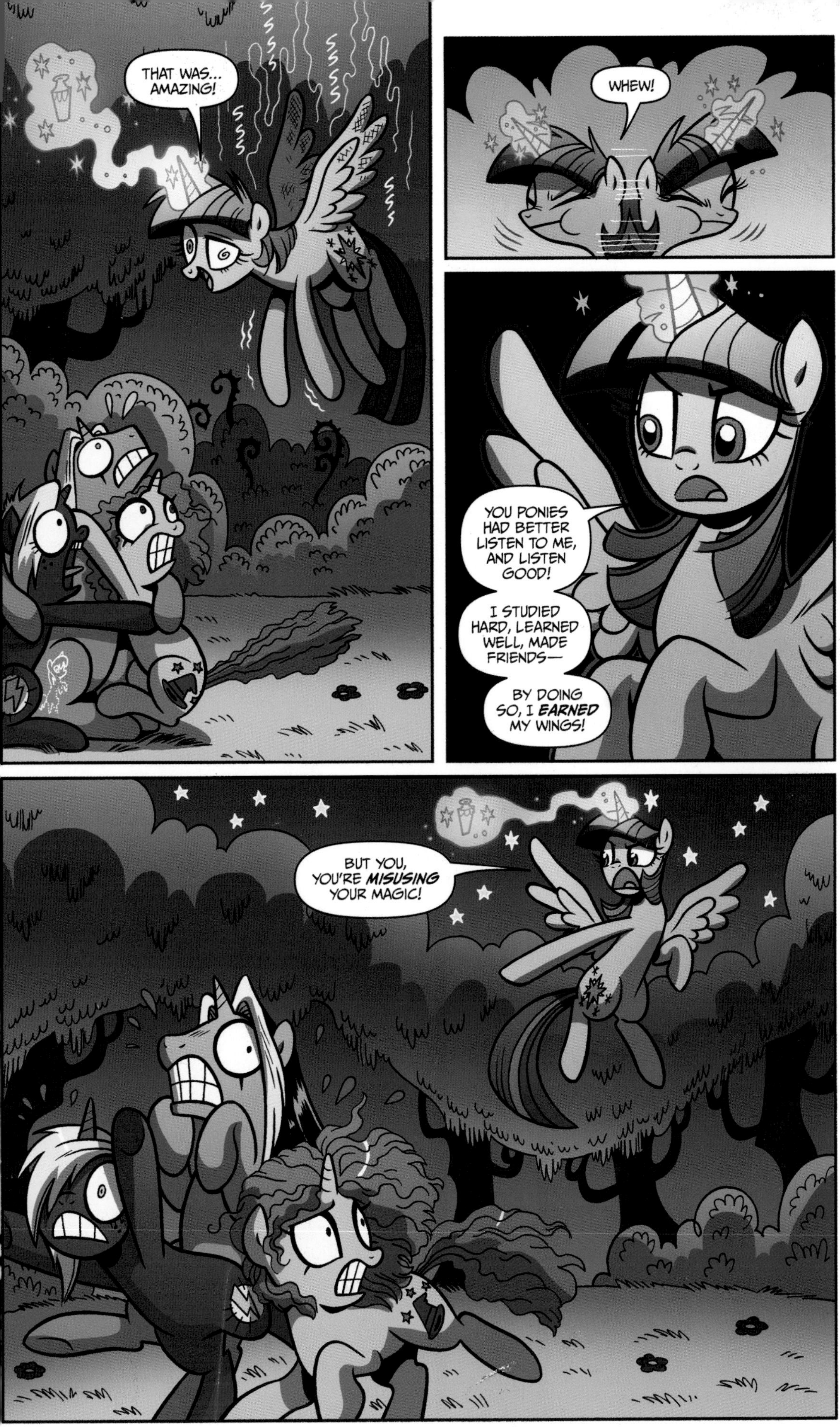
THAT WAS... AMAZING!
WHEW!
YOU PONIES HAD BETTER LISTEN TO ME, AND LISTEN GOOD!
I STUDIED HARD, LEARNED WELL, MADE FRIENDS—
BY DOING SO, I *EARNED* MY WINGS!
BUT YOU, YOU'RE *MISUSING* YOUR MAGIC!

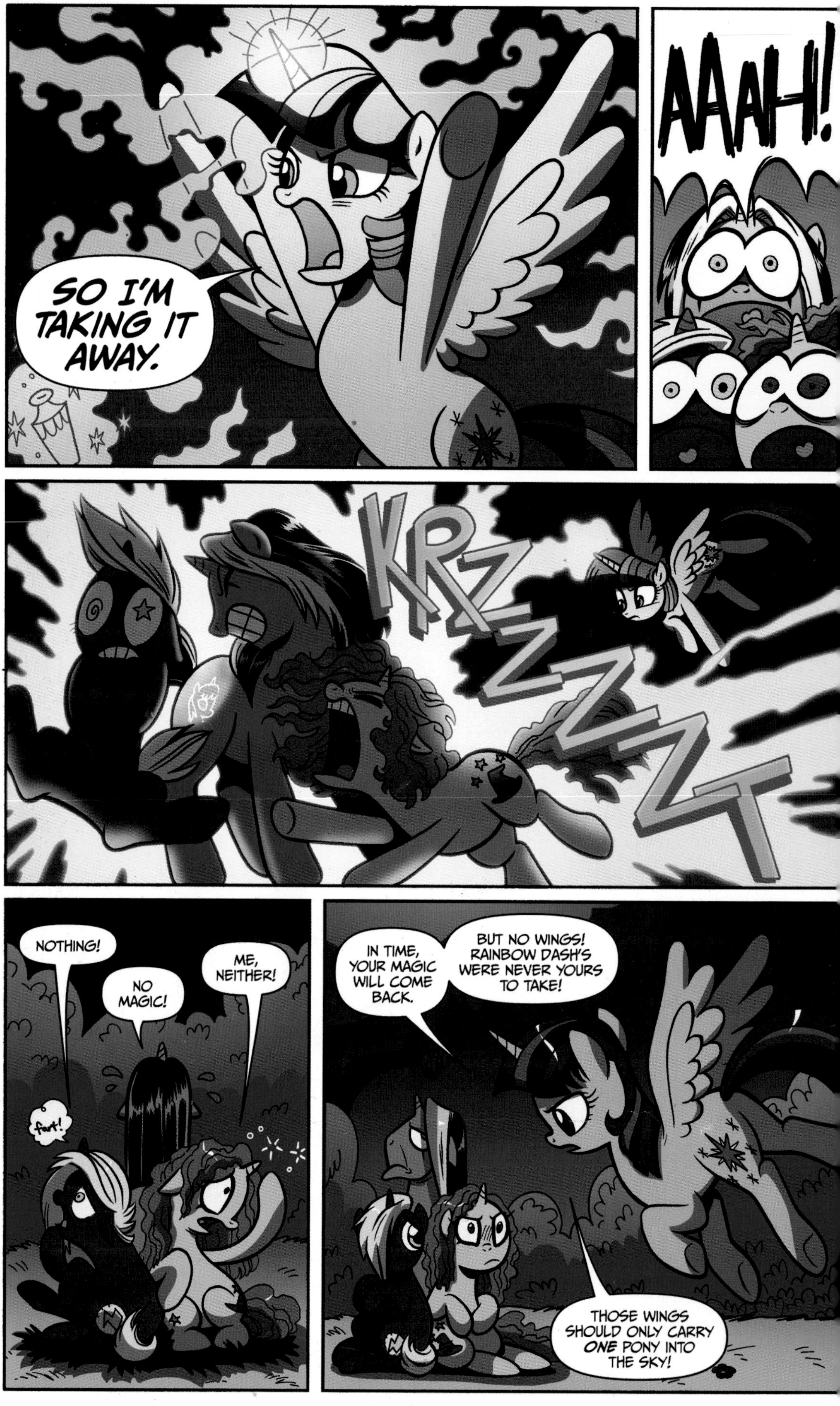
SO I'M TAKING IT AWAY.
AAAH!
KRZZZZT
NOTHING!
fart!
NO MAGIC!
ME, NEITHER!
IN TIME, YOUR MAGIC WILL COME BACK.
BUT NO WINGS! RAINBOW DASH'S WERE NEVER YOURS TO TAKE!
THOSE WINGS SHOULD ONLY CARRY *ONE* PONY INTO THE SKY!

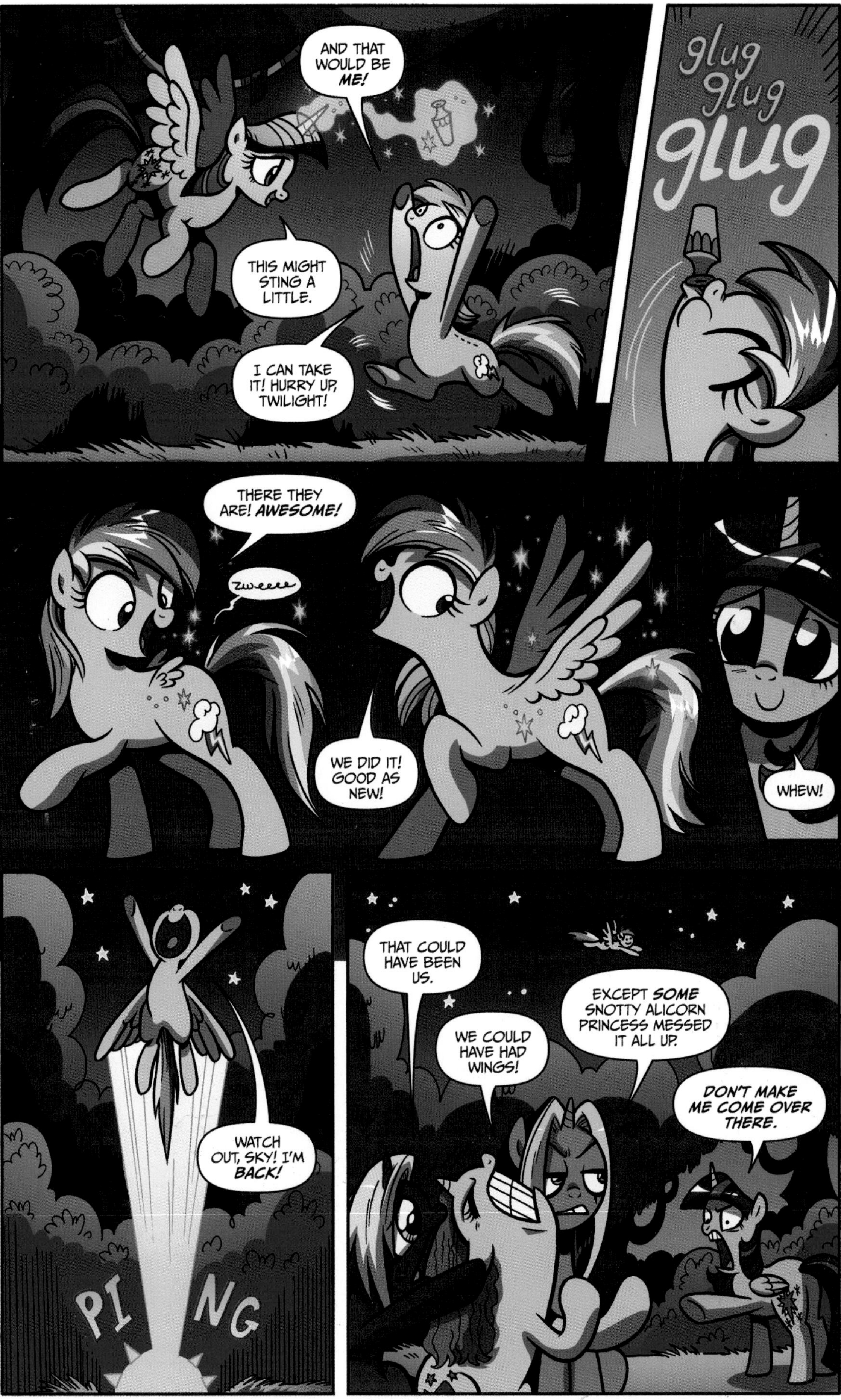
AND THAT WOULD BE ME!
THIS MIGHT STING A LITTLE.
I CAN TAKE IT! HURRY UP, TWILIGHT!
glug glug glug
THERE THEY ARE! AWESOME!
Zweeeee
WE DID IT! GOOD AS NEW!
WHEW!
WATCH OUT, SKY! I'M BACK!
PING
THAT COULD HAVE BEEN US.
WE COULD HAVE HAD WINGS!
EXCEPT SOME SNOTTY ALICORN PRINCESS MESSED IT ALL UP.
DON'T MAKE ME COME OVER THERE.

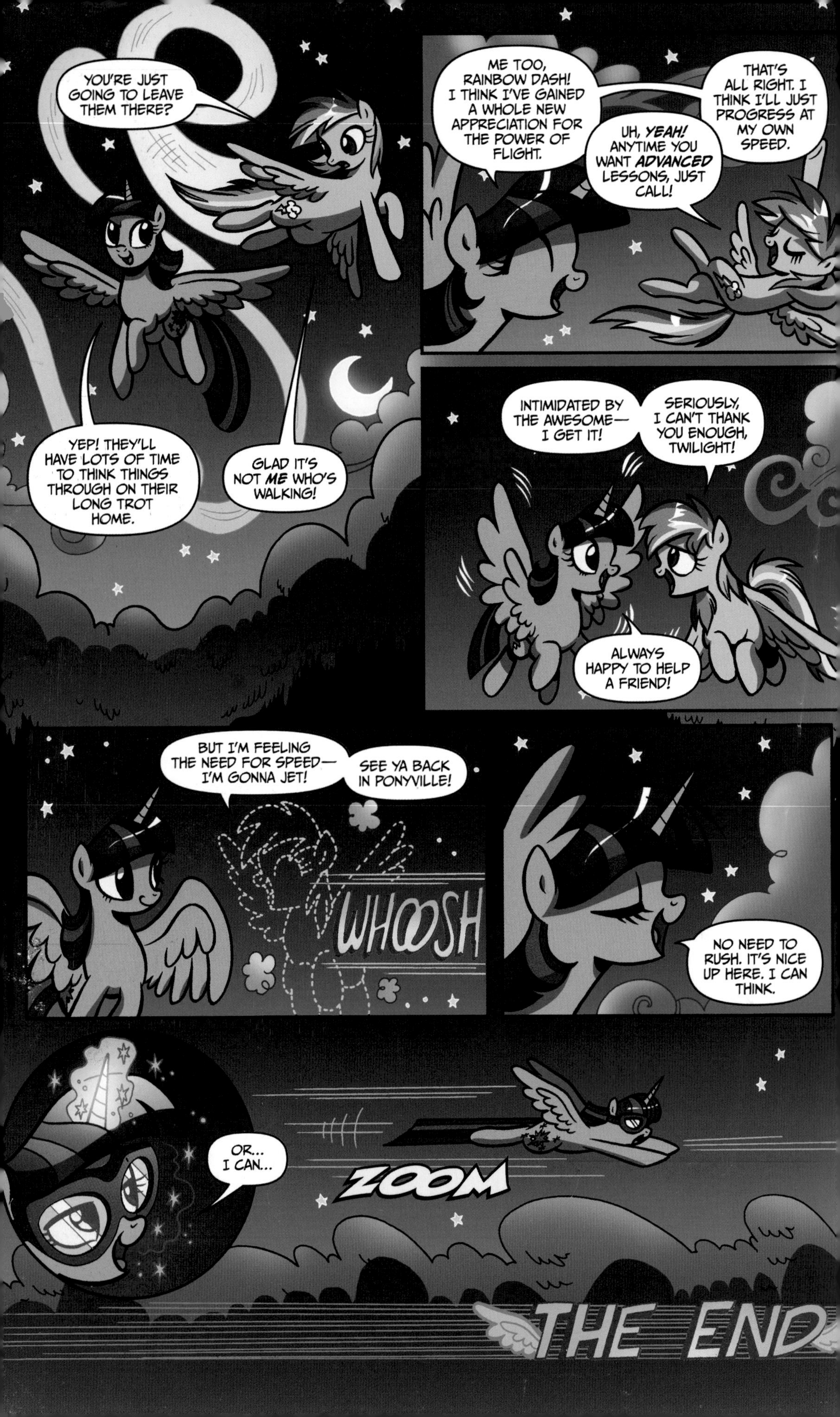
YOU'RE JUST GOING TO LEAVE THEM THERE?
YEP! THEY'LL HAVE LOTS OF TIME TO THINK THINGS THROUGH ON THEIR LONG TROT HOME.
GLAD IT'S NOT ME WHO'S WALKING!
ME TOO, RAINBOW DASH! I THINK I'VE GAINED A WHOLE NEW APPRECIATION FOR THE POWER OF FLIGHT.
UH, YEAH! ANYTIME YOU WANT ADVANCED LESSONS, JUST CALL!
THAT'S ALL RIGHT. I THINK I'LL JUST PROGRESS AT MY OWN SPEED.
INTIMIDATED BY THE AWESOME— I GET IT!
SERIOUSLY, I CAN'T THANK YOU ENOUGH, TWILIGHT!
ALWAYS HAPPY TO HELP A FRIEND!
BUT I'M FEELING THE NEED FOR SPEED— I'M GONNA JET!
SEE YA BACK IN PONYVILLE!
WHOOSH
NO NEED TO RUSH. IT'S NICE UP HERE. I CAN THINK.
OR... I CAN...
ZOOM
THE END

My Little Pony
Friends Forever

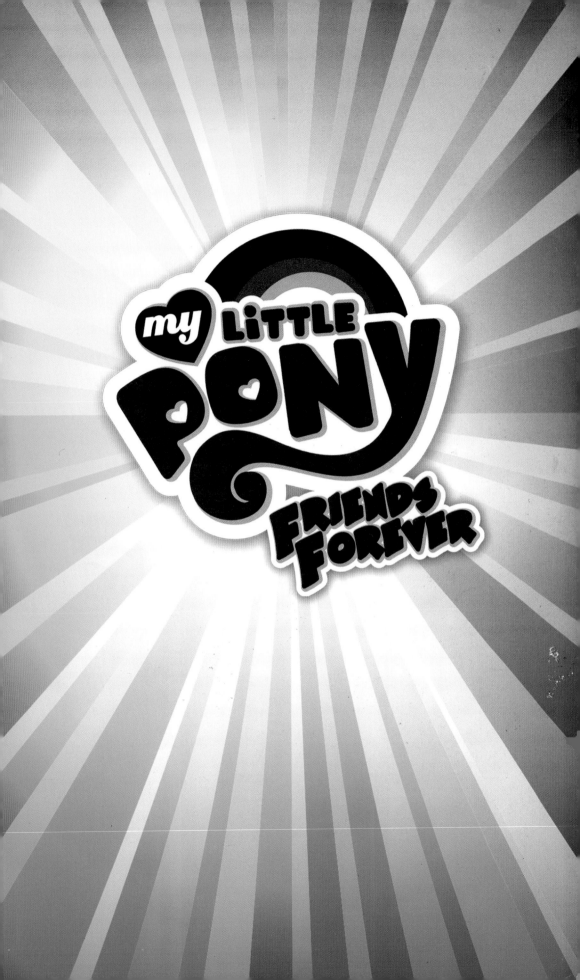

SHINING ARMOR & PRINCE BLUEBLOOD

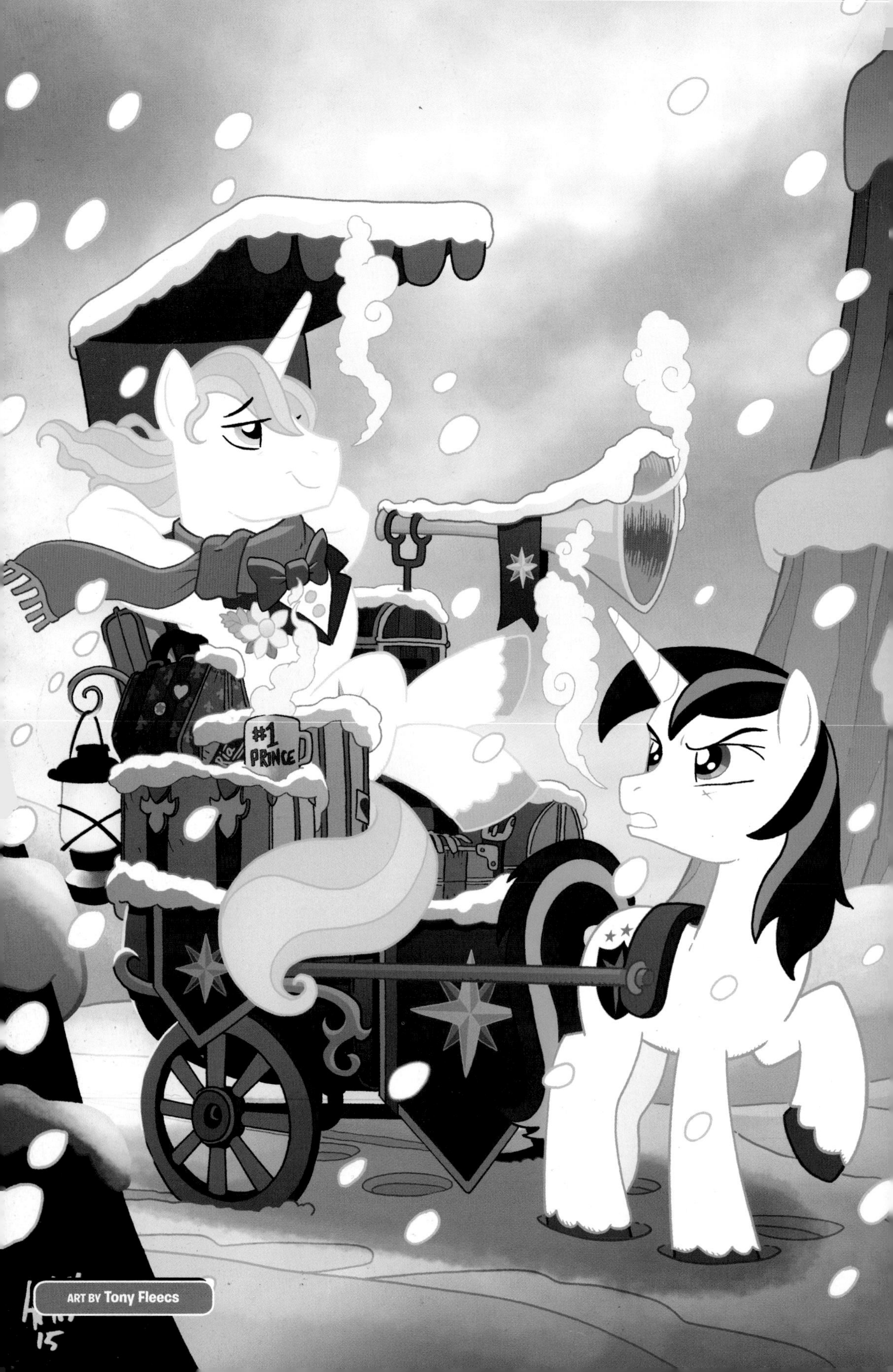
#1
PRINCE

ART BY Tony Fleecs

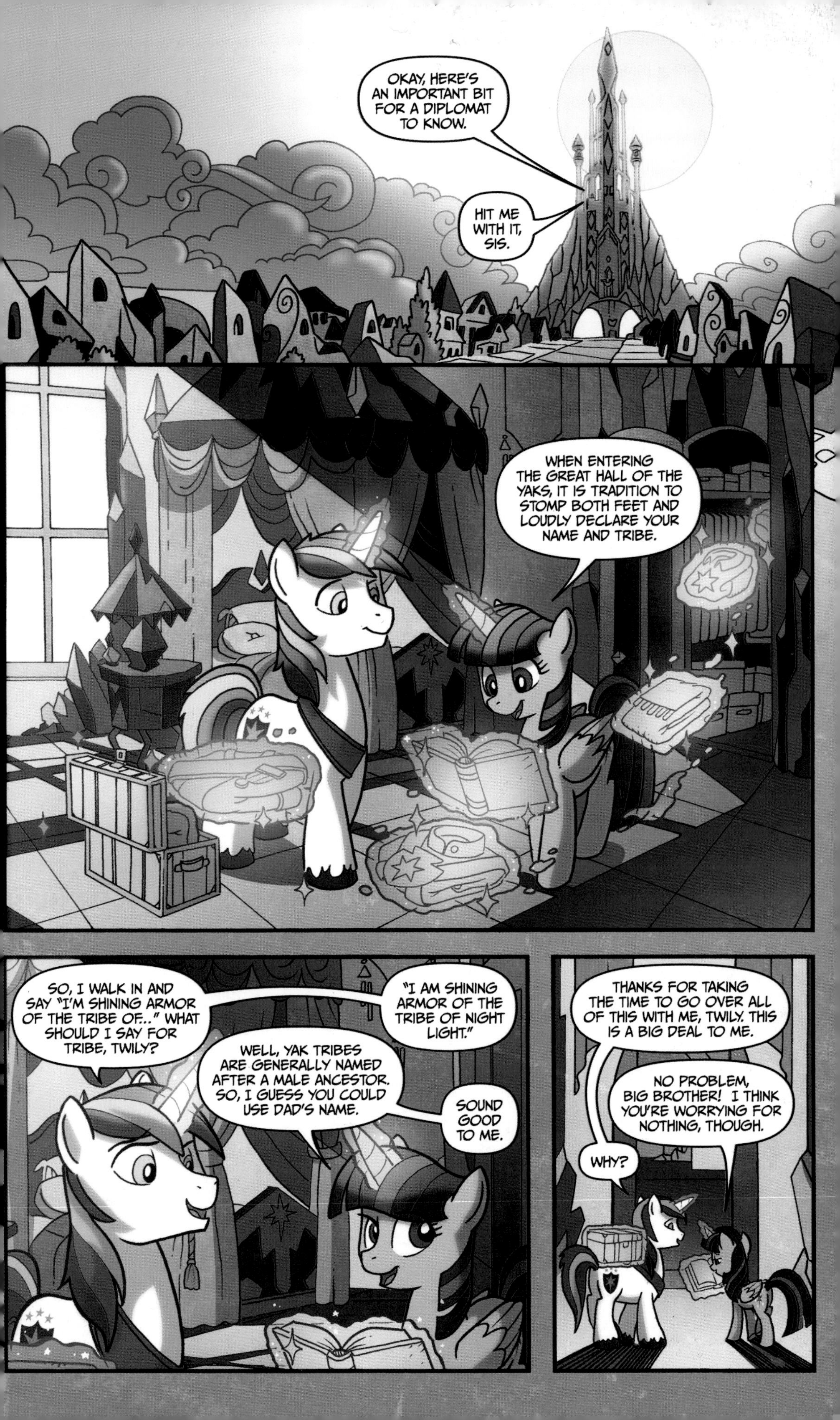
OKAY, HERE'S AN IMPORTANT BIT FOR A DIPLOMAT TO KNOW.
HIT ME WITH IT, SIS.
WHEN ENTERING THE GREAT HALL OF THE YAKS, IT IS TRADITION TO STOMP BOTH FEET AND LOUDLY DECLARE YOUR NAME AND TRIBE.
SO, I WALK IN AND SAY "I'M SHINING ARMOR OF THE TRIBE OF..." WHAT SHOULD I SAY FOR TRIBE, TWILY?
WELL, YAK TRIBES ARE GENERALLY NAMED AFTER A MALE ANCESTOR. SO, I GUESS YOU COULD USE DAD'S NAME.
"I AM SHINING ARMOR OF THE TRIBE OF NIGHT LIGHT."
SOUND GOOD TO ME.
THANKS FOR TAKING THE TIME TO GO OVER ALL OF THIS WITH ME, TWILY. THIS IS A BIG DEAL TO ME.
NO PROBLEM, BIG BROTHER! I THINK YOU'RE WORRYING FOR NOTHING, THOUGH.
WHY?

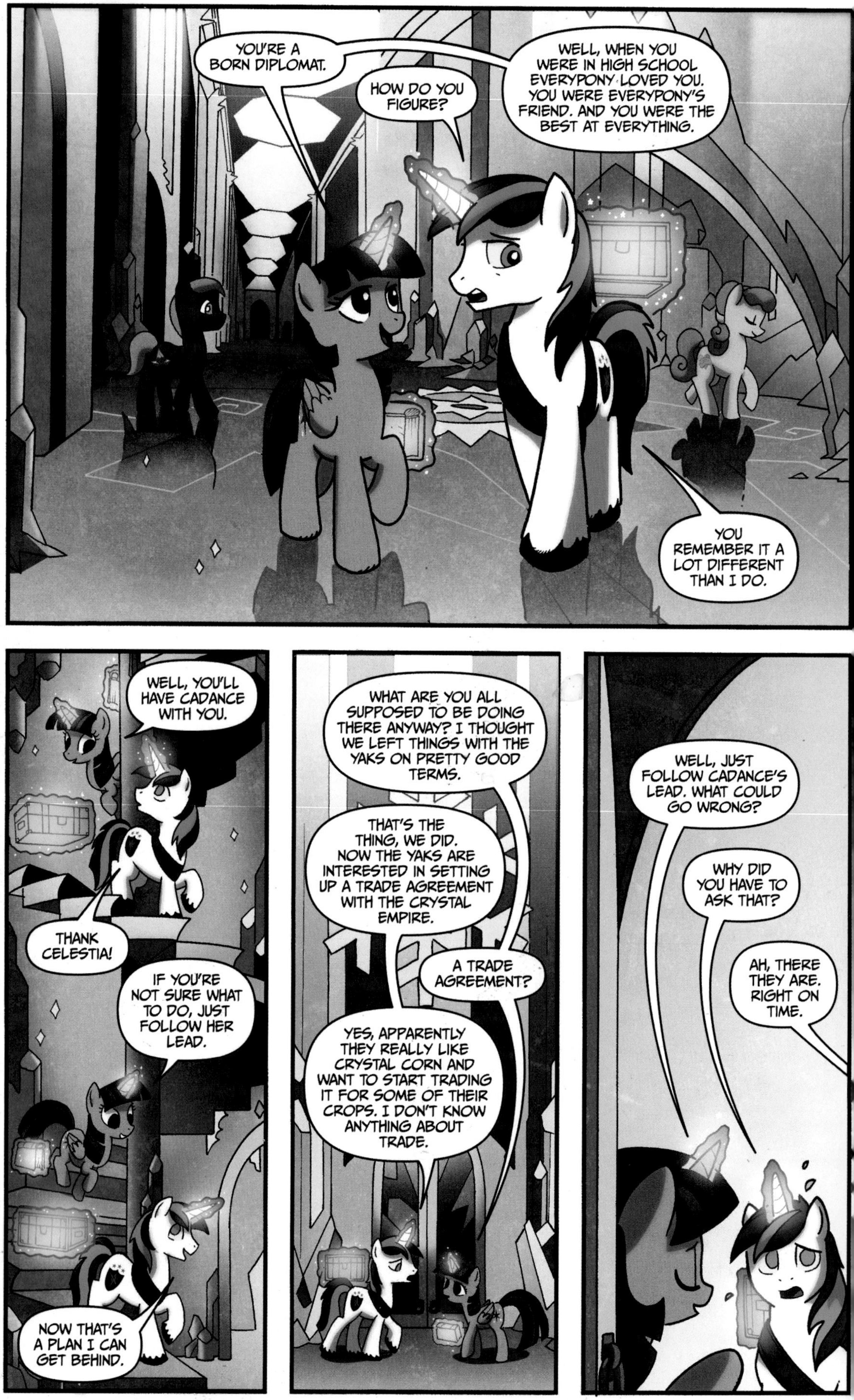

YOU'RE A BORN DIPLOMAT.
HOW DO YOU FIGURE?
WELL, WHEN YOU WERE IN HIGH SCHOOL EVERYPONY LOVED YOU. YOU WERE EVERYPONY'S FRIEND. AND YOU WERE THE BEST AT EVERYTHING.
YOU REMEMBER IT A LOT DIFFERENT THAN I DO.
WELL, YOU'LL HAVE CADANCE WITH YOU.
THANK CELESTIA!
IF YOU'RE NOT SURE WHAT TO DO, JUST FOLLOW HER LEAD.
NOW THAT'S A PLAN I CAN GET BEHIND.
WHAT ARE YOU ALL SUPPOSED TO BE DOING THERE ANYWAY? I THOUGHT WE LEFT THINGS WITH THE YAKS ON PRETTY GOOD TERMS.
THAT'S THE THING, WE DID. NOW THE YAKS ARE INTERESTED IN SETTING UP A TRADE AGREEMENT WITH THE CRYSTAL EMPIRE.
A TRADE AGREEMENT?
YES, APPARENTLY THEY REALLY LIKE CRYSTAL CORN AND WANT TO START TRADING IT FOR SOME OF THEIR CROPS. I DON'T KNOW ANYTHING ABOUT TRADE.
WELL, JUST FOLLOW CADANCE'S LEAD. WHAT COULD GO WRONG?
WHY DID YOU HAVE TO ASK THAT?
AH, THERE THEY ARE. RIGHT ON TIME.

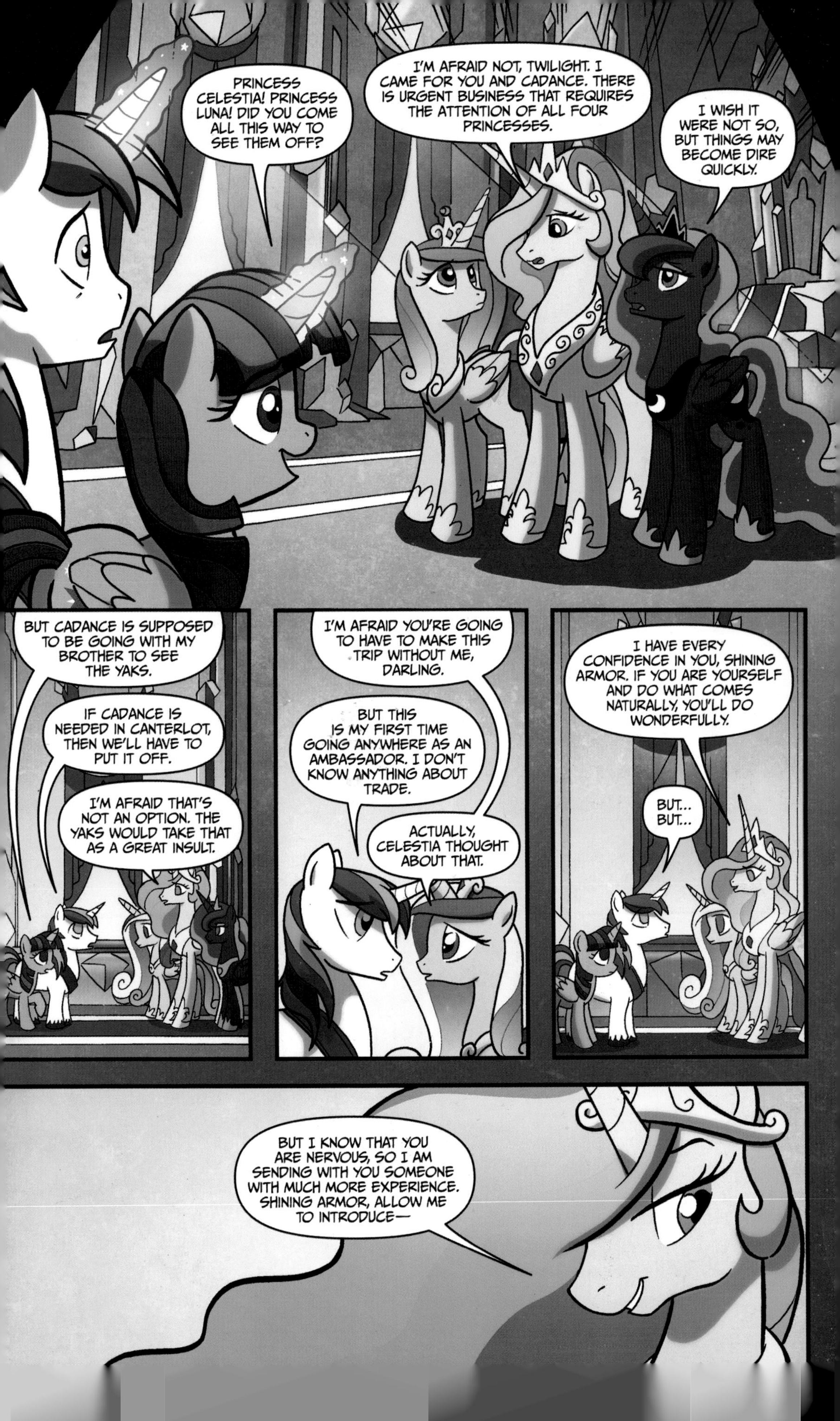
PRINCESS CELESTIA! PRINCESS LUNA! DID YOU COME ALL THIS WAY TO SEE THEM OFF?
I'M AFRAID NOT, TWILIGHT. I CAME FOR YOU AND CADANCE. THERE IS URGENT BUSINESS THAT REQUIRES THE ATTENTION OF ALL FOUR PRINCESSES.
I WISH IT WERE NOT SO, BUT THINGS MAY BECOME DIRE QUICKLY.
BUT CADANCE IS SUPPOSED TO BE GOING WITH MY BROTHER TO SEE THE YAKS.
IF CADANCE IS NEEDED IN CANTERLOT, THEN WE'LL HAVE TO PUT IT OFF.
I'M AFRAID THAT'S NOT AN OPTION. THE YAKS WOULD TAKE THAT AS A GREAT INSULT.
I'M AFRAID YOU'RE GOING TO HAVE TO MAKE THIS TRIP WITHOUT ME, DARLING.
BUT THIS IS MY FIRST TIME GOING ANYWHERE AS AN AMBASSADOR. I DON'T KNOW ANYTHING ABOUT TRADE.
ACTUALLY, CELESTIA THOUGHT ABOUT THAT.
I HAVE EVERY CONFIDENCE IN YOU, SHINING ARMOR. IF YOU ARE YOURSELF AND DO WHAT COMES NATURALLY, YOU'LL DO WONDERFULLY.
BUT... BUT...
BUT I KNOW THAT YOU ARE NERVOUS, SO I AM SENDING WITH YOU SOMEONE WITH MUCH MORE EXPERIENCE. SHINING ARMOR, ALLOW ME TO INTRODUCE—

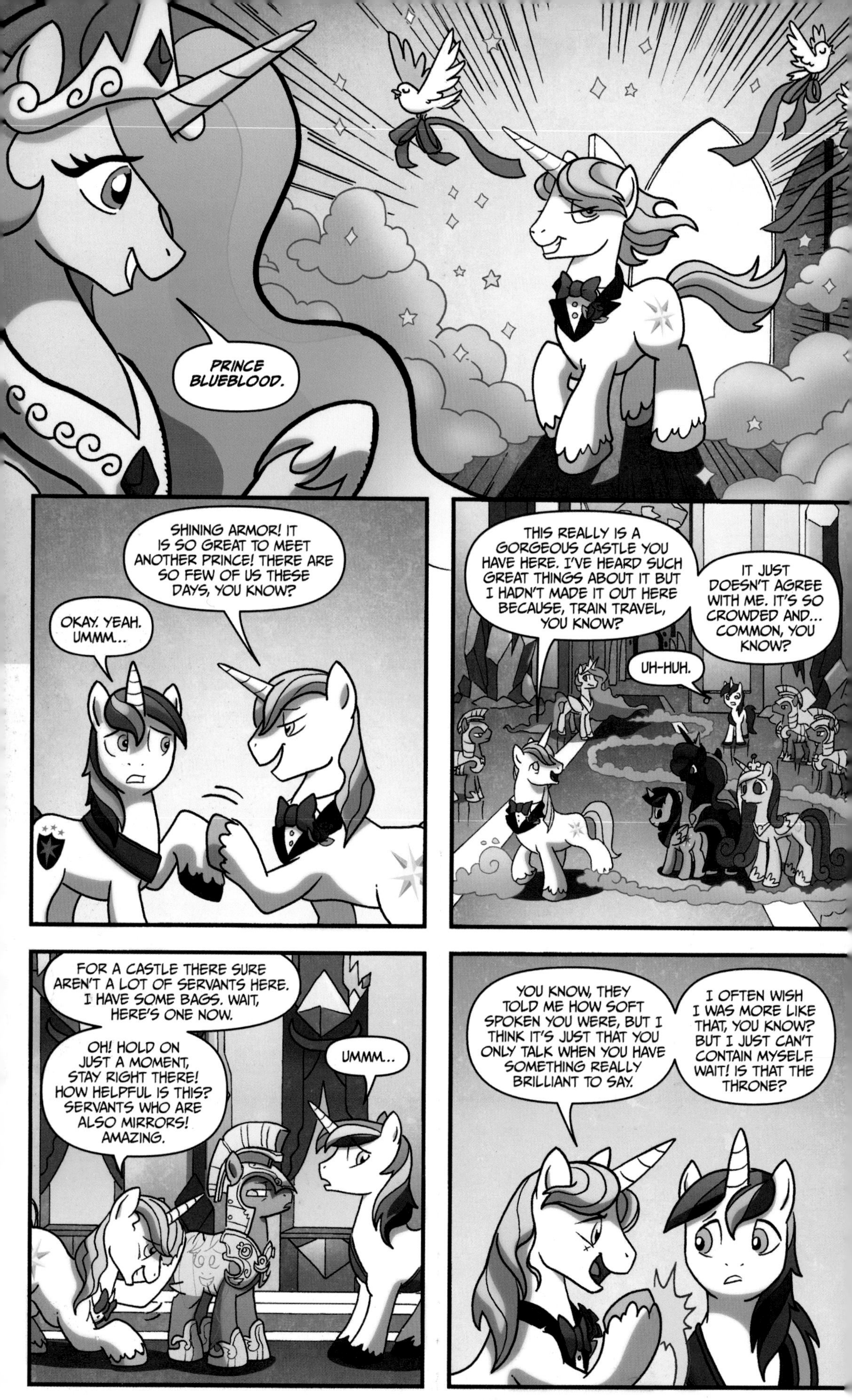
PRINCE BLUEBLOOD.
SHINING ARMOR! IT IS SO GREAT TO MEET ANOTHER PRINCE! THERE ARE SO FEW OF US THESE DAYS, YOU KNOW?
OKAY. YEAH. UMMM...
THIS REALLY IS A GORGEOUS CASTLE YOU HAVE HERE. I'VE HEARD SUCH GREAT THINGS ABOUT IT BUT I HADN'T MADE IT OUT HERE BECAUSE, TRAIN TRAVEL, YOU KNOW?
IT JUST DOESN'T AGREE WITH ME. IT'S SO CROWDED AND... COMMON, YOU KNOW?
UH-HUH.
FOR A CASTLE THERE SURE AREN'T A LOT OF SERVANTS HERE. I HAVE SOME BAGS. WAIT, HERE'S ONE NOW.
OH! HOLD ON JUST A MOMENT, STAY RIGHT THERE! HOW HELPFUL IS THIS? SERVANTS WHO ARE ALSO MIRRORS! AMAZING.
UMMM...
YOU KNOW, THEY TOLD ME HOW SOFT SPOKEN YOU WERE, BUT I THINK IT'S JUST THAT YOU ONLY TALK WHEN YOU HAVE SOMETHING REALLY BRILLIANT TO SAY.
I OFTEN WISH I WAS MORE LIKE THAT, YOU KNOW? BUT I JUST CAN'T CONTAIN MYSELF. WAIT! IS THAT THE THRONE?

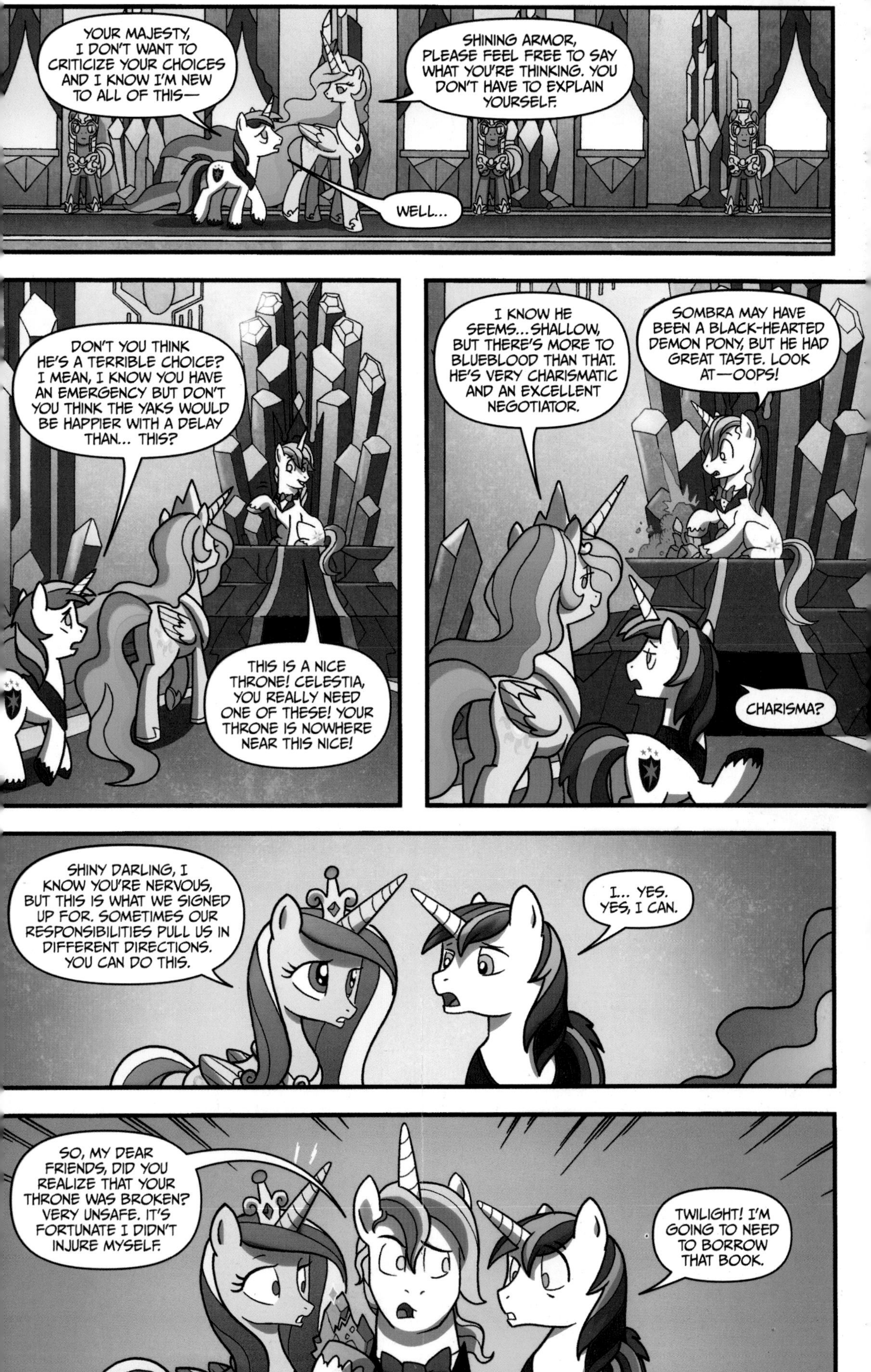
YOUR MAJESTY, I DON'T WANT TO CRITICIZE YOUR CHOICES AND I KNOW I'M NEW TO ALL OF THIS—
SHINING ARMOR, PLEASE FEEL FREE TO SAY WHAT YOU'RE THINKING. YOU DON'T HAVE TO EXPLAIN YOURSELF.
WELL...
DON'T YOU THINK HE'S A TERRIBLE CHOICE? I MEAN, I KNOW YOU HAVE AN EMERGENCY BUT DON'T YOU THINK THE YAKS WOULD BE HAPPIER WITH A DELAY THAN... THIS?
THIS IS A NICE THRONE! CELESTIA, YOU REALLY NEED ONE OF THESE! YOUR THRONE IS NOWHERE NEAR THIS NICE!
I KNOW HE SEEMS...SHALLOW, BUT THERE'S MORE TO BLUEBLOOD THAN THAT. HE'S VERY CHARISMATIC AND AN EXCELLENT NEGOTIATOR.
SOMBRA MAY HAVE BEEN A BLACK-HEARTED DEMON PONY, BUT HE HAD GREAT TASTE. LOOK AT—OOPS!
CHARISMA?
SHINY DARLING, I KNOW YOU'RE NERVOUS, BUT THIS IS WHAT WE SIGNED UP FOR. SOMETIMES OUR RESPONSIBILITIES PULL US IN DIFFERENT DIRECTIONS. YOU CAN DO THIS.
I... YES. YES, I CAN.
SO, MY DEAR FRIENDS, DID YOU REALIZE THAT YOUR THRONE WAS BROKEN? VERY UNSAFE. IT'S FORTUNATE I DIDN'T INJURE MYSELF.
TWILIGHT! I'M GOING TO NEED TO BORROW THAT BOOK.

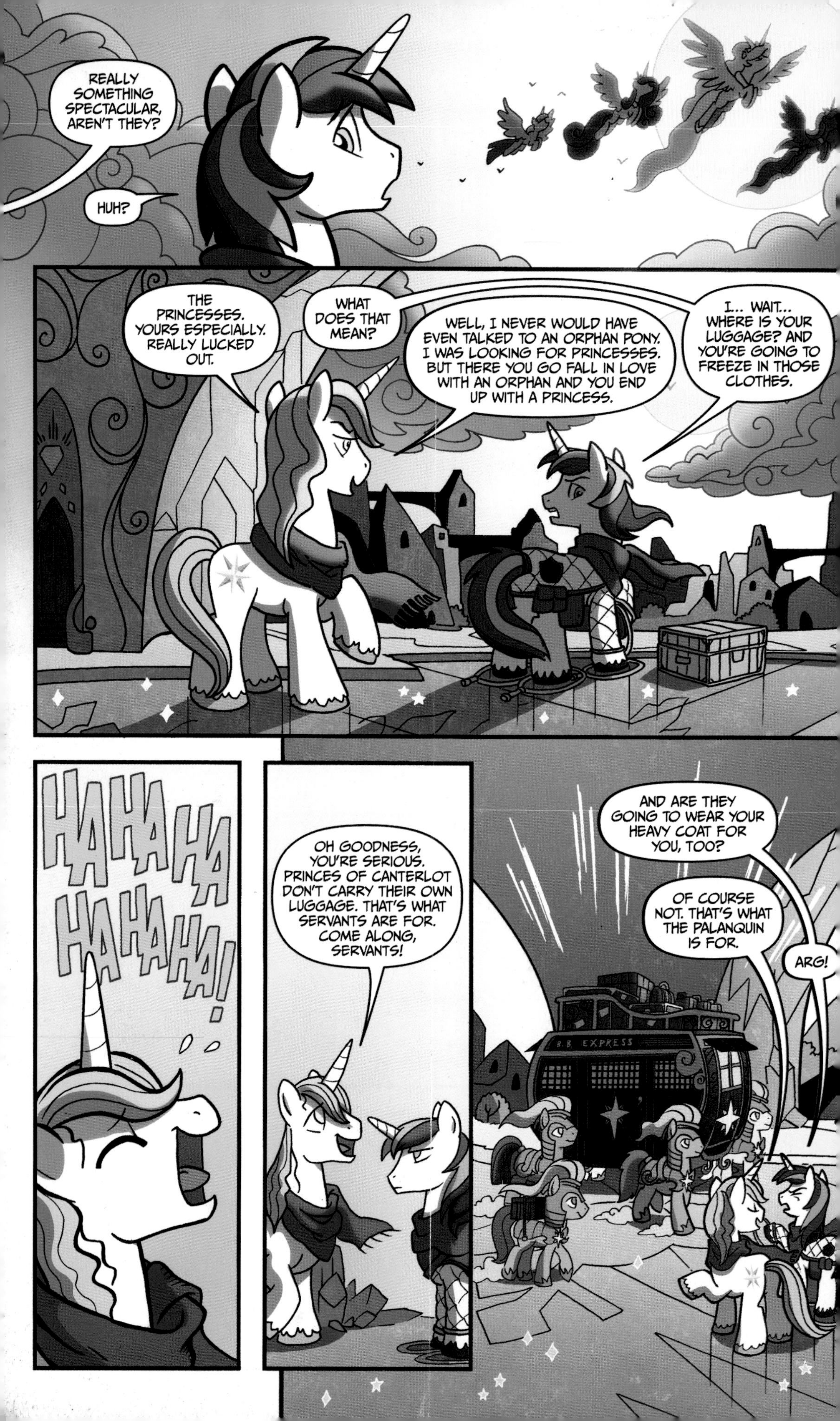
REALLY SOMETHING SPECTACULAR, AREN'T THEY?
HUH?
THE PRINCESSES. YOURS ESPECIALLY. REALLY LUCKED OUT.
WHAT DOES THAT MEAN?
WELL, I NEVER WOULD HAVE EVEN TALKED TO AN ORPHAN PONY. I WAS LOOKING FOR PRINCESSES. BUT THERE YOU GO FALL IN LOVE WITH AN ORPHAN AND YOU END UP WITH A PRINCESS.
I... WAIT... WHERE IS YOUR LUGGAGE? AND YOU'RE GOING TO FREEZE IN THOSE CLOTHES.
HAHAHAHA HAHAHAHA!
OH GOODNESS, YOU'RE SERIOUS. PRINCES OF CANTERLOT DON'T CARRY THEIR OWN LUGGAGE. THAT'S WHAT SERVANTS ARE FOR. COME ALONG, SERVANTS!
B.B EXPRESS
AND ARE THEY GOING TO WEAR YOUR HEAVY COAT FOR YOU, TOO?
OF COURSE NOT. THAT'S WHAT THE PALANQUIN IS FOR.
ARG!

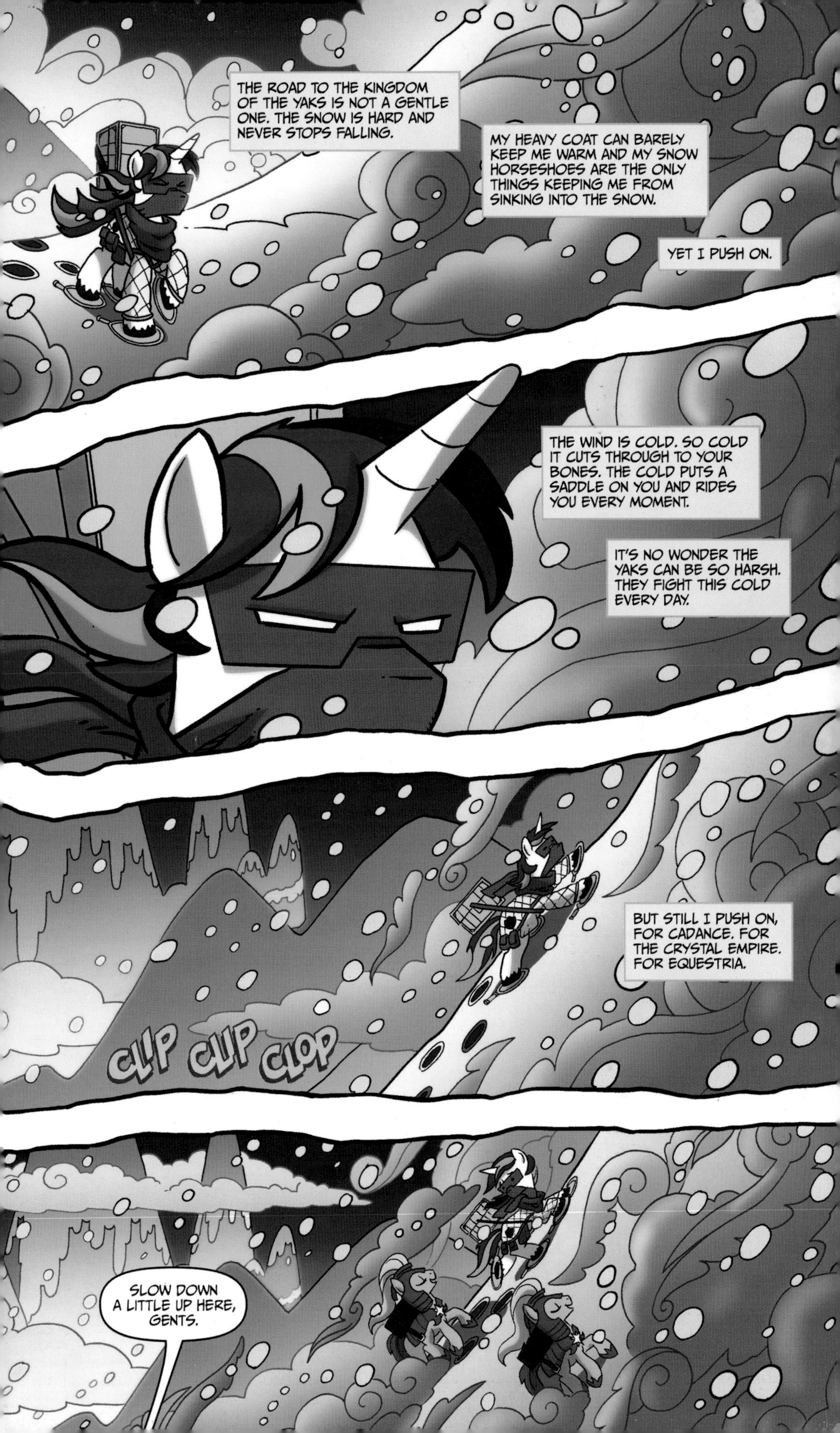
THE ROAD TO THE KINGDOM OF THE YAKS IS NOT A GENTLE ONE. THE SNOW IS HARD AND NEVER STOPS FALLING.
MY HEAVY COAT CAN BARELY KEEP ME WARM AND MY SNOW HORSESHOES ARE THE ONLY THINGS KEEPING ME FROM SINKING INTO THE SNOW.
YET I PUSH ON.
THE WIND IS COLD. SO COLD IT CUTS THROUGH TO YOUR BONES. THE COLD PUTS A SADDLE ON YOU AND RIDES YOU EVERY MOMENT.
IT'S NO WONDER THE YAKS CAN BE SO HARSH. THEY FIGHT THIS COLD EVERY DAY.
BUT STILL I PUSH ON, FOR CADANCE. FOR THE CRYSTAL EMPIRE. FOR EQUESTRIA.
CLIP CLIP CLOP
SLOW DOWN A LITTLE UP HERE, GENTS.

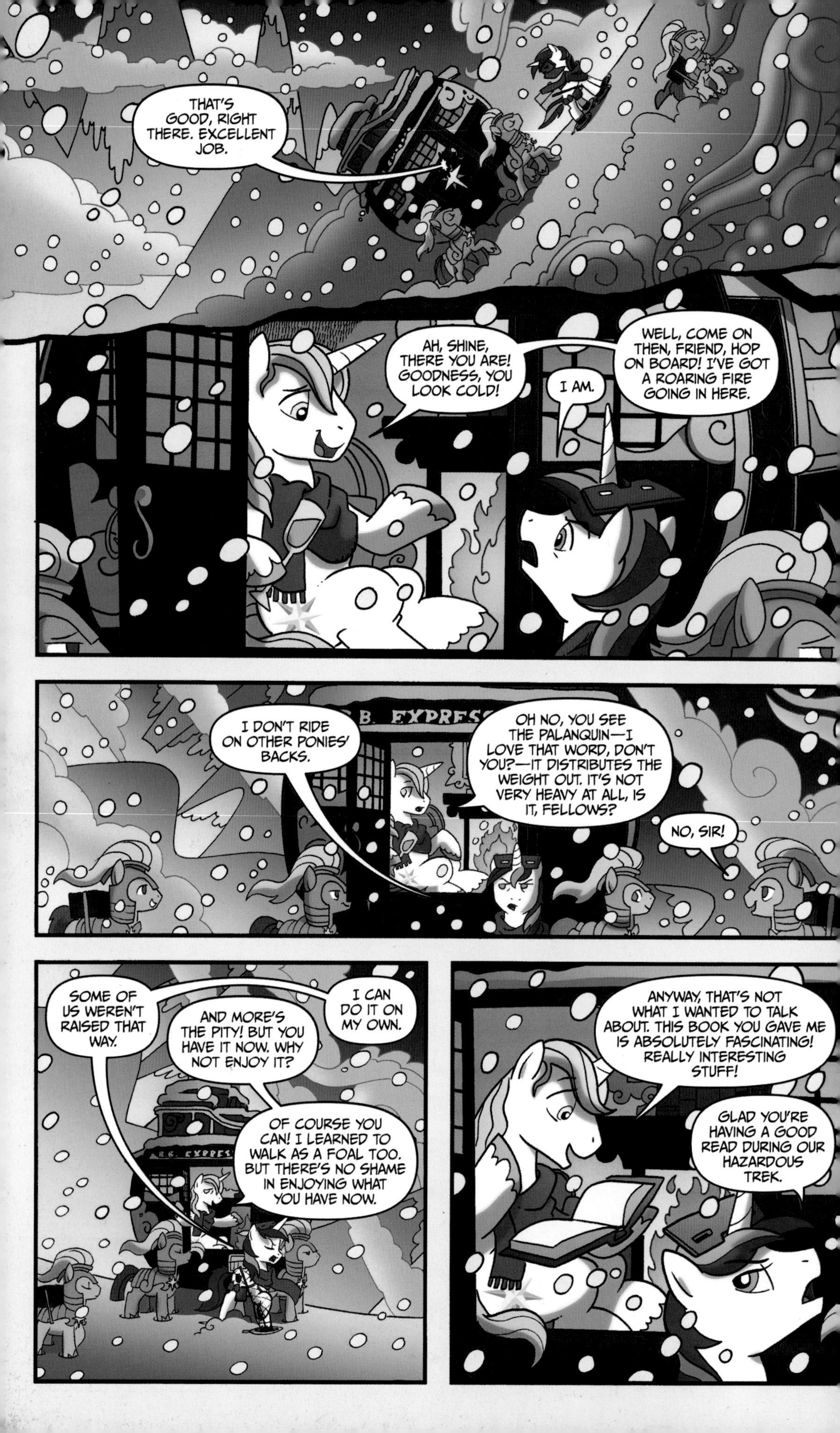
THAT'S GOOD, RIGHT THERE. EXCELLENT JOB.
AH, SHINE, THERE YOU ARE! GOODNESS, YOU LOOK COLD!
I AM.
WELL, COME ON THEN, FRIEND, HOP ON BOARD! I'VE GOT A ROARING FIRE GOING IN HERE.
I DON'T RIDE ON OTHER PONIES' BACKS.
OH NO, YOU SEE THE PALANQUIN—I LOVE THAT WORD, DON'T YOU?—IT DISTRIBUTES THE WEIGHT OUT. IT'S NOT VERY HEAVY AT ALL, IS IT, FELLOWS?
NO, SIR!
SOME OF US WEREN'T RAISED THAT WAY.
AND MORE'S THE PITY! BUT YOU HAVE IT NOW. WHY NOT ENJOY IT?
I CAN DO IT ON MY OWN.
OF COURSE YOU CAN! I LEARNED TO WALK AS A FOAL TOO. BUT THERE'S NO SHAME IN ENJOYING WHAT YOU HAVE NOW.
ANYWAY, THAT'S NOT WHAT I WANTED TO TALK ABOUT. THIS BOOK YOU GAVE ME IS ABSOLUTELY FASCINATING! REALLY INTERESTING STUFF!
GLAD YOU'RE HAVING A GOOD READ DURING OUR HAZARDOUS TREK.

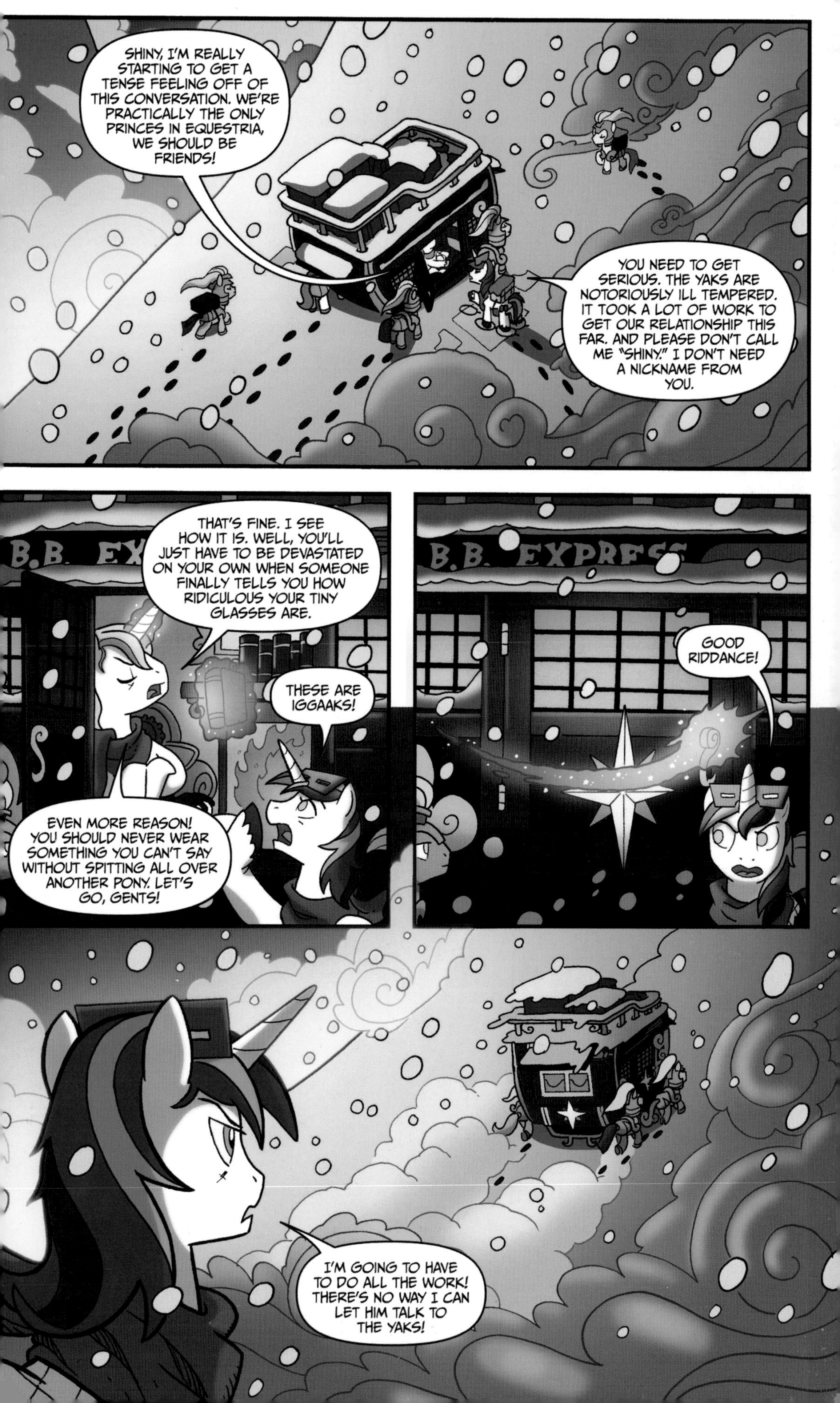
SHINY, I'M REALLY STARTING TO GET A TENSE FEELING OFF OF THIS CONVERSATION. WE'RE PRACTICALLY THE ONLY PRINCES IN EQUESTRIA, WE SHOULD BE FRIENDS!
YOU NEED TO GET SERIOUS. THE YAKS ARE NOTORIOUSLY ILL TEMPERED. IT TOOK A LOT OF WORK TO GET OUR RELATIONSHIP THIS FAR. AND PLEASE DON'T CALL ME "SHINY." I DON'T NEED A NICKNAME FROM YOU.
B.B. EX
THAT'S FINE. I SEE HOW IT IS. WELL, YOU'LL JUST HAVE TO BE DEVASTATED ON YOUR OWN WHEN SOMEONE FINALLY TELLS YOU HOW RIDICULOUS YOUR TINY GLASSES ARE.
THESE ARE IGGAAKS!
EVEN MORE REASON! YOU SHOULD NEVER WEAR SOMETHING YOU CAN'T SAY WITHOUT SPITTING ALL OVER ANOTHER PONY. LET'S GO, GENTS!
B.B. EXPRESS
GOOD RIDDANCE!
I'M GOING TO HAVE TO DO ALL THE WORK! THERE'S NO WAY I CAN LET HIM TALK TO THE YAKS!

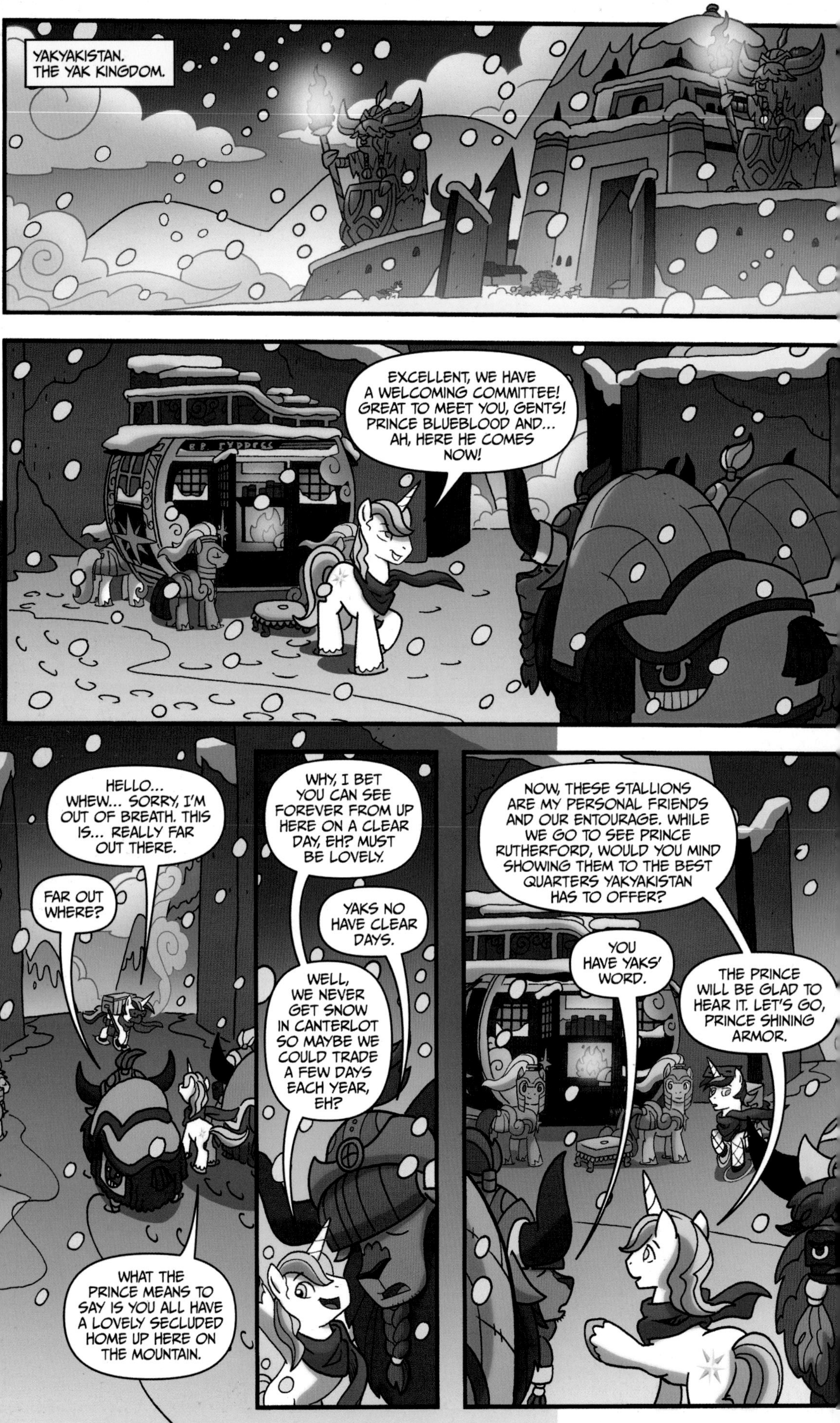
YAKYAKISTAN. THE YAK KINGDOM.
EXCELLENT, WE HAVE A WELCOMING COMMITTEE! GREAT TO MEET YOU, GENTS! PRINCE BLUEBLOOD AND... AH, HERE HE COMES NOW!
HELLO... WHEW... SORRY, I'M OUT OF BREATH. THIS IS... REALLY FAR OUT THERE.
FAR OUT WHERE?
WHAT THE PRINCE MEANS TO SAY IS YOU ALL HAVE A LOVELY SECLUDED HOME UP HERE ON THE MOUNTAIN.
WHY, I BET YOU CAN SEE FOREVER FROM UP HERE ON A CLEAR DAY, EH? MUST BE LOVELY.
YAKS NO HAVE CLEAR DAYS.
WELL, WE NEVER GET SNOW IN CANTERLOT SO MAYBE WE COULD TRADE A FEW DAYS EACH YEAR, EH?
NOW, THESE STALLIONS ARE MY PERSONAL FRIENDS AND OUR ENTOURAGE. WHILE WE GO TO SEE PRINCE RUTHERFORD, WOULD YOU MIND SHOWING THEM TO THE BEST QUARTERS YAKYAKISTAN HAS TO OFFER?
YOU HAVE YAKS' WORD.
THE PRINCE WILL BE GLAD TO HEAR IT. LET'S GO, PRINCE SHINING ARMOR.

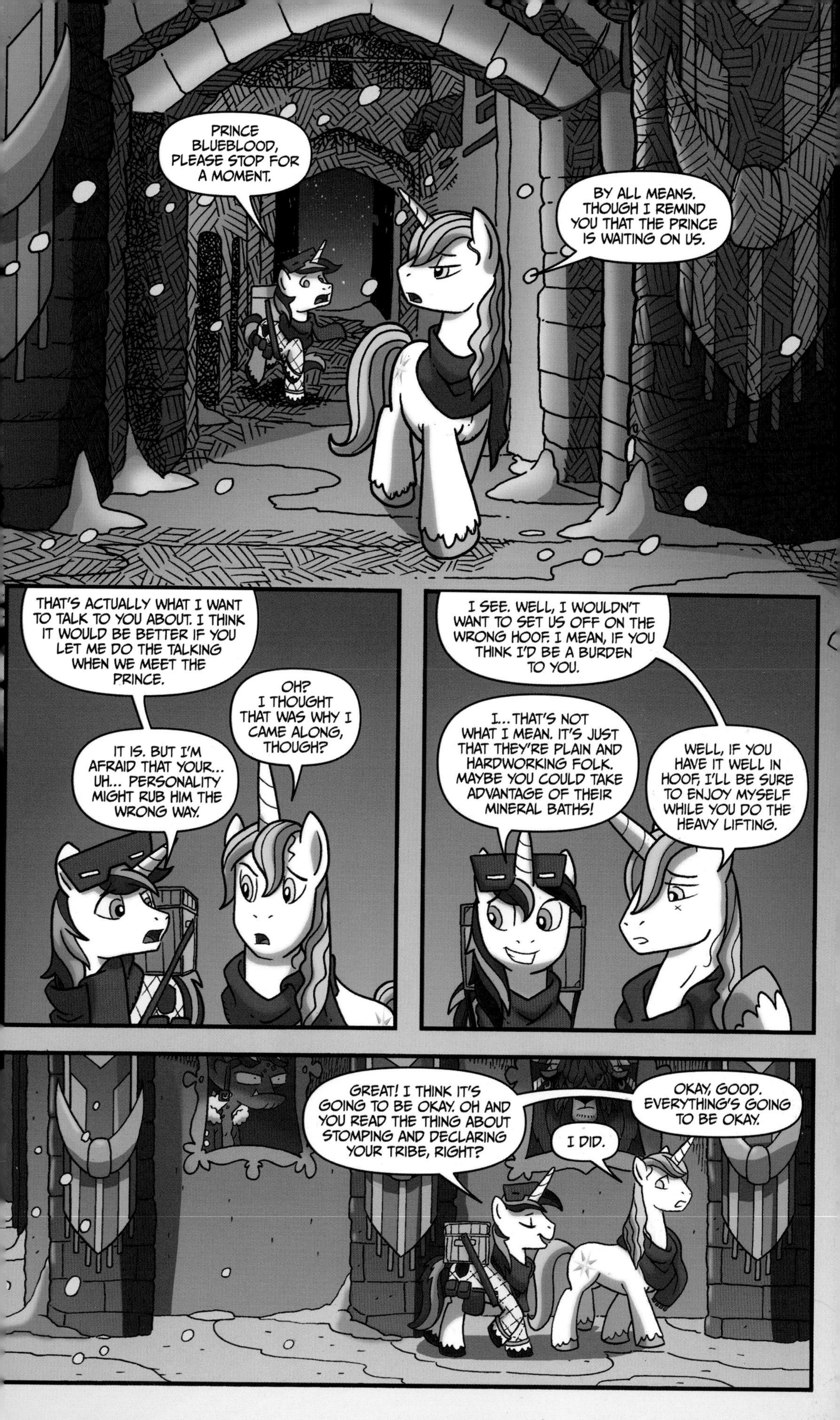
PRINCE BLUEBLOOD, PLEASE STOP FOR A MOMENT.
BY ALL MEANS. THOUGH I REMIND YOU THAT THE PRINCE IS WAITING ON US.
THAT'S ACTUALLY WHAT I WANT TO TALK TO YOU ABOUT. I THINK IT WOULD BE BETTER IF YOU LET ME DO THE TALKING WHEN WE MEET THE PRINCE.
OH? I THOUGHT THAT WAS WHY I CAME ALONG, THOUGH?
IT IS. BUT I'M AFRAID THAT YOUR... UH... PERSONALITY MIGHT RUB HIM THE WRONG WAY.
I SEE. WELL, I WOULDN'T WANT TO SET US OFF ON THE WRONG HOOF. I MEAN, IF YOU THINK I'D BE A BURDEN TO YOU.
I...THAT'S NOT WHAT I MEAN. IT'S JUST THAT THEY'RE PLAIN AND HARDWORKING FOLK. MAYBE YOU COULD TAKE ADVANTAGE OF THEIR MINERAL BATHS!
WELL, IF YOU HAVE IT WELL IN HOOF, I'LL BE SURE TO ENJOY MYSELF WHILE YOU DO THE HEAVY LIFTING.
GREAT! I THINK IT'S GOING TO BE OKAY. OH AND YOU READ THE THING ABOUT STOMPING AND DECLARING YOUR TRIBE, RIGHT?
I DID.
OKAY, GOOD. EVERYTHING'S GOING TO BE OKAY.

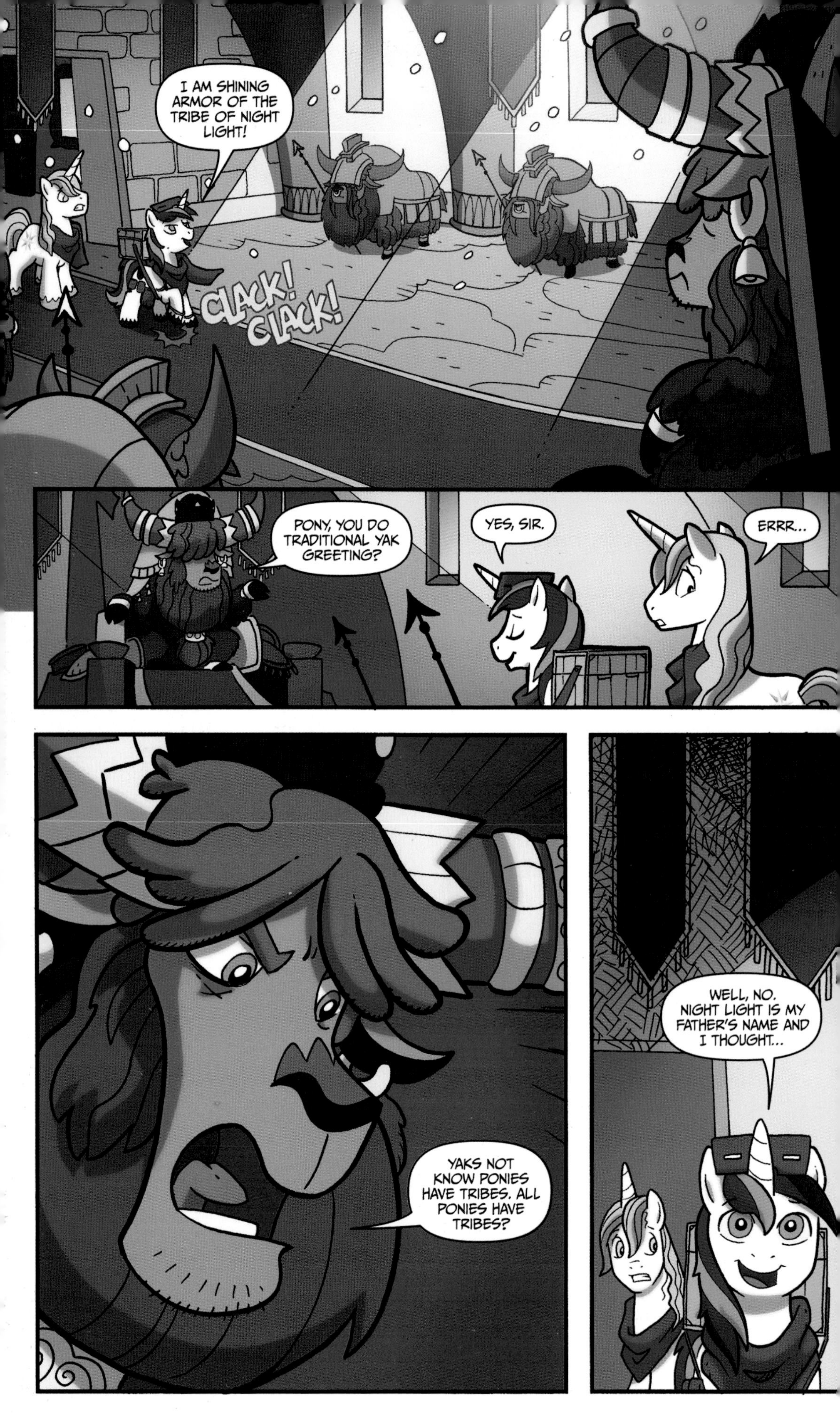
I AM SHINING ARMOR OF THE TRIBE OF NIGHT LIGHT!
CLACK! CLACK!
PONY, YOU DO TRADITIONAL YAK GREETING?
YES, SIR.
ERRR...
YAKS NOT KNOW PONIES HAVE TRIBES. ALL PONIES HAVE TRIBES?
WELL, NO. NIGHT LIGHT IS MY FATHER'S NAME AND I THOUGHT...

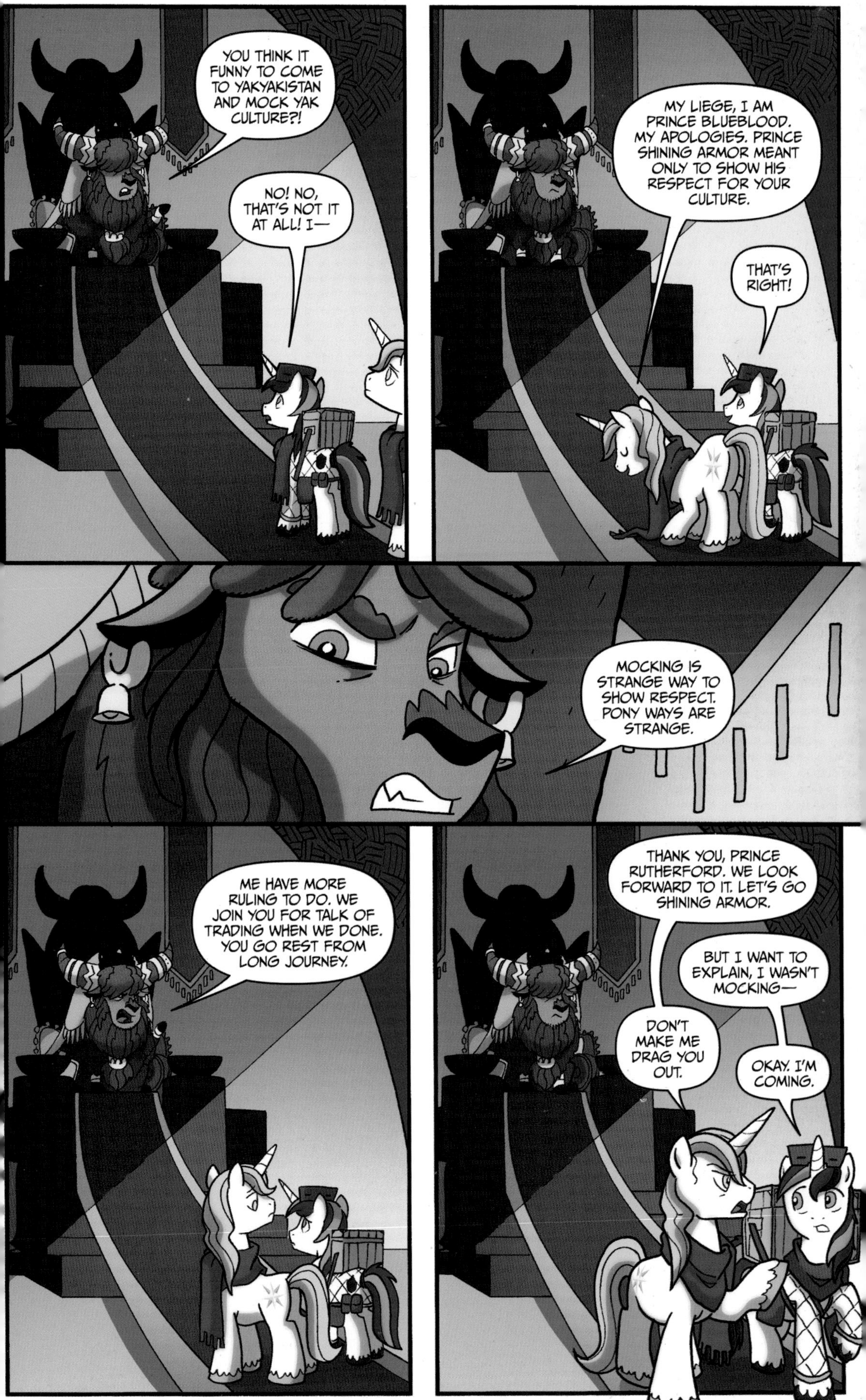
YOU THINK IT FUNNY TO COME TO YAKYAKISTAN AND MOCK YAK CULTURE?!
NO! NO, THAT'S NOT IT AT ALL! I—
MY LIEGE, I AM PRINCE BLUEBLOOD. MY APOLOGIES. PRINCE SHINING ARMOR MEANT ONLY TO SHOW HIS RESPECT FOR YOUR CULTURE.
THAT'S RIGHT!
MOCKING IS STRANGE WAY TO SHOW RESPECT. PONY WAYS ARE STRANGE.
ME HAVE MORE RULING TO DO. WE JOIN YOU FOR TALK OF TRADING WHEN WE DONE. YOU GO REST FROM LONG JOURNEY.
THANK YOU, PRINCE RUTHERFORD. WE LOOK FORWARD TO IT. LET'S GO SHINING ARMOR.
BUT I WANT TO EXPLAIN, I WASN'T MOCKING—
DON'T MAKE ME DRAG YOU OUT.
OKAY. I'M COMING.

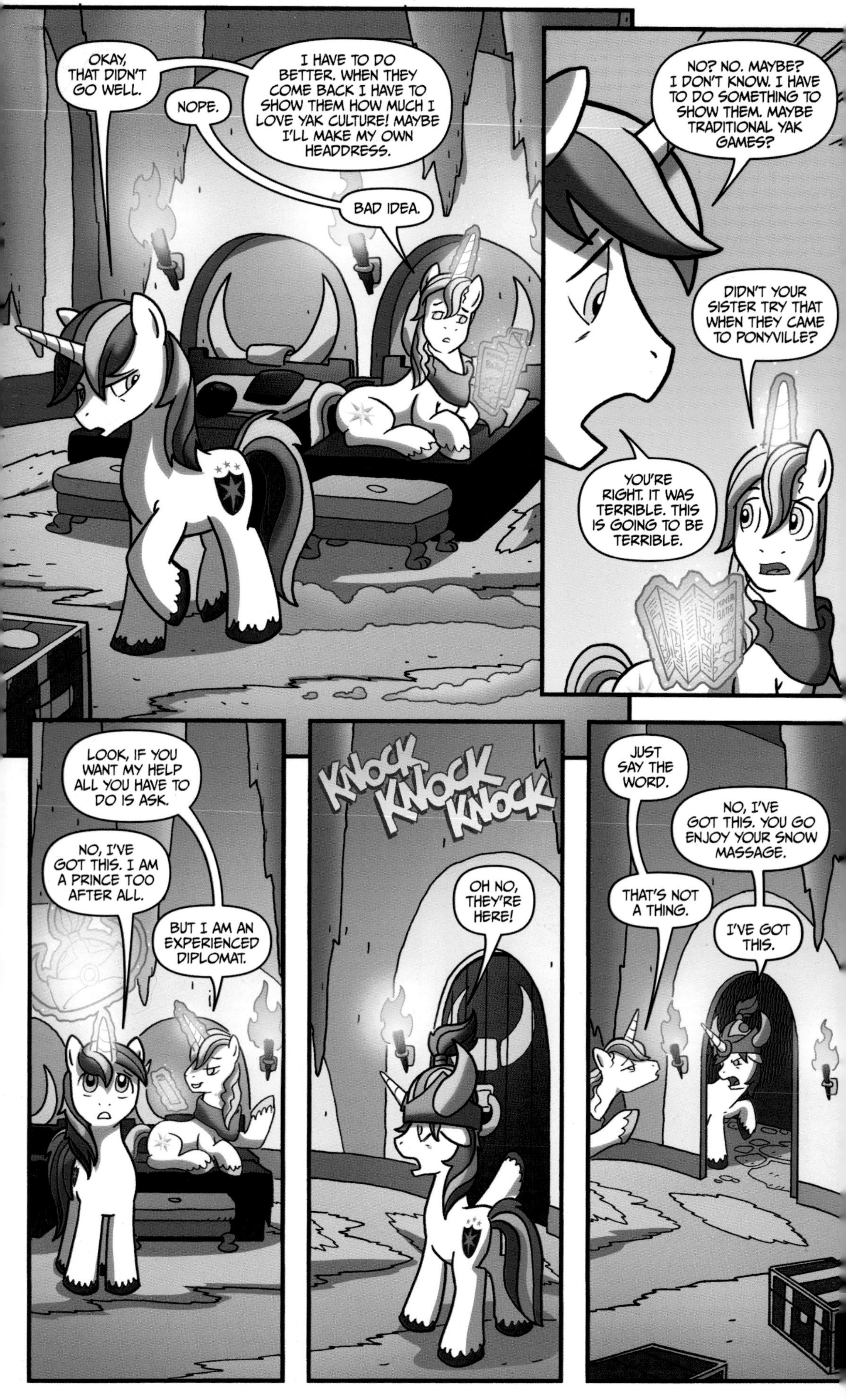
OKAY, THAT DIDN'T GO WELL.
NOPE.
I HAVE TO DO BETTER. WHEN THEY COME BACK I HAVE TO SHOW THEM HOW MUCH I LOVE YAK CULTURE! MAYBE I'LL MAKE MY OWN HEADDRESS.
BAD IDEA.
NO? NO. MAYBE? I DON'T KNOW. I HAVE TO DO SOMETHING TO SHOW THEM. MAYBE TRADITIONAL YAK GAMES?
DIDN'T YOUR SISTER TRY THAT WHEN THEY CAME TO PONYVILLE?
YOU'RE RIGHT. IT WAS TERRIBLE. THIS IS GOING TO BE TERRIBLE.
LOOK, IF YOU WANT MY HELP ALL YOU HAVE TO DO IS ASK.
NO, I'VE GOT THIS. I AM A PRINCE TOO AFTER ALL.
BUT I AM AN EXPERIENCED DIPLOMAT.
KNOCK KNOCK KNOCK
OH NO, THEY'RE HERE!
JUST SAY THE WORD.
NO, I'VE GOT THIS. YOU GO ENJOY YOUR SNOW MASSAGE.
THAT'S NOT A THING.
I'VE GOT THIS.

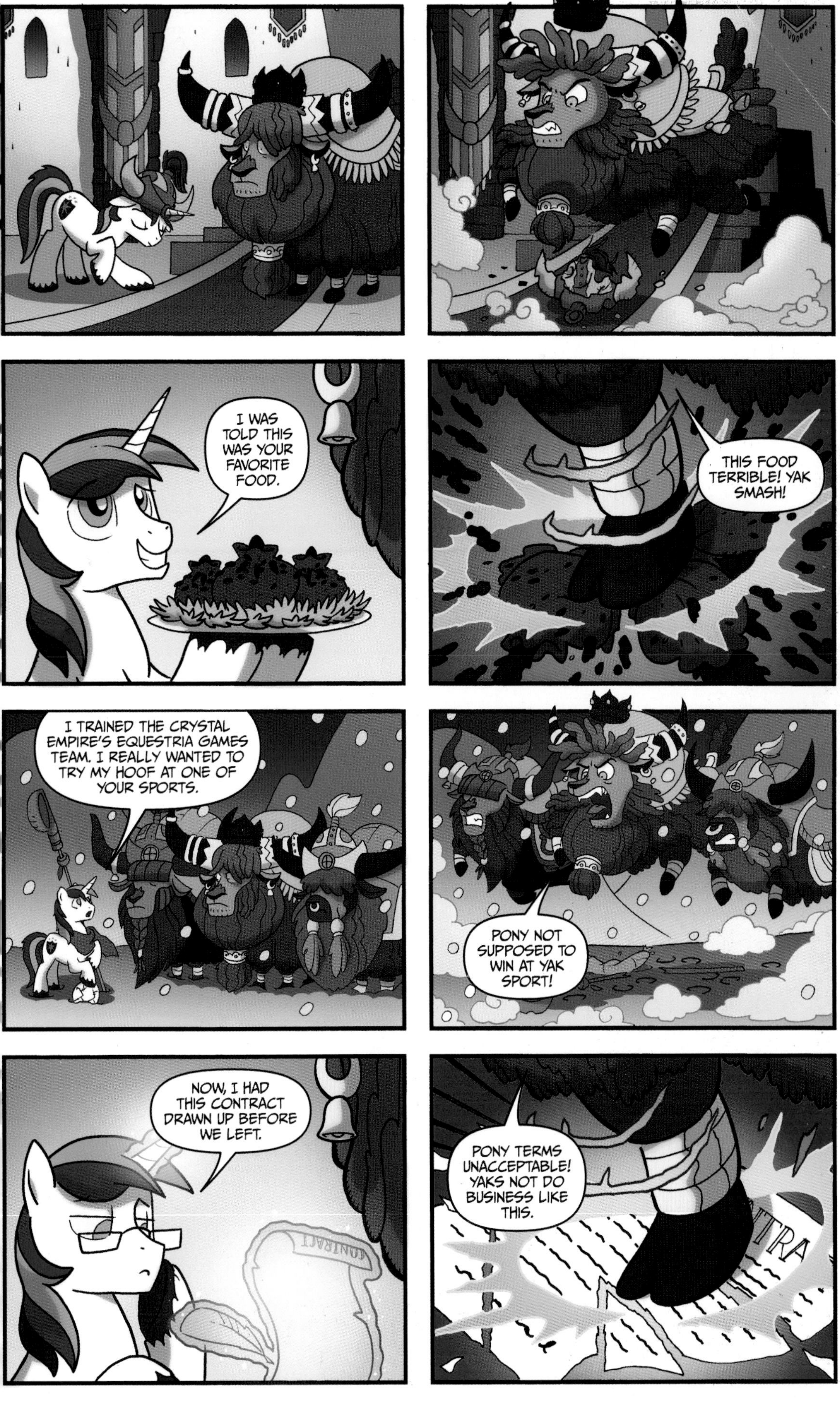
I WAS TOLD THIS WAS YOUR FAVORITE FOOD.
THIS FOOD TERRIBLE! YAK SMASH!
I TRAINED THE CRYSTAL EMPIRE'S EQUESTRIA GAMES TEAM. I REALLY WANTED TO TRY MY HOOF AT ONE OF YOUR SPORTS.
PONY NOT SUPPOSED TO WIN AT YAK SPORT!
NOW, I HAD THIS CONTRACT DRAWN UP BEFORE WE LEFT.
PONY TERMS UNACCEPTABLE! YAKS NOT DO BUSINESS LIKE THIS.

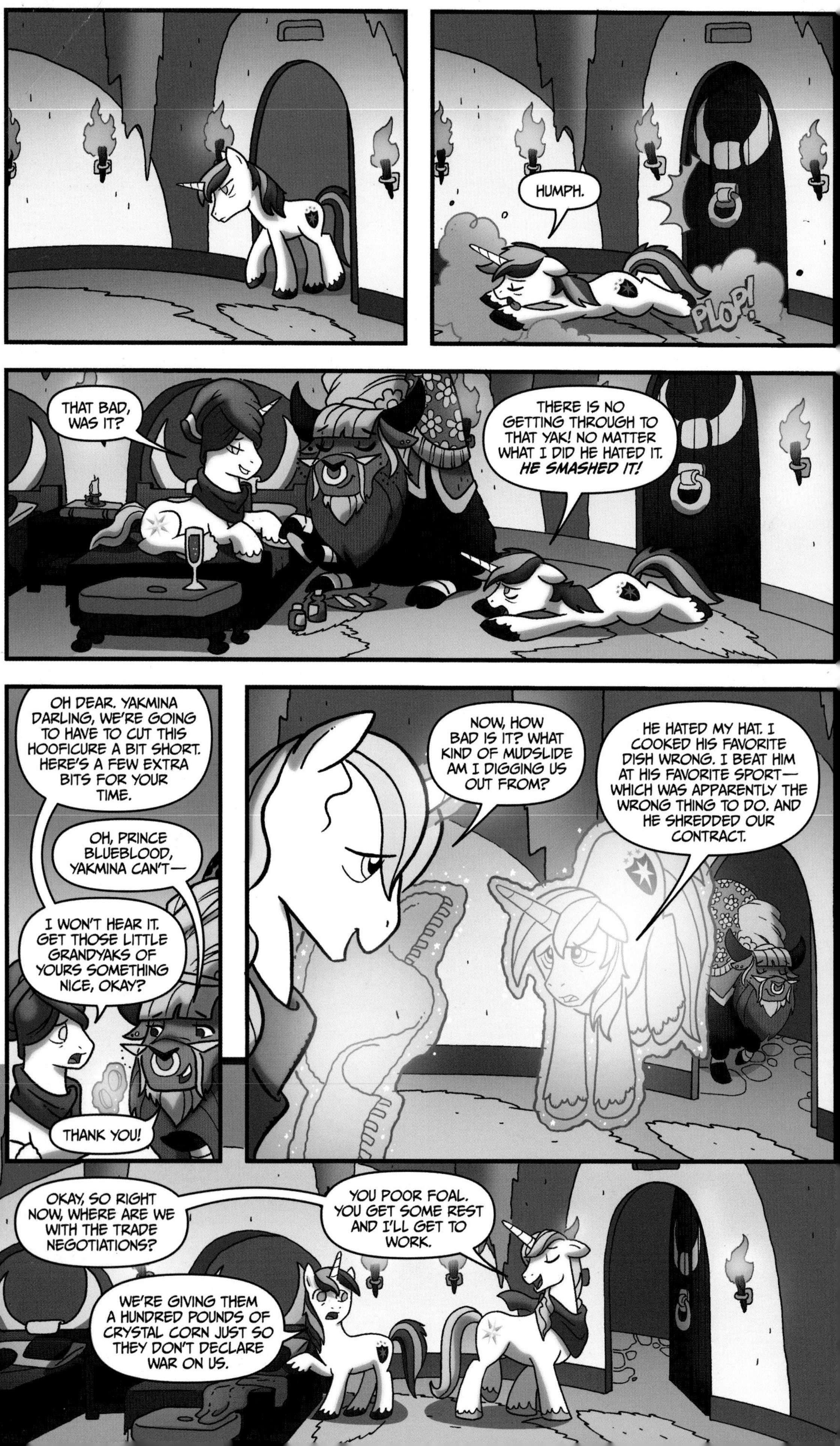
HUMPH.
PLOP!
THAT BAD, WAS IT?
THERE IS NO GETTING THROUGH TO THAT YAK! NO MATTER WHAT I DID HE HATED IT. *HE SMASHED IT!*
OH DEAR. YAKMINA DARLING, WE'RE GOING TO HAVE TO CUT THIS HOOFICURE A BIT SHORT. HERE'S A FEW EXTRA BITS FOR YOUR TIME.
OH, PRINCE BLUEBLOOD, YAKMINA CAN'T—
I WON'T HEAR IT. GET THOSE LITTLE GRANDYAKS OF YOURS SOMETHING NICE, OKAY?
THANK YOU!
NOW, HOW BAD IS IT? WHAT KIND OF MUDSLIDE AM I DIGGING US OUT FROM?
HE HATED MY HAT. I COOKED HIS FAVORITE DISH WRONG. I BEAT HIM AT HIS FAVORITE SPORT—WHICH WAS APPARENTLY THE WRONG THING TO DO. AND HE SHREDDED OUR CONTRACT.
YOU POOR FOAL. YOU GET SOME REST AND I'LL GET TO WORK.
OKAY, SO RIGHT NOW, WHERE ARE WE WITH THE TRADE NEGOTIATIONS?
WE'RE GIVING THEM A HUNDRED POUNDS OF CRYSTAL CORN JUST SO THEY DON'T DECLARE WAR ON US.

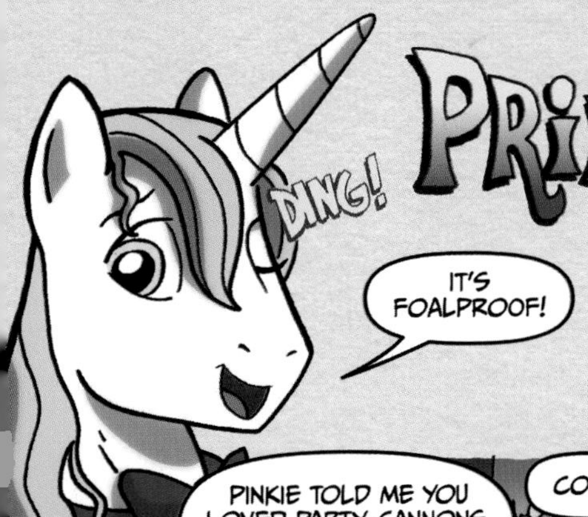
DING!
IT'S FOALPROOF!

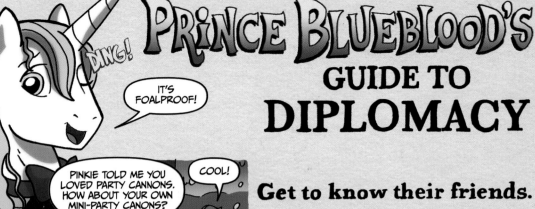

PRINCE BLUEBLOOD'S GUIDE TO DIPLOMACY

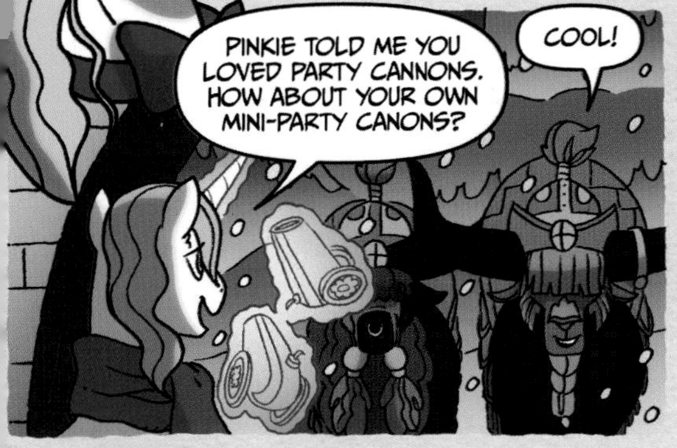
PINKIE TOLD ME YOU LOVED PARTY CANNONS. HOW ABOUT YOUR OWN MINI-PARTY CANONS?
COOL!

Get to know their friends.

Winning over a diplomat's friends means they're hearing good things about you when you're not around.

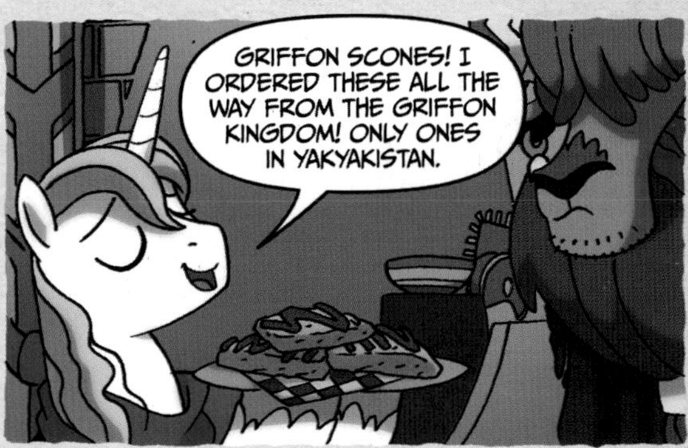
GRIFFON SCONES! I ORDERED THESE ALL THE WAY FROM THE GRIFFON KINGDOM! ONLY ONES IN YAKYAKISTAN.

Bring food.

But don't bring their food and don't claim it's the best. Make it something they'll be curious about.

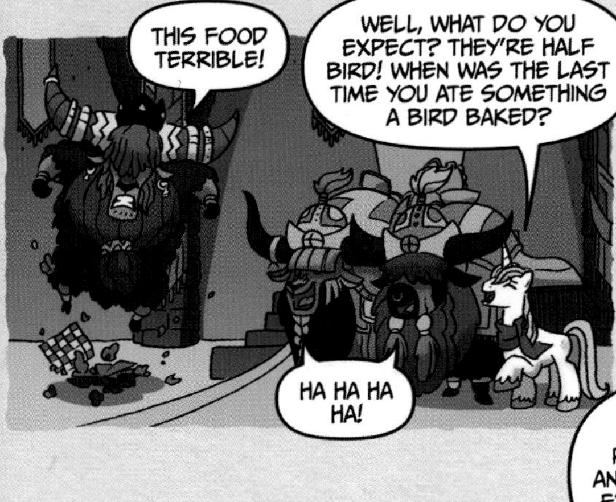
THIS FOOD TERRIBLE!
WELL, WHAT DO YOU EXPECT? THEY'RE HALF BIRD! WHEN WAS THE LAST TIME YOU ATE SOMETHING A BIRD BAKED?
HA HA HA HA!

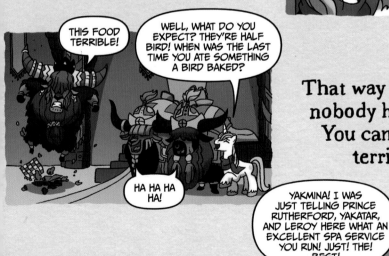

That way if they hate them, nobody has to be insulted. You can bond over how terrible they are.

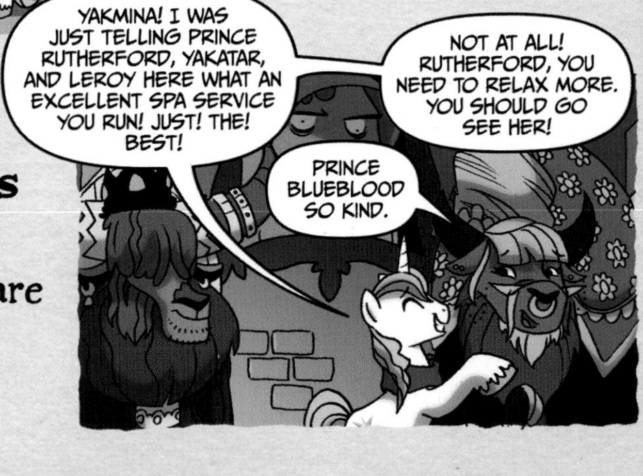
YAKMINA! I WAS JUST TELLING PRINCE RUTHERFORD, YAKATAR, AND LEROY HERE WHAT AN EXCELLENT SPA SERVICE YOU RUN! JUST! THE! BEST!
NOT AT ALL! RUTHERFORD, YOU NEED TO RELAX MORE. YOU SHOULD GO SEE HER!
PRINCE BLUEBLOOD SO KIND.

Remember everypony's name all the time.

It shows ponies that you care (even if you don't).

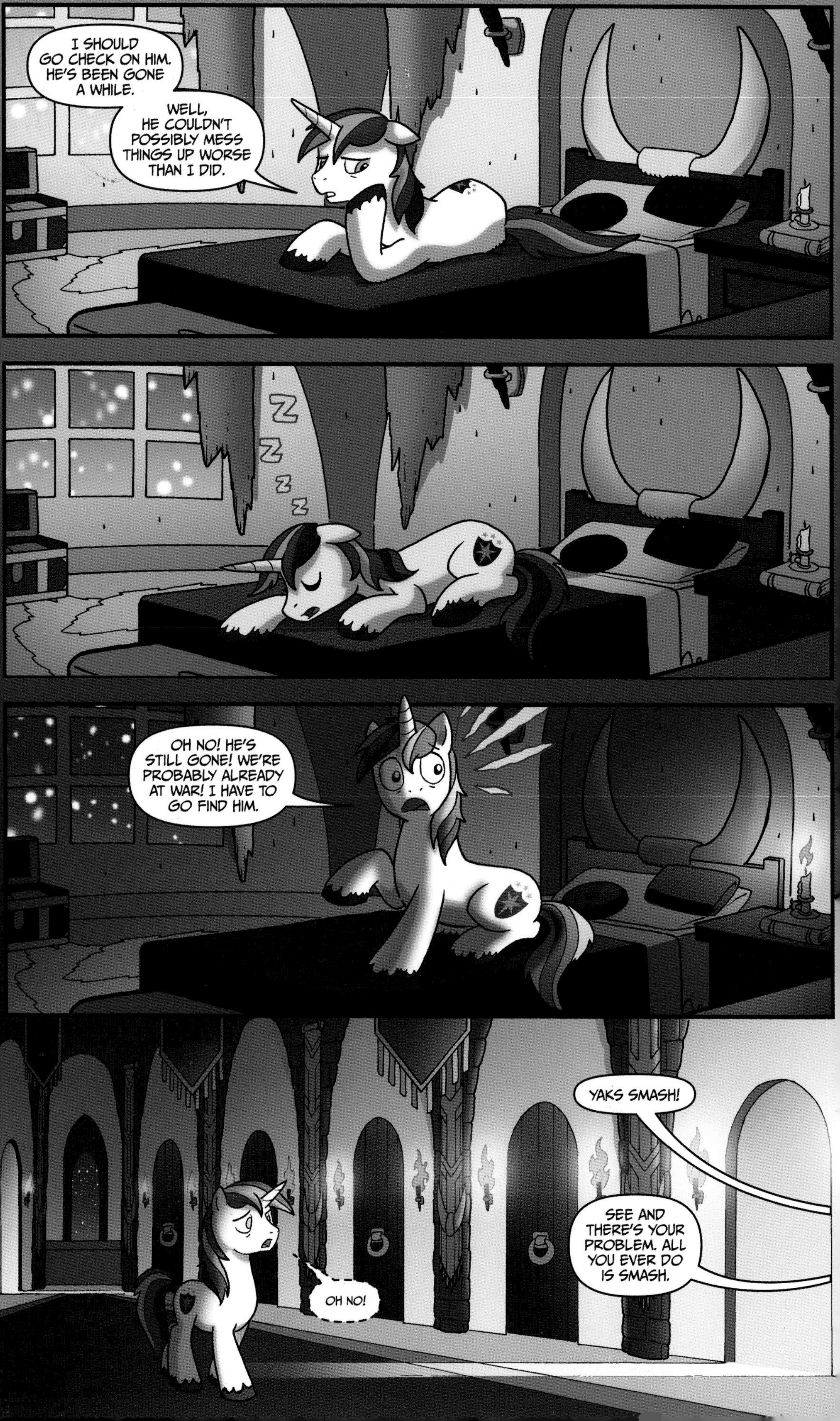
I SHOULD GO CHECK ON HIM. HE'S BEEN GONE A WHILE.
WELL, HE COULDN'T POSSIBLY MESS THINGS UP WORSE THAN I DID.
Z Z Z Z
OH NO! HE'S STILL GONE! WE'RE PROBABLY ALREADY AT WAR! I HAVE TO GO FIND HIM.
YAKS SMASH!
SEE AND THERE'S YOUR PROBLEM. ALL YOU EVER DO IS SMASH.
OH NO!

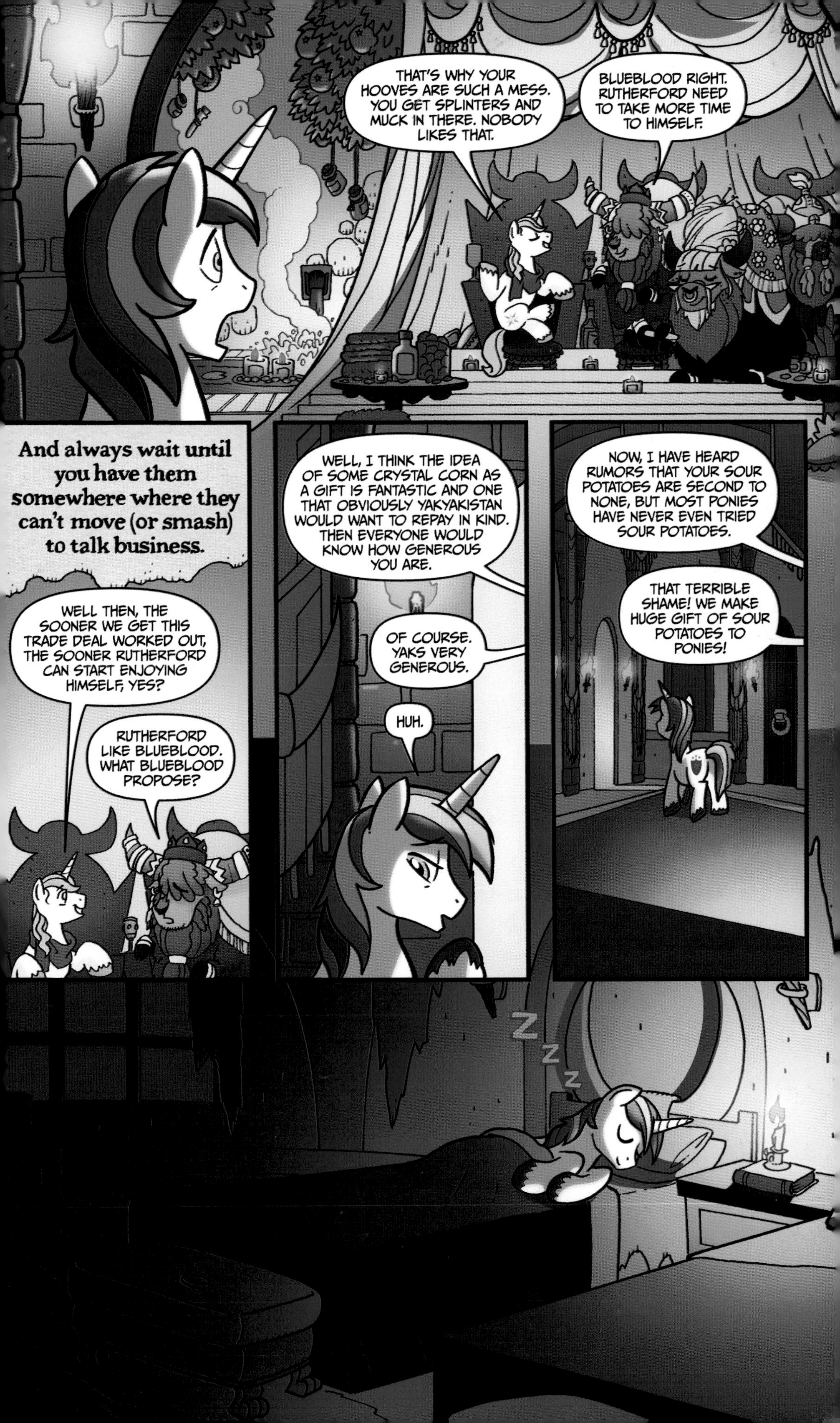
THAT'S WHY YOUR HOOVES ARE SUCH A MESS. YOU GET SPLINTERS AND MUCK IN THERE. NOBODY LIKES THAT.
BLUEBLOOD RIGHT. RUTHERFORD NEED TO TAKE MORE TIME TO HIMSELF.
And always wait until you have them somewhere where they can't move (or smash) to talk business.
WELL THEN, THE SOONER WE GET THIS TRADE DEAL WORKED OUT, THE SOONER RUTHERFORD CAN START ENJOYING HIMSELF, YES?
RUTHERFORD LIKE BLUEBLOOD. WHAT BLUEBLOOD PROPOSE?
WELL, I THINK THE IDEA OF SOME CRYSTAL CORN AS A GIFT IS FANTASTIC AND ONE THAT OBVIOUSLY YAKYAKISTAN WOULD WANT TO REPAY IN KIND. THEN EVERYONE WOULD KNOW HOW GENEROUS YOU ARE.
OF COURSE. YAKS VERY GENEROUS.
HUH.
NOW, I HAVE HEARD RUMORS THAT YOUR SOUR POTATOES ARE SECOND TO NONE, BUT MOST PONIES HAVE NEVER EVEN TRIED SOUR POTATOES.
THAT TERRIBLE SHAME! WE MAKE HUGE GIFT OF SOUR POTATOES TO PONIES!
Z Z Z

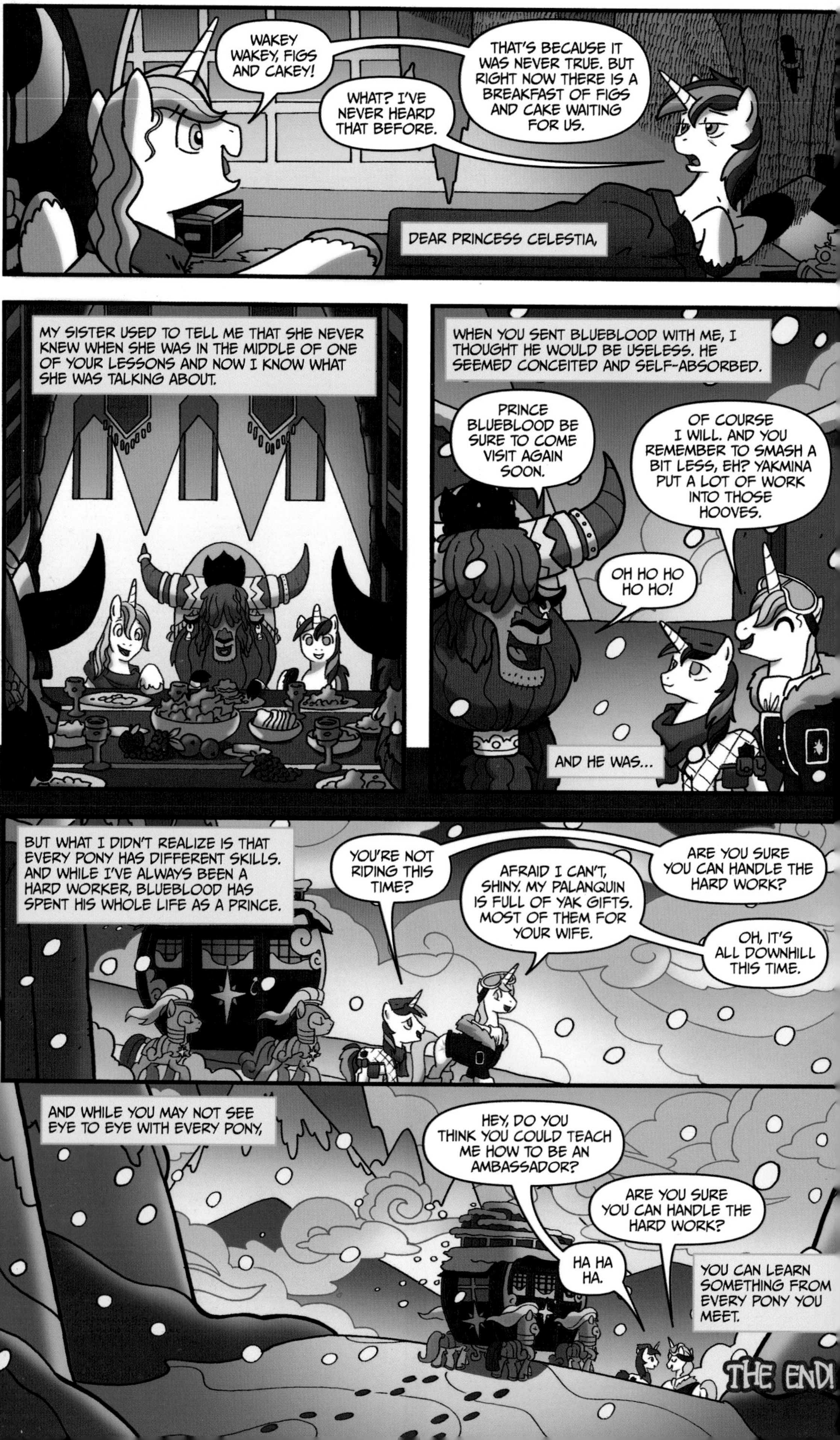
WAKEY WAKEY, FIGS AND CAKEY!
WHAT? I'VE NEVER HEARD THAT BEFORE.
THAT'S BECAUSE IT WAS NEVER TRUE. BUT RIGHT NOW THERE IS A BREAKFAST OF FIGS AND CAKE WAITING FOR US.
DEAR PRINCESS CELESTIA,
MY SISTER USED TO TELL ME THAT SHE NEVER KNEW WHEN SHE WAS IN THE MIDDLE OF ONE OF YOUR LESSONS AND NOW I KNOW WHAT SHE WAS TALKING ABOUT.
WHEN YOU SENT BLUEBLOOD WITH ME, I THOUGHT HE WOULD BE USELESS. HE SEEMED CONCEITED AND SELF-ABSORBED.
PRINCE BLUEBLOOD BE SURE TO COME VISIT AGAIN SOON.
OF COURSE I WILL. AND YOU REMEMBER TO SMASH A BIT LESS, EH? YAKMINA PUT A LOT OF WORK INTO THOSE HOOVES.
OH HO HO HO HO!
AND HE WAS...
BUT WHAT I DIDN'T REALIZE IS THAT EVERY PONY HAS DIFFERENT SKILLS. AND WHILE I'VE ALWAYS BEEN A HARD WORKER, BLUEBLOOD HAS SPENT HIS WHOLE LIFE AS A PRINCE.
YOU'RE NOT RIDING THIS TIME?
AFRAID I CAN'T, SHINY. MY PALANQUIN IS FULL OF YAK GIFTS. MOST OF THEM FOR YOUR WIFE.
ARE YOU SURE YOU CAN HANDLE THE HARD WORK?
OH, IT'S ALL DOWNHILL THIS TIME.
AND WHILE YOU MAY NOT SEE EYE TO EYE WITH EVERY PONY,
HEY, DO YOU THINK YOU COULD TEACH ME HOW TO BE AN AMBASSADOR?
ARE YOU SURE YOU CAN HANDLE THE HARD WORK?
HA HA HA.
YOU CAN LEARN SOMETHING FROM EVERY PONY YOU MEET.
THE END!

my LITTLE PONY

FRIENDS FOREVER

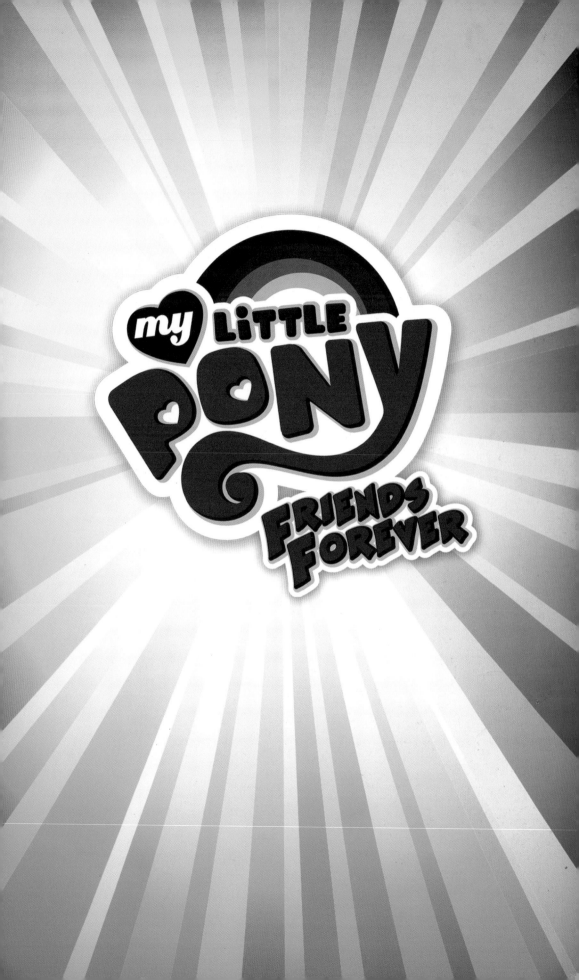

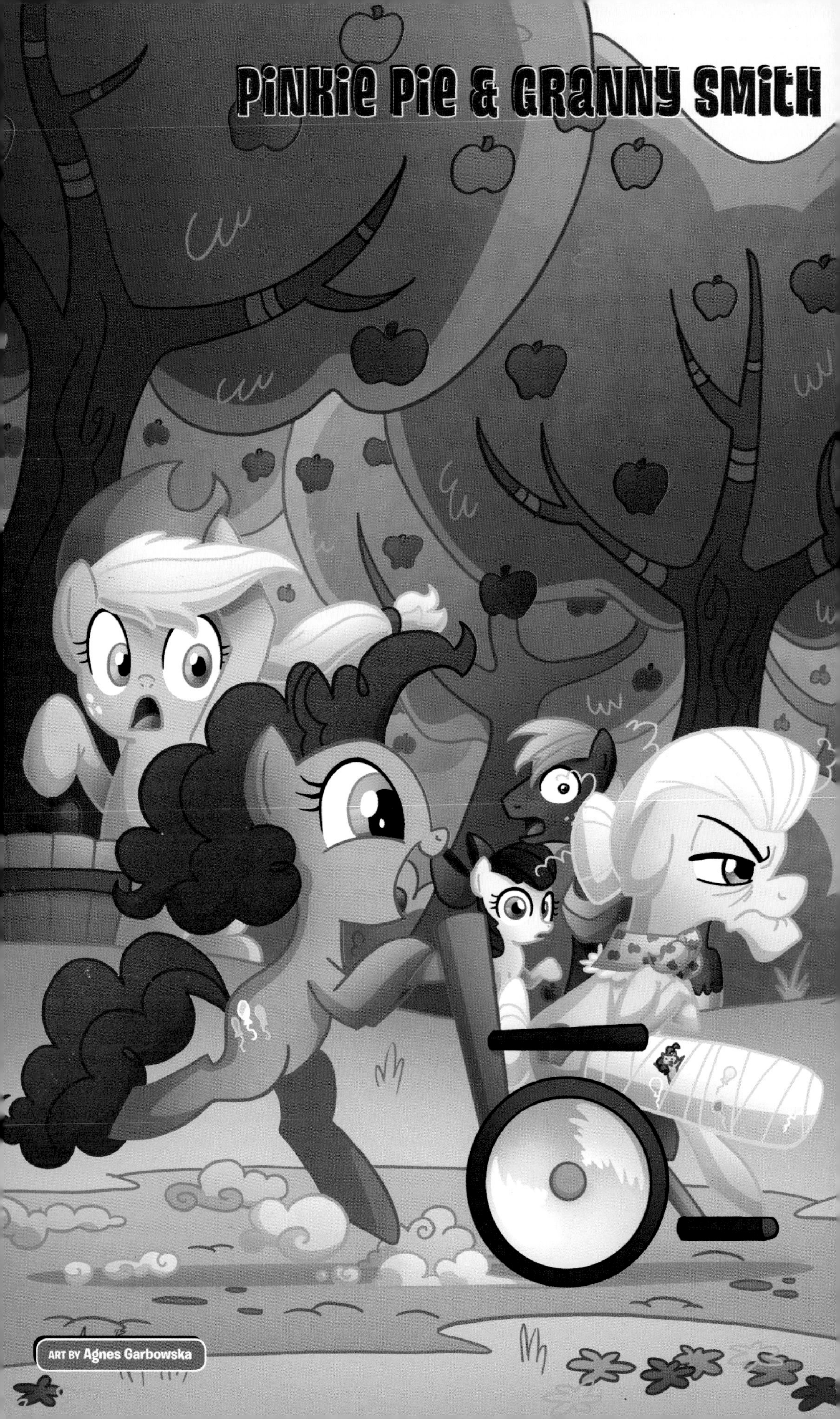
Pinkie Pie & Granny Smith
ART BY Agnes Garbowska

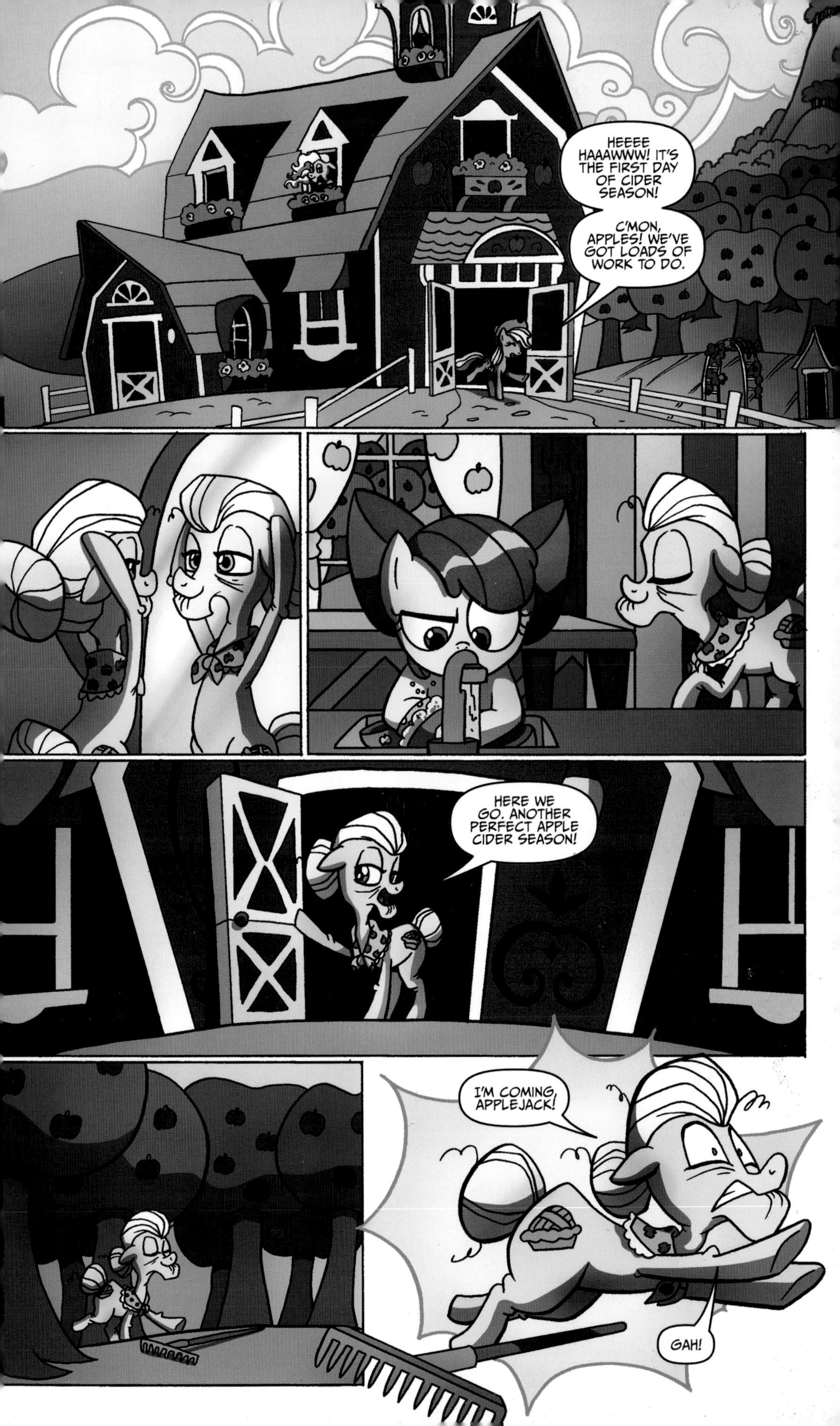
HEEEE HAAAWWW! IT'S THE FIRST DAY OF CIDER SEASON!
C'MON, APPLES! WE'VE GOT LOADS OF WORK TO DO.
HERE WE GO. ANOTHER PERFECT APPLE CIDER SEASON!
I'M COMING, APPLEJACK!
GAH!

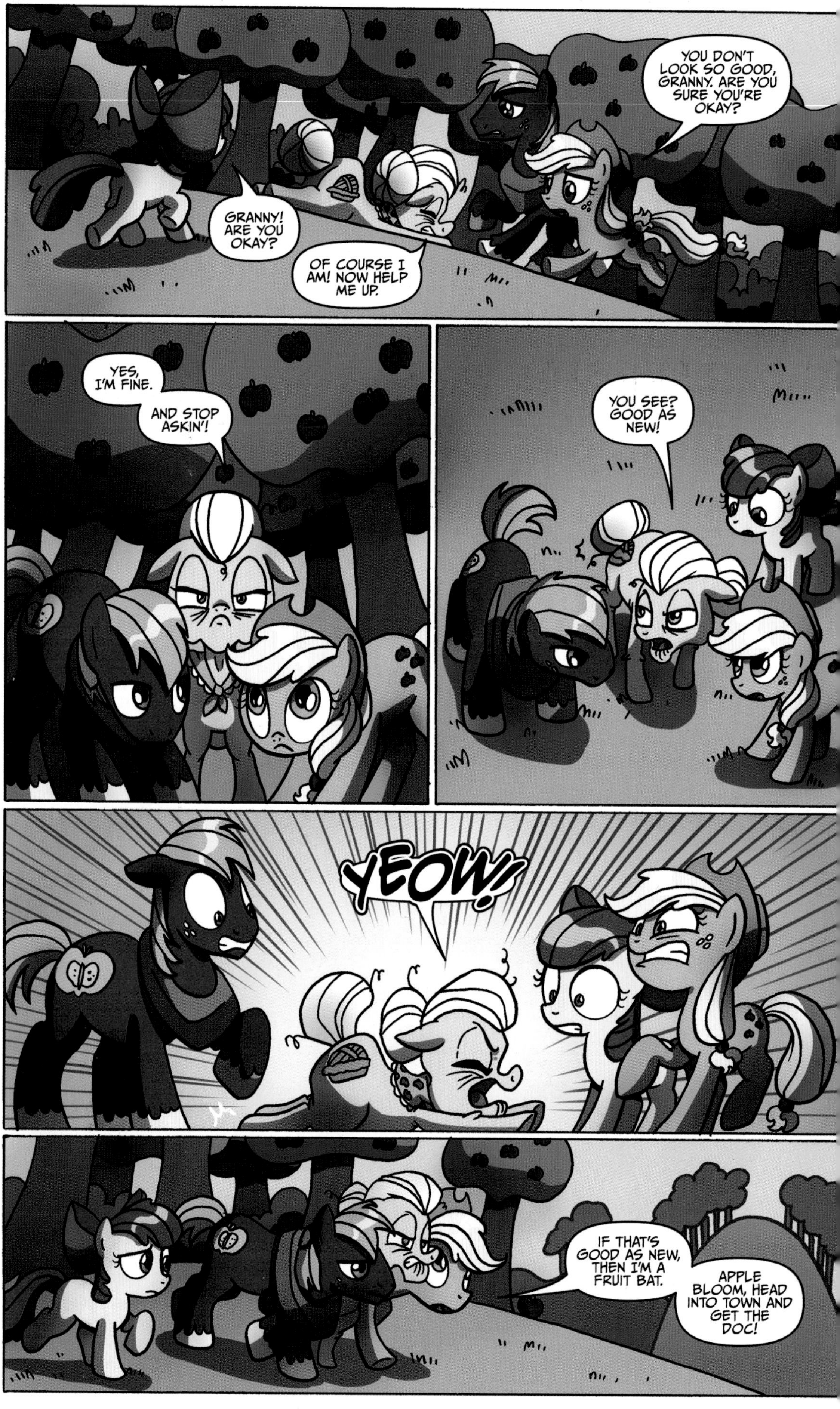
YOU DON'T LOOK SO GOOD, GRANNY. ARE YOU SURE YOU'RE OKAY?
GRANNY! ARE YOU OKAY?
OF COURSE I AM! NOW HELP ME UP.
YES, I'M FINE.
AND STOP ASKIN'!
YOU SEE? GOOD AS NEW!
YEOW!
IF THAT'S GOOD AS NEW, THEN I'M A FRUIT BAT.
APPLE BLOOM, HEAD INTO TOWN AND GET THE DOC!

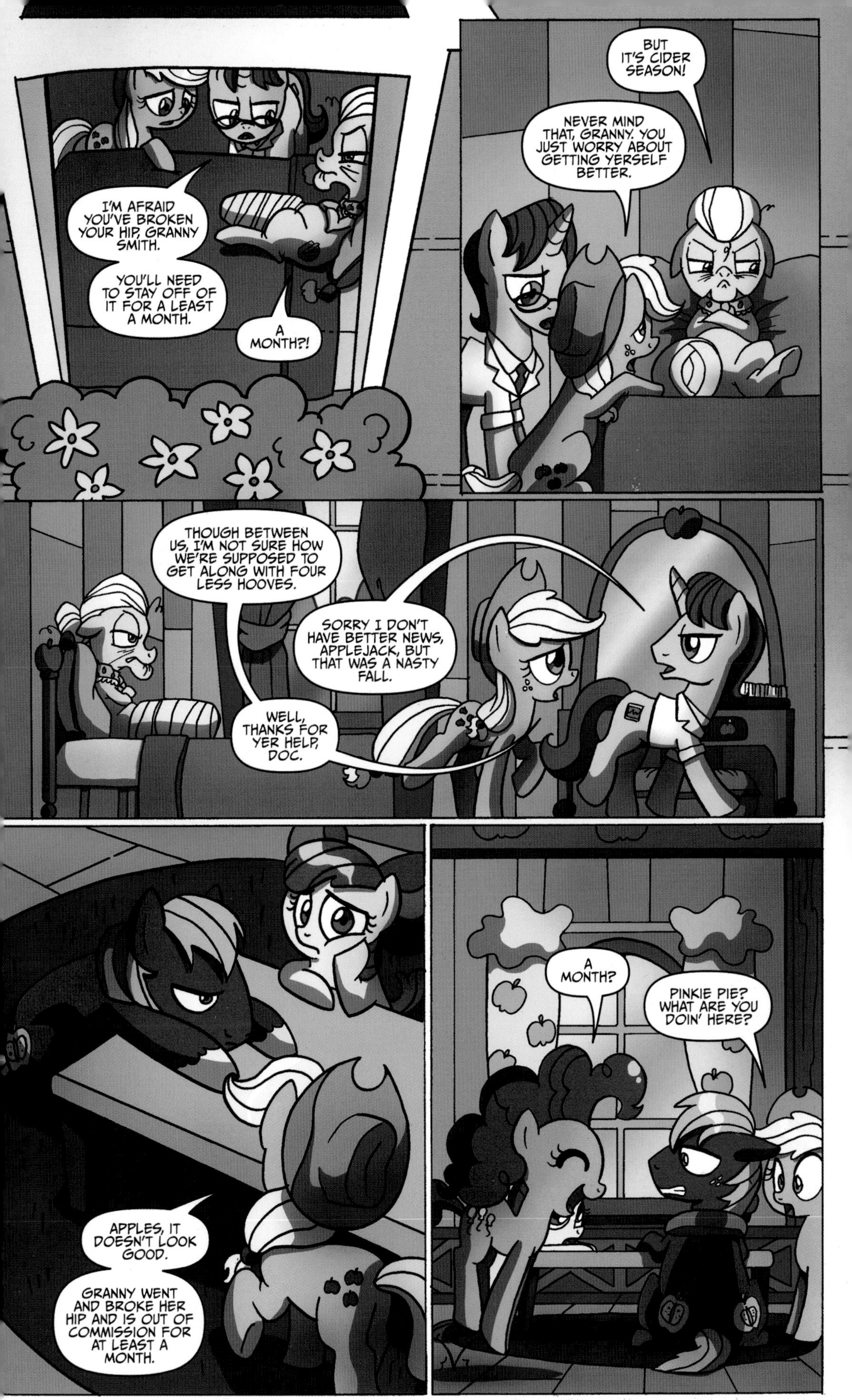
I'M AFRAID YOU'VE BROKEN YOUR HIP, GRANNY SMITH.
YOU'LL NEED TO STAY OFF OF IT FOR A LEAST A MONTH.
A MONTH?!
BUT IT'S CIDER SEASON!
NEVER MIND THAT, GRANNY. YOU JUST WORRY ABOUT GETTING YERSELF BETTER.
THOUGH BETWEEN US, I'M NOT SURE HOW WE'RE SUPPOSED TO GET ALONG WITH FOUR LESS HOOVES.
SORRY I DON'T HAVE BETTER NEWS, APPLEJACK, BUT THAT WAS A NASTY FALL.
WELL, THANKS FOR YER HELP, DOC.
APPLES, IT DOESN'T LOOK GOOD.
GRANNY WENT AND BROKE HER HIP AND IS OUT OF COMMISSION FOR AT LEAST A MONTH.
A MONTH?
PINKIE PIE? WHAT ARE YOU DOIN' HERE?

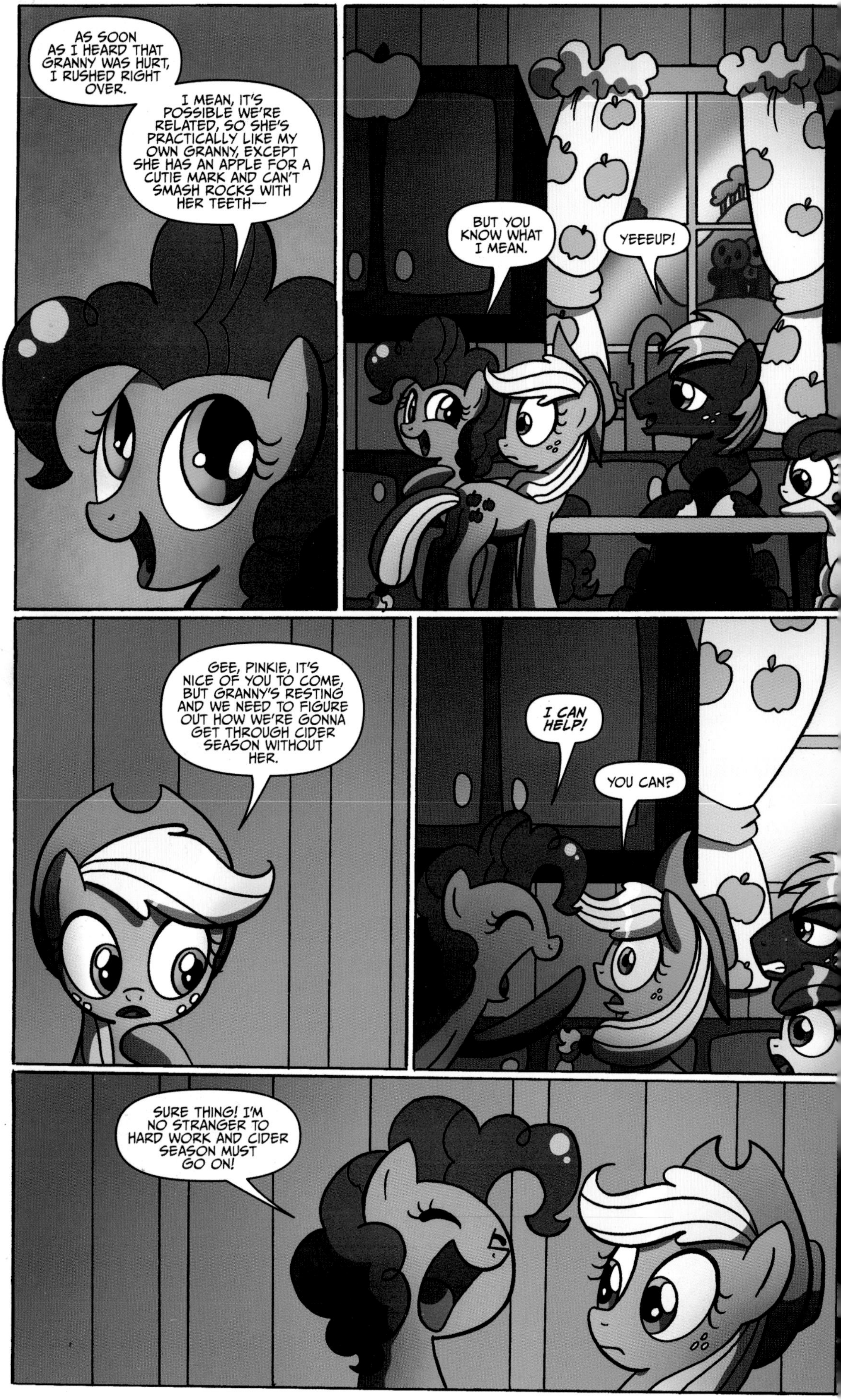
AS SOON AS I HEARD THAT GRANNY WAS HURT, I RUSHED RIGHT OVER.
I MEAN, IT'S POSSIBLE WE'RE RELATED, SO SHE'S PRACTICALLY LIKE MY OWN GRANNY, EXCEPT SHE HAS AN APPLE FOR A CUTIE MARK AND CAN'T SMASH ROCKS WITH HER TEETH—
BUT YOU KNOW WHAT I MEAN.
YEEEUP!
GEE, PINKIE, IT'S NICE OF YOU TO COME, BUT GRANNY'S RESTING AND WE NEED TO FIGURE OUT HOW WE'RE GONNA GET THROUGH CIDER SEASON WITHOUT HER.
I CAN HELP!
YOU CAN?
SURE THING! I'M NO STRANGER TO HARD WORK AND CIDER SEASON MUST GO ON!

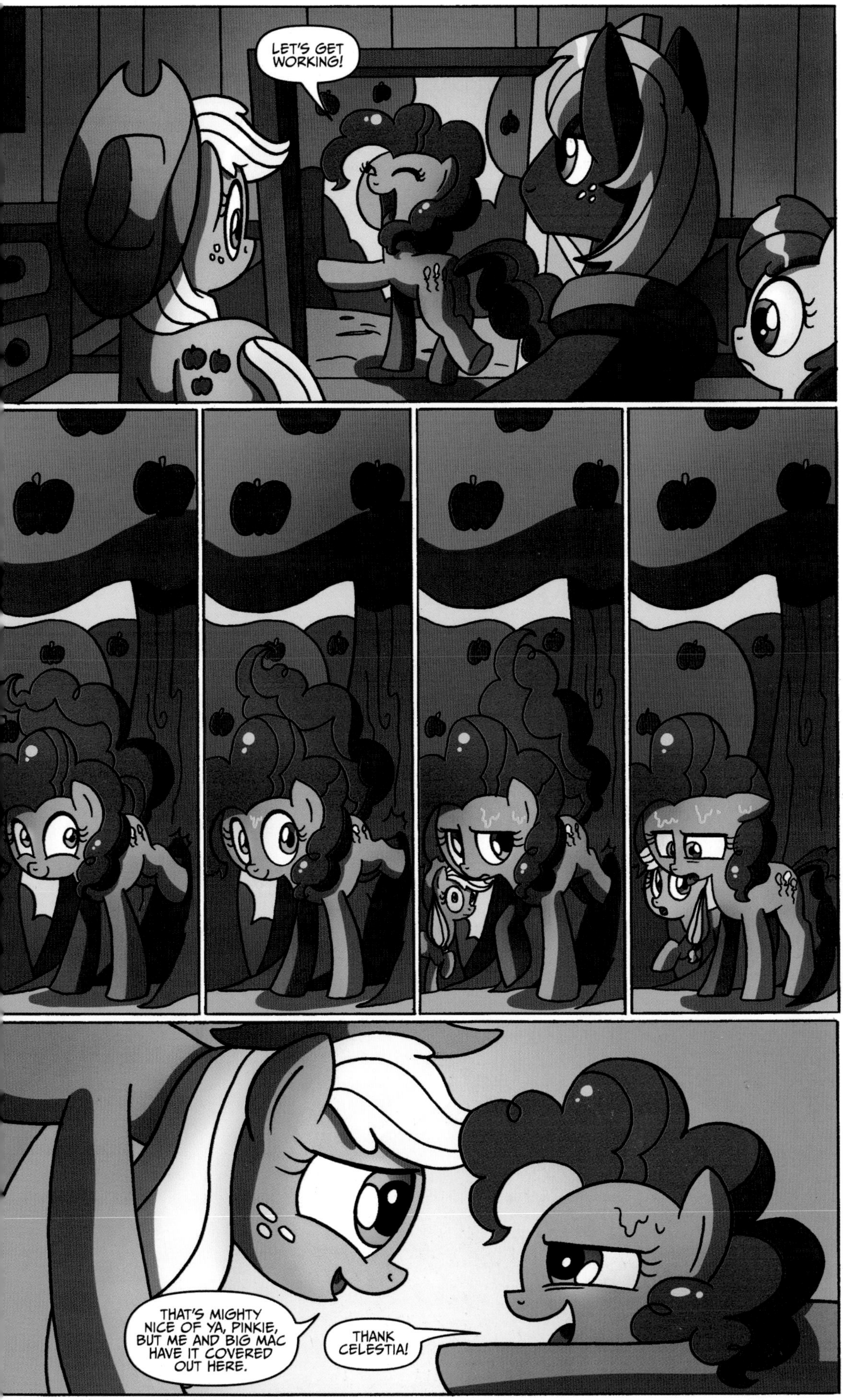

LET'S GET WORKING!
THAT'S MIGHTY NICE OF YA, PINKIE, BUT ME AND BIG MAC HAVE IT COVERED OUT HERE.
THANK CELESTIA!

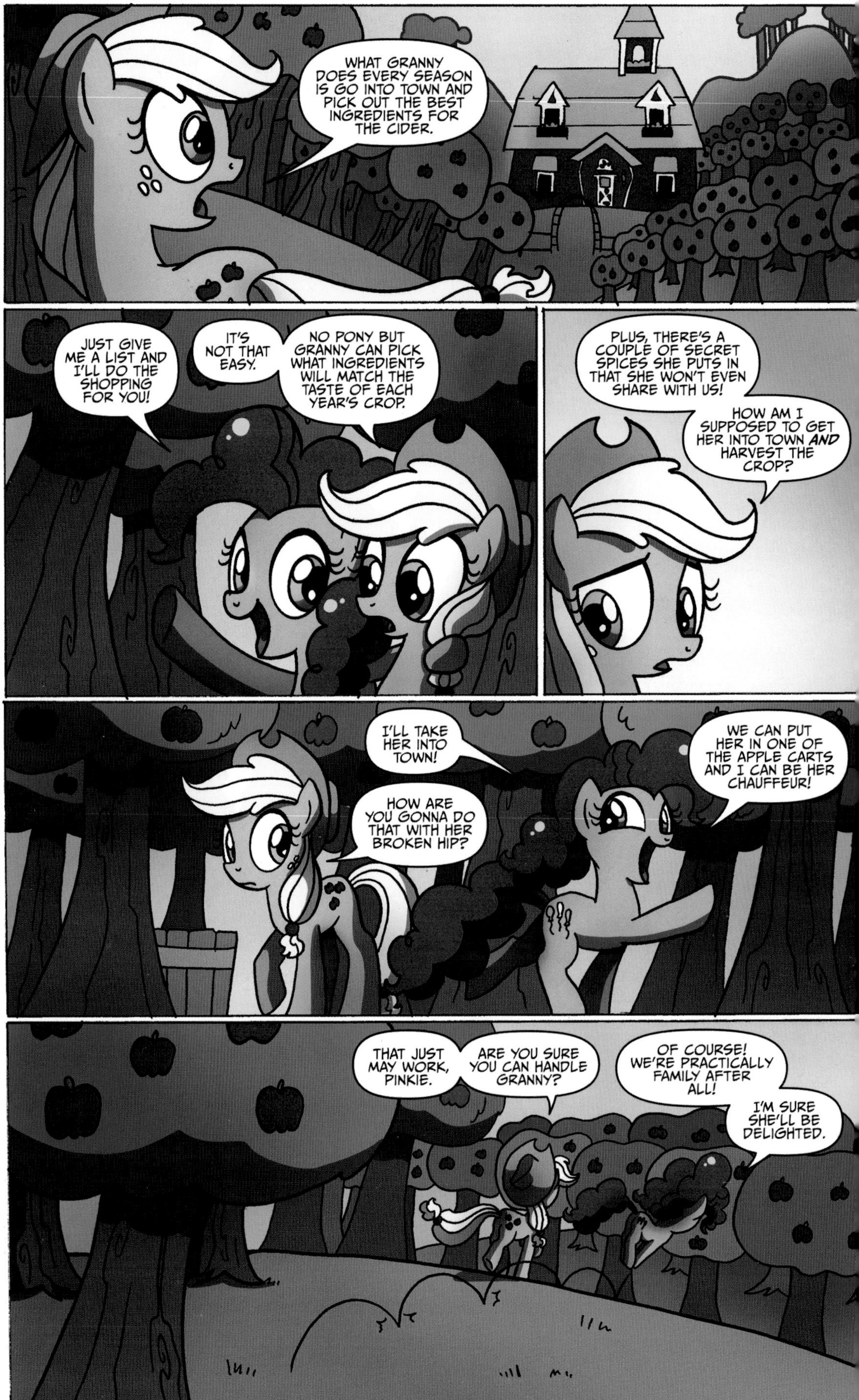
WHAT GRANNY DOES EVERY SEASON IS GO INTO TOWN AND PICK OUT THE BEST INGREDIENTS FOR THE CIDER.
JUST GIVE ME A LIST AND I'LL DO THE SHOPPING FOR YOU!
IT'S NOT THAT EASY.
NO PONY BUT GRANNY CAN PICK WHAT INGREDIENTS WILL MATCH THE TASTE OF EACH YEAR'S CROP.
PLUS, THERE'S A COUPLE OF SECRET SPICES SHE PUTS IN THAT SHE WON'T EVEN SHARE WITH US!
HOW AM I SUPPOSED TO GET HER INTO TOWN AND HARVEST THE CROP?
I'LL TAKE HER INTO TOWN!
HOW ARE YOU GONNA DO THAT WITH HER BROKEN HIP?
WE CAN PUT HER IN ONE OF THE APPLE CARTS AND I CAN BE HER CHAUFFEUR!
THAT JUST MAY WORK, PINKIE.
ARE YOU SURE YOU CAN HANDLE GRANNY?
OF COURSE! WE'RE PRACTICALLY FAMILY AFTER ALL!
I'M SURE SHE'LL BE DELIGHTED.

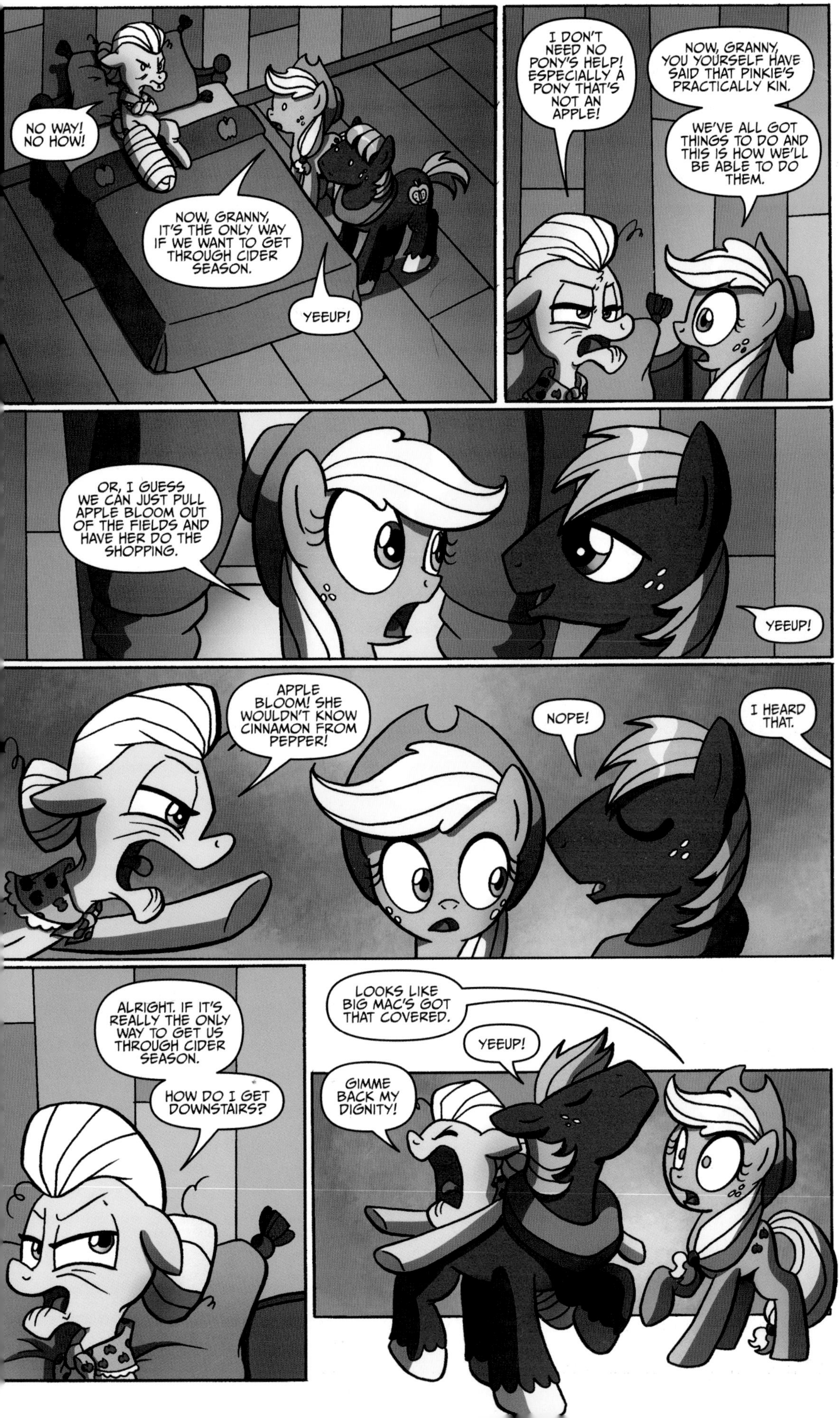
NO WAY! NO HOW!
NOW, GRANNY, IT'S THE ONLY WAY IF WE WANT TO GET THROUGH CIDER SEASON.
YEEUP!
I DON'T NEED NO PONY'S HELP! ESPECIALLY A PONY THAT'S NOT AN APPLE!
NOW, GRANNY, YOU YOURSELF HAVE SAID THAT PINKIE'S PRACTICALLY KIN.
WE'VE ALL GOT THINGS TO DO AND THIS IS HOW WE'LL BE ABLE TO DO THEM.
OR, I GUESS WE CAN JUST PULL APPLE BLOOM OUT OF THE FIELDS AND HAVE HER DO THE SHOPPING.
YEEUP!
APPLE BLOOM! SHE WOULDN'T KNOW CINNAMON FROM PEPPER!
NOPE!
I HEARD THAT.
ALRIGHT. IF IT'S REALLY THE ONLY WAY TO GET US THROUGH CIDER SEASON.
HOW DO I GET DOWNSTAIRS?
LOOKS LIKE BIG MAC'S GOT THAT COVERED.
YEEUP!
GIMME BACK MY DIGNITY!

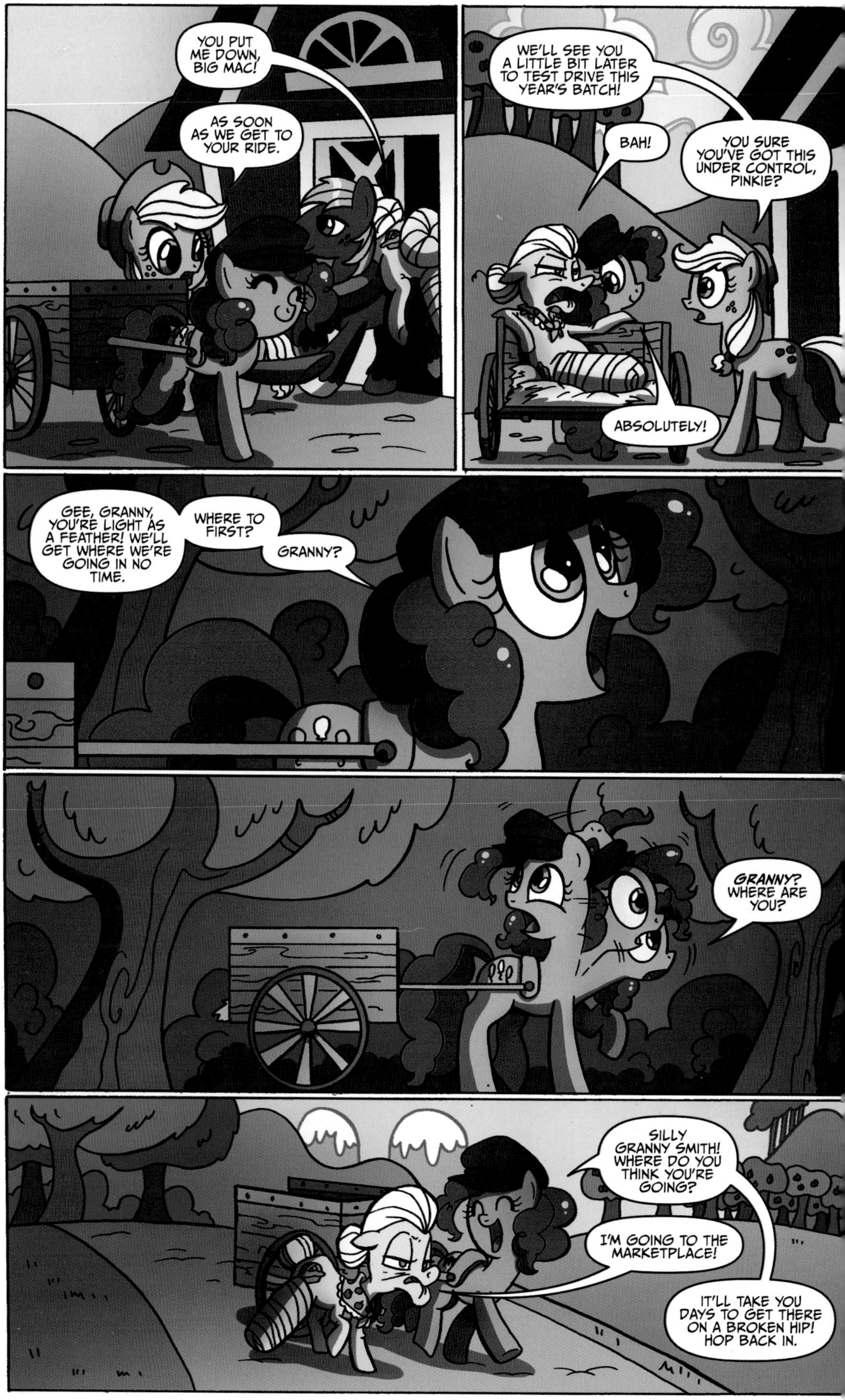
YOU PUT ME DOWN, BIG MAC!
AS SOON AS WE GET TO YOUR RIDE.
WE'LL SEE YOU A LITTLE BIT LATER TO TEST DRIVE THIS YEAR'S BATCH!
BAH!
YOU SURE YOU'VE GOT THIS UNDER CONTROL, PINKIE?
ABSOLUTELY!
GEE, GRANNY, YOU'RE LIGHT AS A FEATHER! WE'LL GET WHERE WE'RE GOING IN NO TIME.
WHERE TO FIRST?
GRANNY?
GRANNY? WHERE ARE YOU?
SILLY GRANNY SMITH! WHERE DO YOU THINK YOU'RE GOING?
I'M GOING TO THE MARKETPLACE!
IT'LL TAKE YOU DAYS TO GET THERE ON A BROKEN HIP! HOP BACK IN.

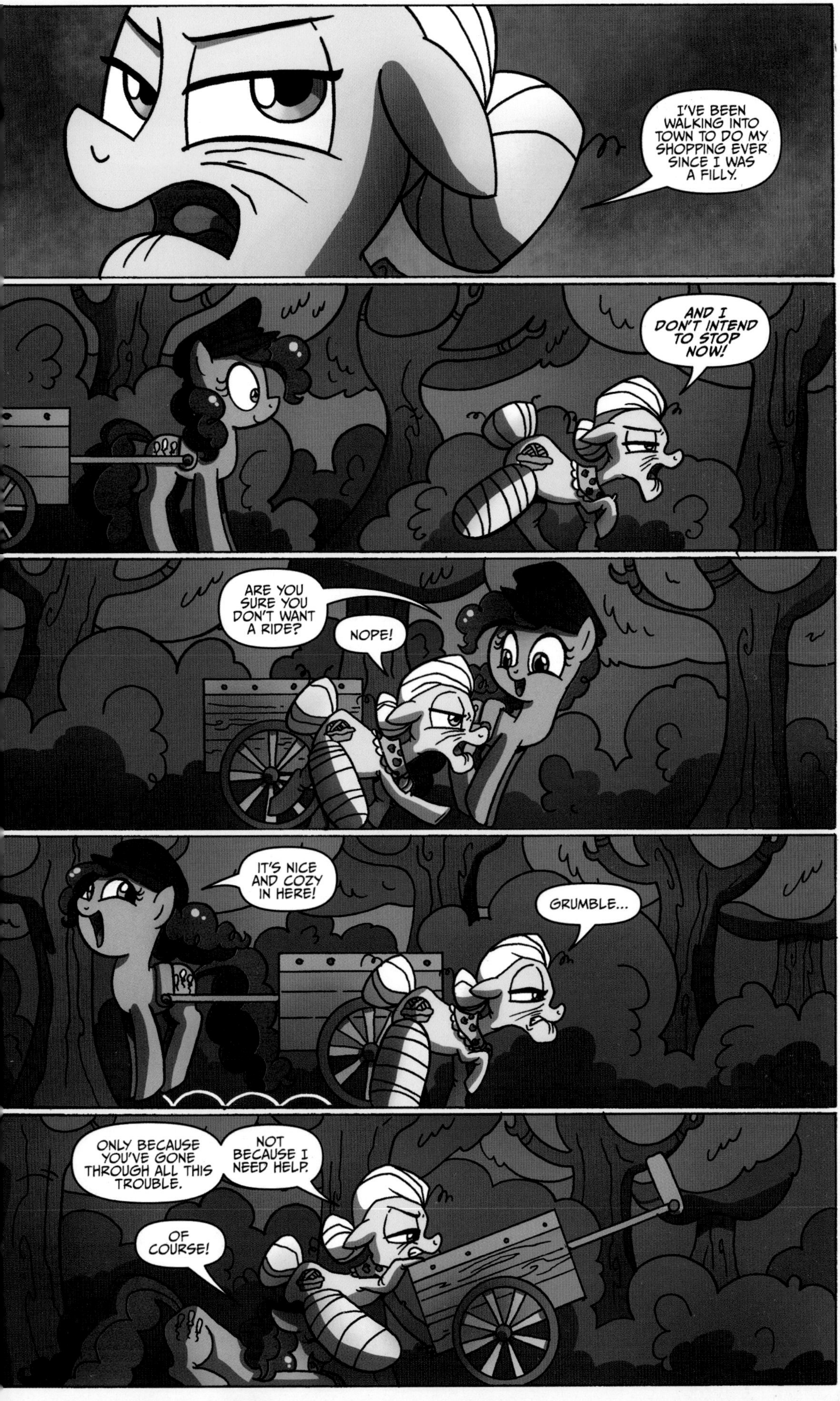
I'VE BEEN WALKING INTO TOWN TO DO MY SHOPPING EVER SINCE I WAS A FILLY.
AND I DON'T INTEND TO STOP NOW!
ARE YOU SURE YOU DON'T WANT A RIDE?
NOPE!
IT'S NICE AND COZY IN HERE!
GRUMBLE...
ONLY BECAUSE YOU'VE GONE THROUGH ALL THIS TROUBLE.
NOT BECAUSE I NEED HELP.
OF COURSE!

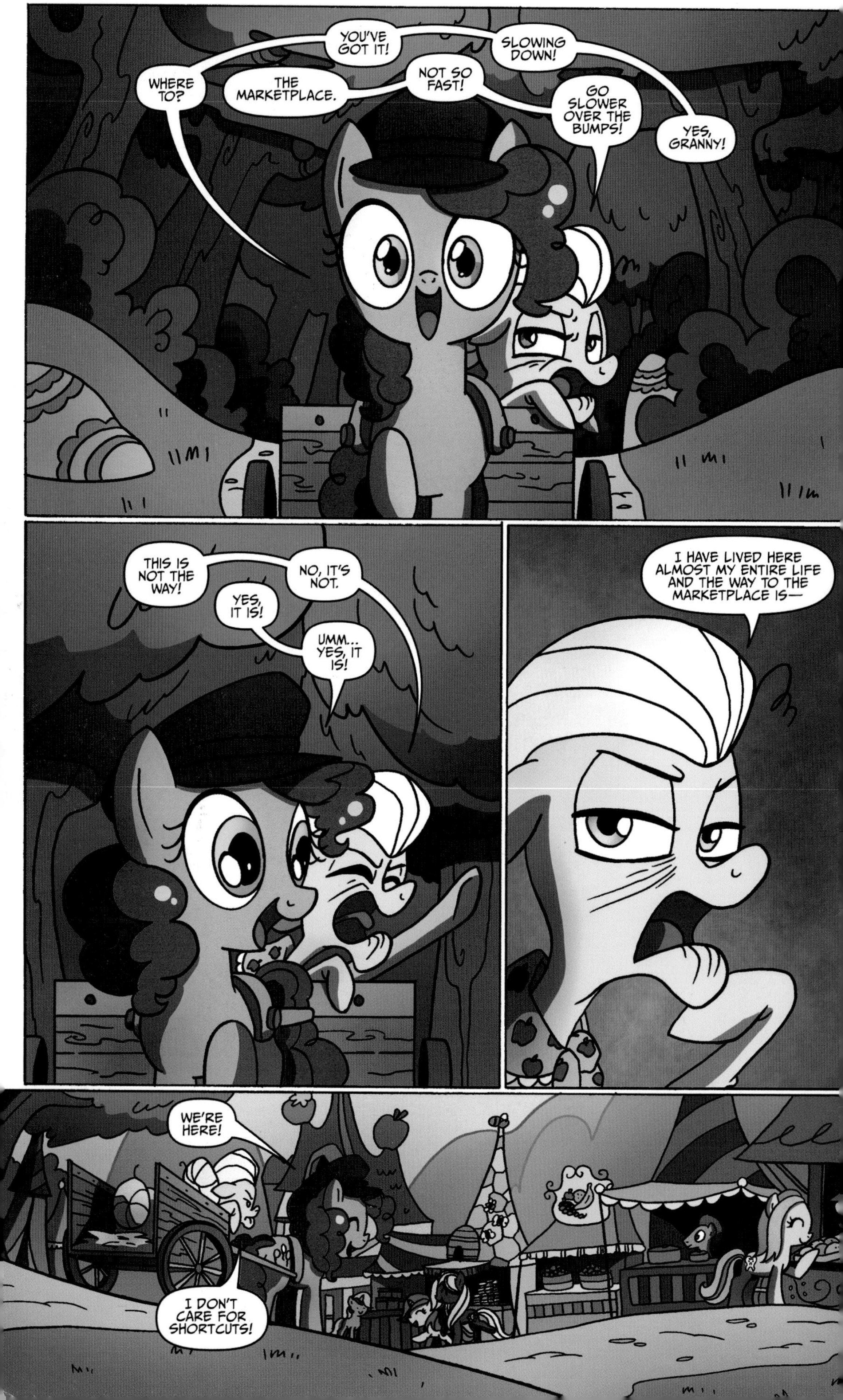
WHERE TO?
THE MARKETPLACE.
YOU'VE GOT IT!
NOT SO FAST!
SLOWING DOWN!
GO SLOWER OVER THE BUMPS!
YES, GRANNY!
THIS IS NOT THE WAY!
YES, IT IS!
NO, IT'S NOT.
UMM... YES, IT IS!
I HAVE LIVED HERE ALMOST MY ENTIRE LIFE AND THE WAY TO THE MARKETPLACE IS—
WE'RE HERE!
I DON'T CARE FOR SHORTCUTS!

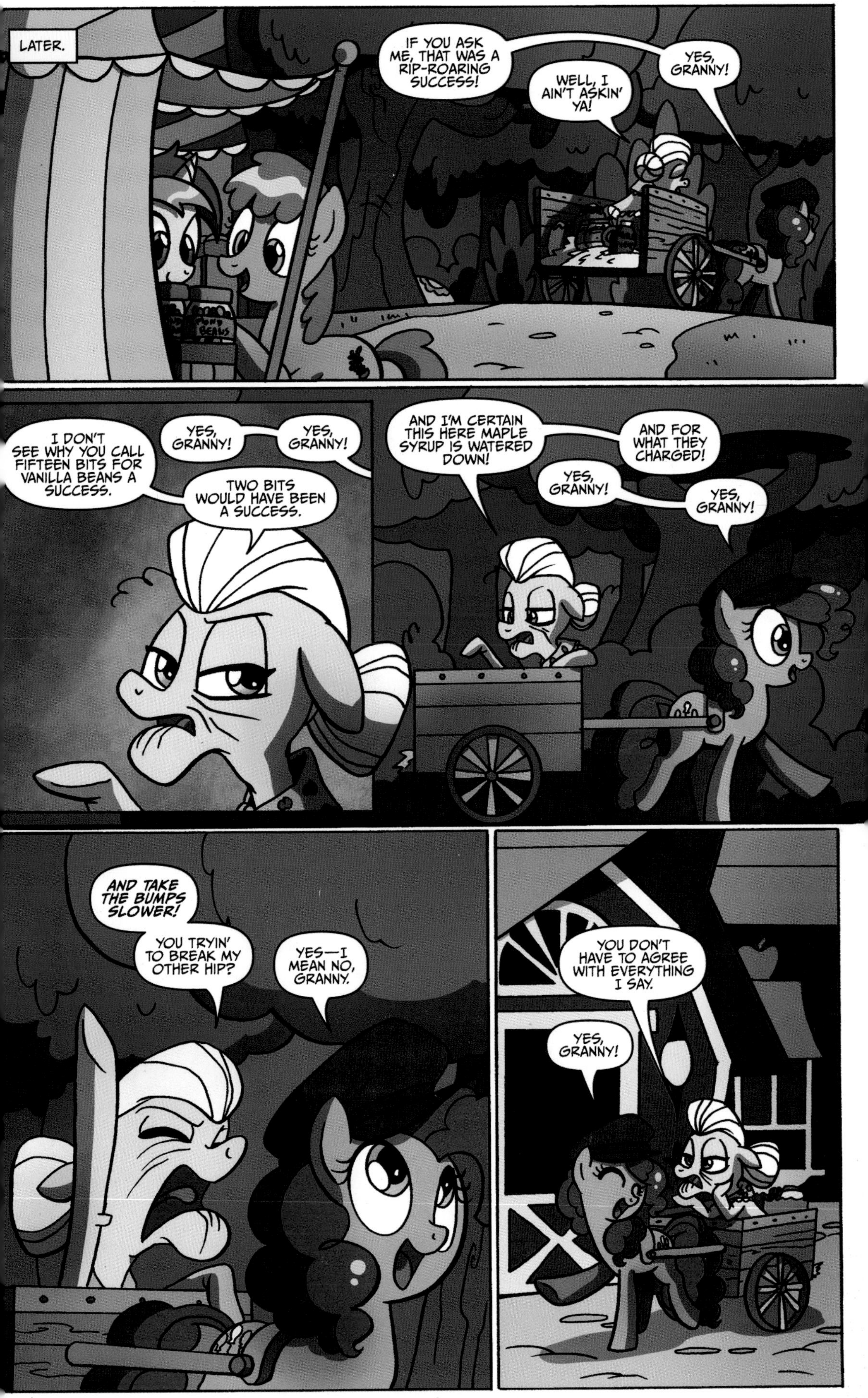
LATER.
IF YOU ASK ME, THAT WAS A RIP-ROARING SUCCESS!
WELL, I AIN'T ASKIN' YA!
YES, GRANNY!
I DON'T SEE WHY YOU CALL FIFTEEN BITS FOR VANILLA BEANS A SUCCESS.
YES, GRANNY!
YES, GRANNY!
TWO BITS WOULD HAVE BEEN A SUCCESS.
AND I'M CERTAIN THIS HERE MAPLE SYRUP IS WATERED DOWN!
YES, GRANNY!
AND FOR WHAT THEY CHARGED!
YES, GRANNY!
AND TAKE THE BUMPS SLOWER!
YOU TRYIN' TO BREAK MY OTHER HIP?
YES—I MEAN NO, GRANNY.
YOU DON'T HAVE TO AGREE WITH EVERYTHING I SAY.
YES, GRANNY!

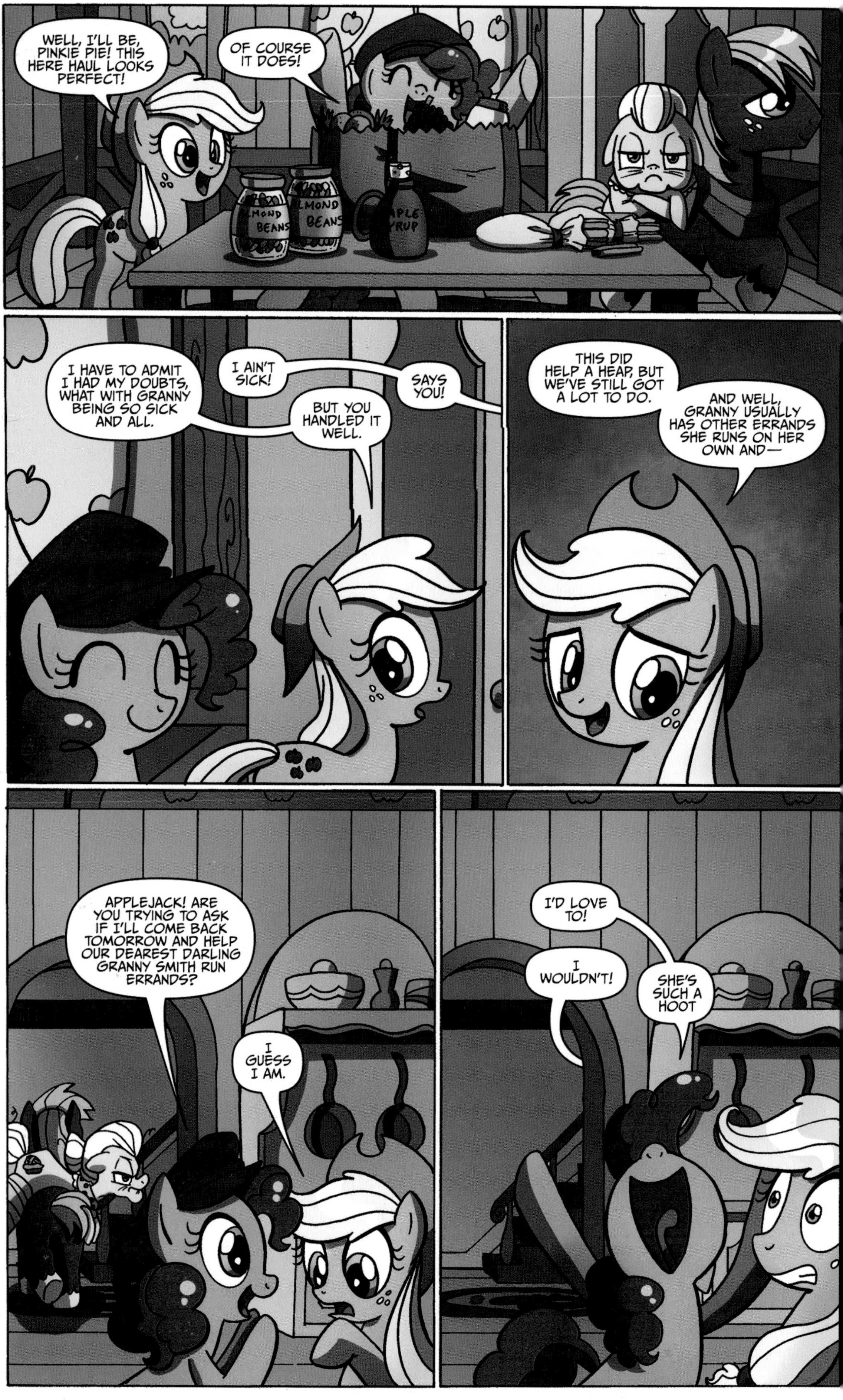
WELL, I'LL BE, PINKIE PIE! THIS HERE HAUL LOOKS PERFECT!
OF COURSE IT DOES!
ALMOND BEANS
ALMOND BEANS
APLE YRUP
I HAVE TO ADMIT I HAD MY DOUBTS, WHAT WITH GRANNY BEING SO SICK AND ALL.
I AIN'T SICK!
SAYS YOU!
BUT YOU HANDLED IT WELL.
THIS DID HELP A HEAP, BUT WE'VE STILL GOT A LOT TO DO.
AND WELL, GRANNY USUALLY HAS OTHER ERRANDS SHE RUNS ON HER OWN AND—
APPLEJACK! ARE YOU TRYING TO ASK IF I'LL COME BACK TOMORROW AND HELP OUR DEAREST DARLING GRANNY SMITH RUN ERRANDS?
I GUESS I AM.
I'D LOVE TO!
I WOULDN'T!
SHE'S SUCH A HOOT

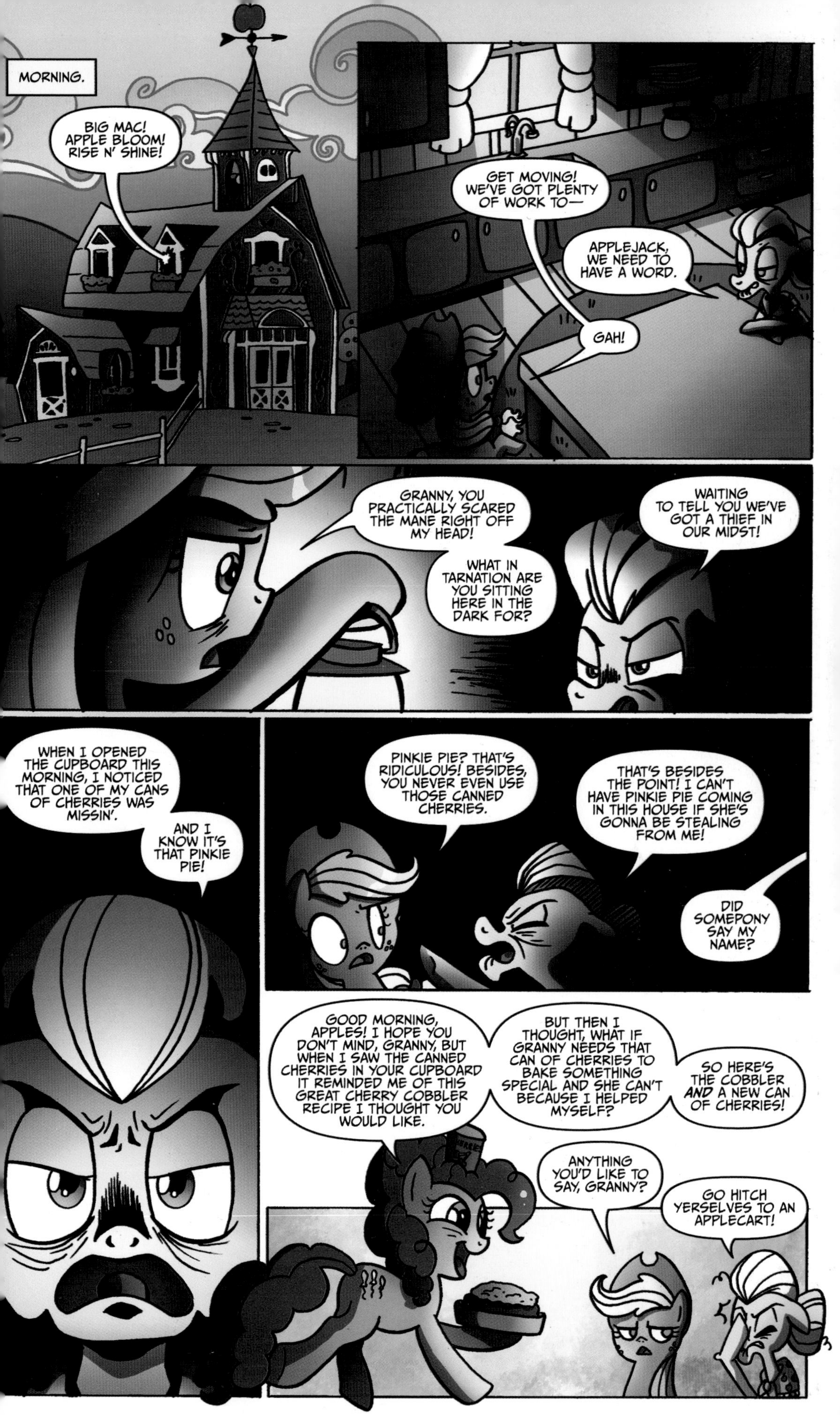
MORNING.
BIG MAC! APPLE BLOOM! RISE N' SHINE!
GET MOVING! WE'VE GOT PLENTY OF WORK TO—
APPLEJACK, WE NEED TO HAVE A WORD.
GAH!
GRANNY, YOU PRACTICALLY SCARED THE MANE RIGHT OFF MY HEAD!
WHAT IN TARNATION ARE YOU SITTING HERE IN THE DARK FOR?
WAITING TO TELL YOU WE'VE GOT A THIEF IN OUR MIDST!
WHEN I OPENED THE CUPBOARD THIS MORNING, I NOTICED THAT ONE OF MY CANS OF CHERRIES WAS MISSIN'.
AND I KNOW IT'S THAT PINKIE PIE!
PINKIE PIE? THAT'S RIDICULOUS! BESIDES, YOU NEVER EVEN USE THOSE CANNED CHERRIES.
THAT'S BESIDES THE POINT! I CAN'T HAVE PINKIE PIE COMING IN THIS HOUSE IF SHE'S GONNA BE STEALING FROM ME!
DID SOMEPONY SAY MY NAME?
GOOD MORNING, APPLES! I HOPE YOU DON'T MIND, GRANNY, BUT WHEN I SAW THE CANNED CHERRIES IN YOUR CUPBOARD IT REMINDED ME OF THIS GREAT CHERRY COBBLER RECIPE I THOUGHT YOU WOULD LIKE.
BUT THEN I THOUGHT, WHAT IF GRANNY NEEDS THAT CAN OF CHERRIES TO BAKE SOMETHING SPECIAL AND SHE CAN'T BECAUSE I HELPED MYSELF?
SO HERE'S THE COBBLER *AND* A NEW CAN OF CHERRIES!
ANYTHING YOU'D LIKE TO SAY, GRANNY?
GO HITCH YERSELVES TO AN APPLECART!

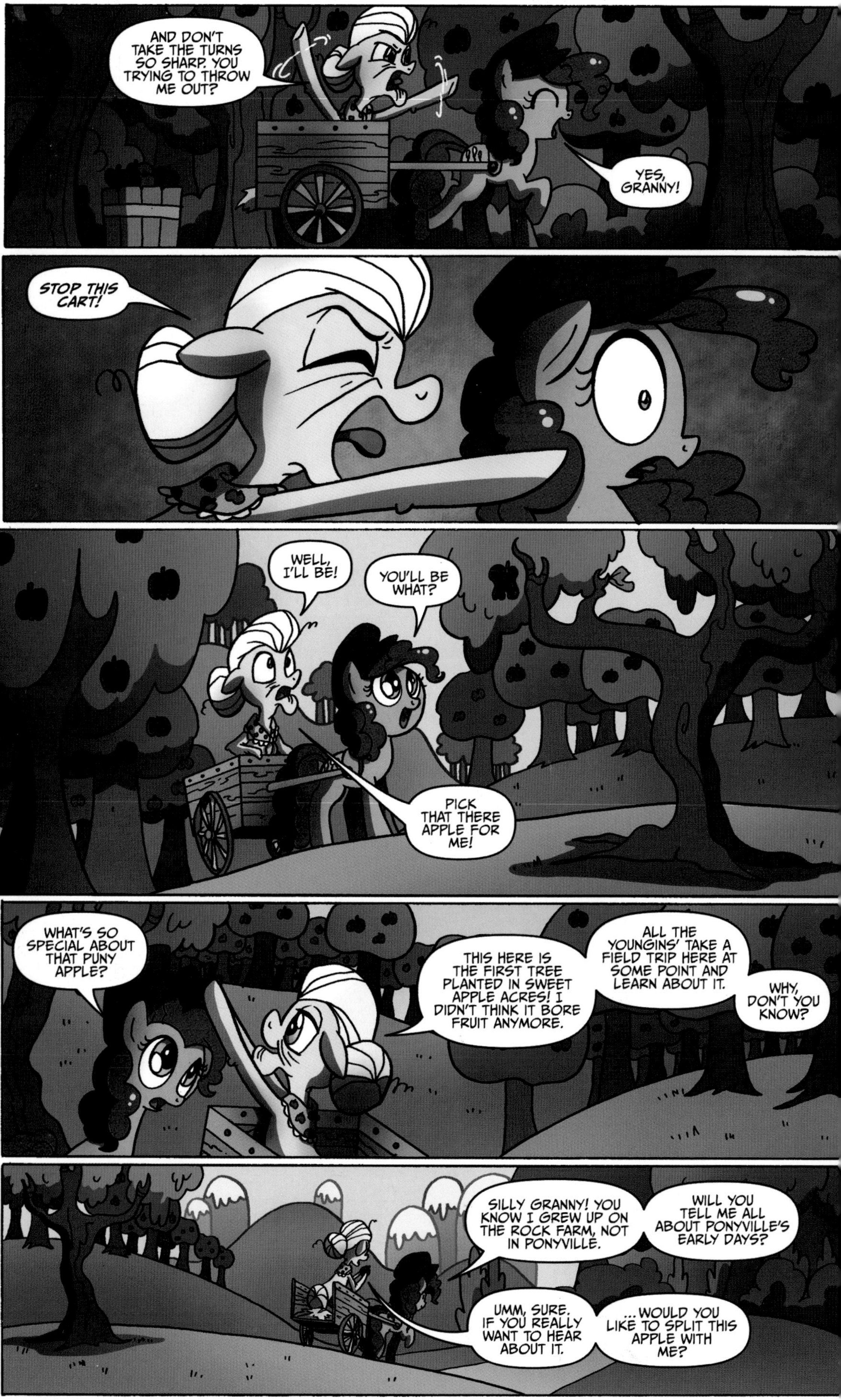
AND DON'T TAKE THE TURNS SO SHARP. YOU TRYING TO THROW ME OUT?
YES, GRANNY!
STOP THIS CART!
WELL, I'LL BE!
YOU'LL BE WHAT?
PICK THAT THERE APPLE FOR ME!
WHAT'S SO SPECIAL ABOUT THAT PUNY APPLE?
THIS HERE IS THE FIRST TREE PLANTED IN SWEET APPLE ACRES! I DIDN'T THINK IT BORE FRUIT ANYMORE.
ALL THE YOUNGINS' TAKE A FIELD TRIP HERE AT SOME POINT AND LEARN ABOUT IT.
WHY, DON'T YOU KNOW?
SILLY GRANNY! YOU KNOW I GREW UP ON THE ROCK FARM, NOT IN PONYVILLE.
WILL YOU TELL ME ALL ABOUT PONYVILLE'S EARLY DAYS?
UMM, SURE. IF YOU REALLY WANT TO HEAR ABOUT IT.
...WOULD YOU LIKE TO SPLIT THIS APPLE WITH ME?

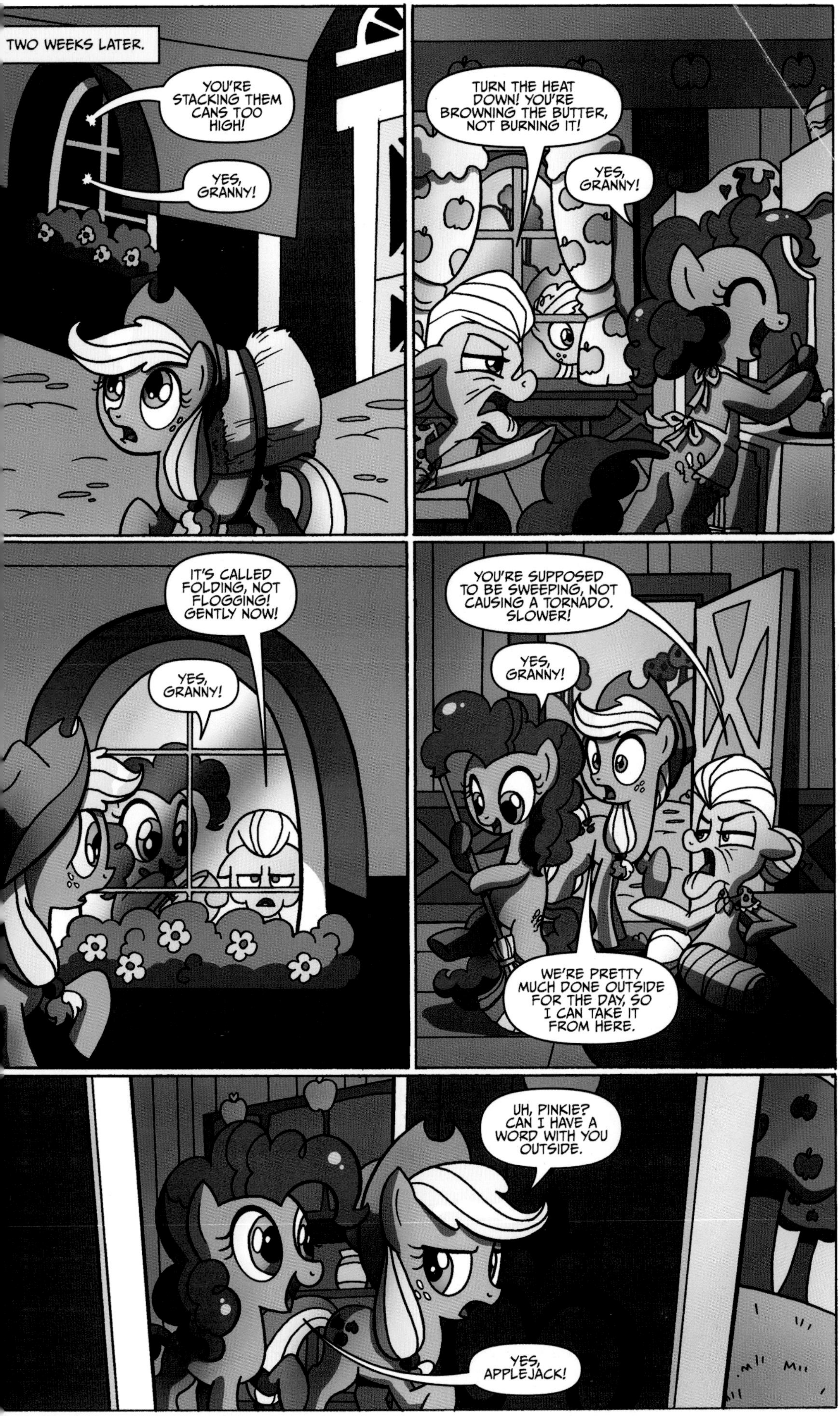
TWO WEEKS LATER.
YOU'RE STACKING THEM CANS TOO HIGH!
YES, GRANNY!
TURN THE HEAT DOWN! YOU'RE BROWNING THE BUTTER, NOT BURNING IT!
YES, GRANNY!
IT'S CALLED FOLDING, NOT FLOGGING! GENTLY NOW!
YES, GRANNY!
YOU'RE SUPPOSED TO BE SWEEPING, NOT CAUSING A TORNADO. SLOWER!
YES, GRANNY!
WE'RE PRETTY MUCH DONE OUTSIDE FOR THE DAY, SO I CAN TAKE IT FROM HERE.
UH, PINKIE? CAN I HAVE A WORD WITH YOU OUTSIDE.
YES, APPLEJACK!

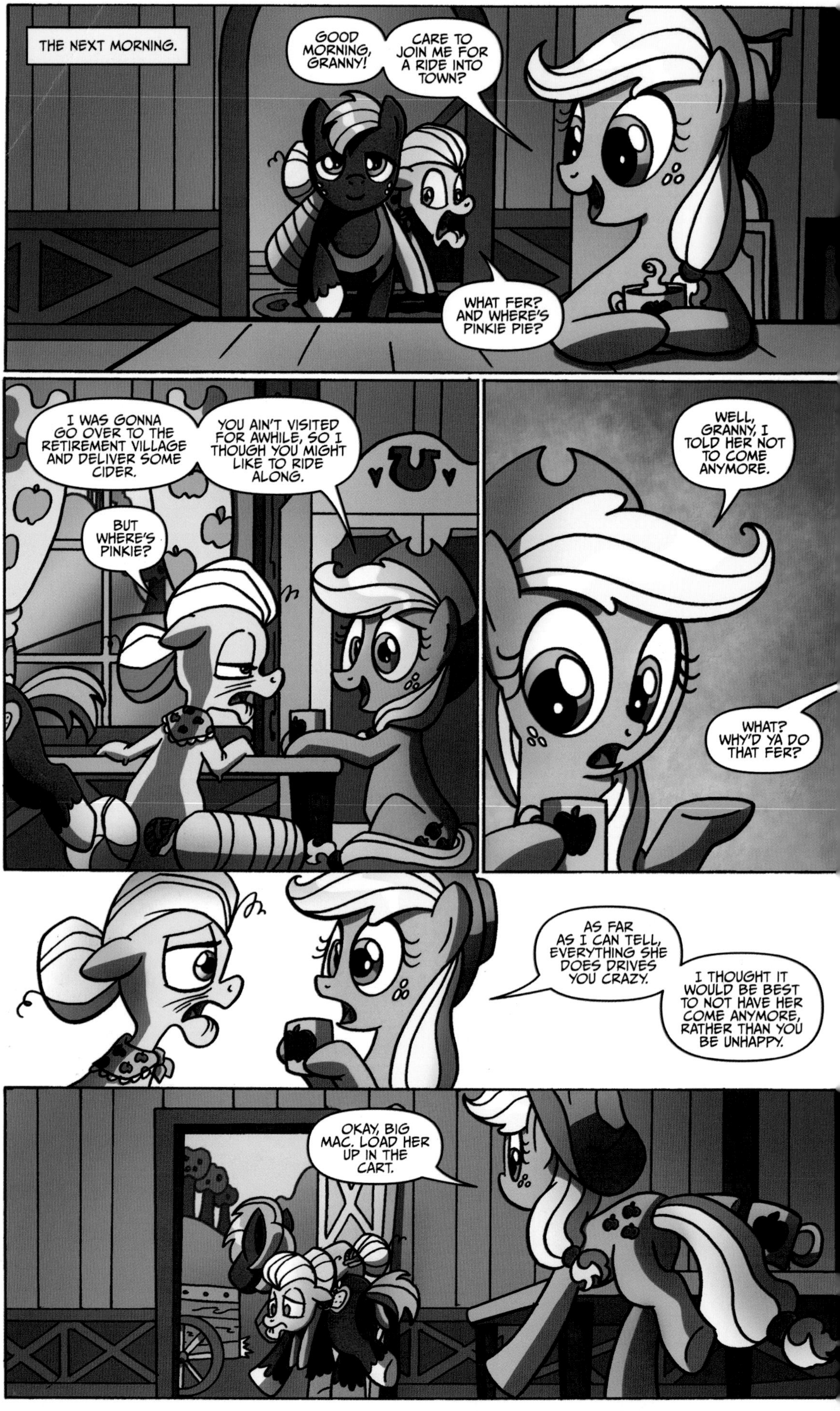
THE NEXT MORNING.
GOOD MORNING, GRANNY!
CARE TO JOIN ME FOR A RIDE INTO TOWN?
WHAT FER? AND WHERE'S PINKIE PIE?
I WAS GONNA GO OVER TO THE RETIREMENT VILLAGE AND DELIVER SOME CIDER.
YOU AIN'T VISITED FOR AWHILE, SO I THOUGH YOU MIGHT LIKE TO RIDE ALONG.
BUT WHERE'S PINKIE?
WELL, GRANNY, I TOLD HER NOT TO COME ANYMORE.
WHAT? WHY'D YA DO THAT FER?
AS FAR AS I CAN TELL, EVERYTHING SHE DOES DRIVES YOU CRAZY.
I THOUGHT IT WOULD BE BEST TO NOT HAVE HER COME ANYMORE, RATHER THAN YOU BE UNHAPPY.
OKAY, BIG MAC. LOAD HER UP IN THE CART.

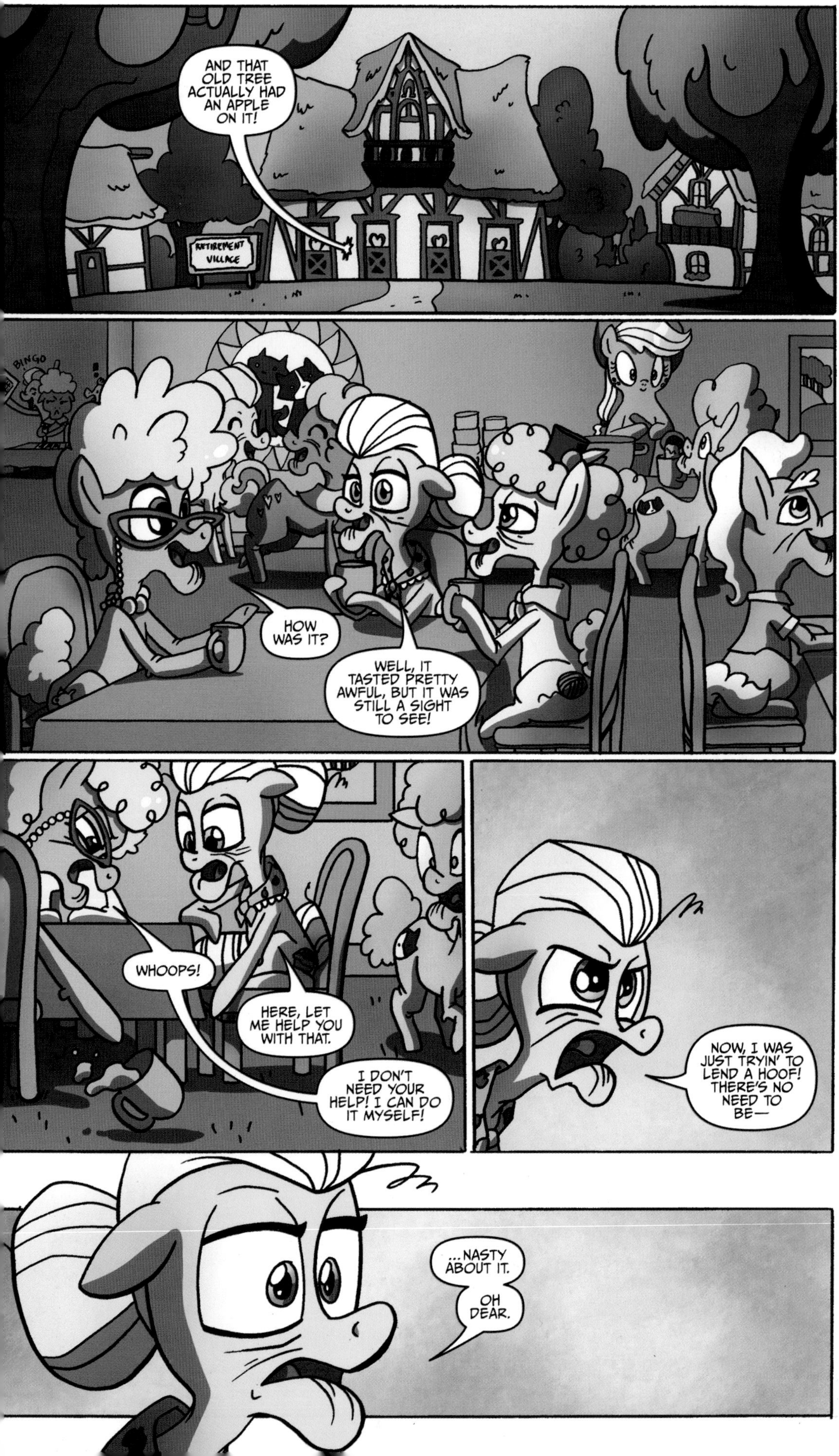
AND THAT OLD TREE ACTUALLY HAD AN APPLE ON IT!
RETIREMENT VILLAGE
BINGO
HOW WAS IT?
WELL, IT TASTED PRETTY AWFUL, BUT IT WAS STILL A SIGHT TO SEE!
WHOOPS!
HERE, LET ME HELP YOU WITH THAT.
I DON'T NEED YOUR HELP! I CAN DO IT MYSELF!
NOW, I WAS JUST TRYIN' TO LEND A HOOF! THERE'S NO NEED TO BE—
...NASTY ABOUT IT.
OH DEAR.

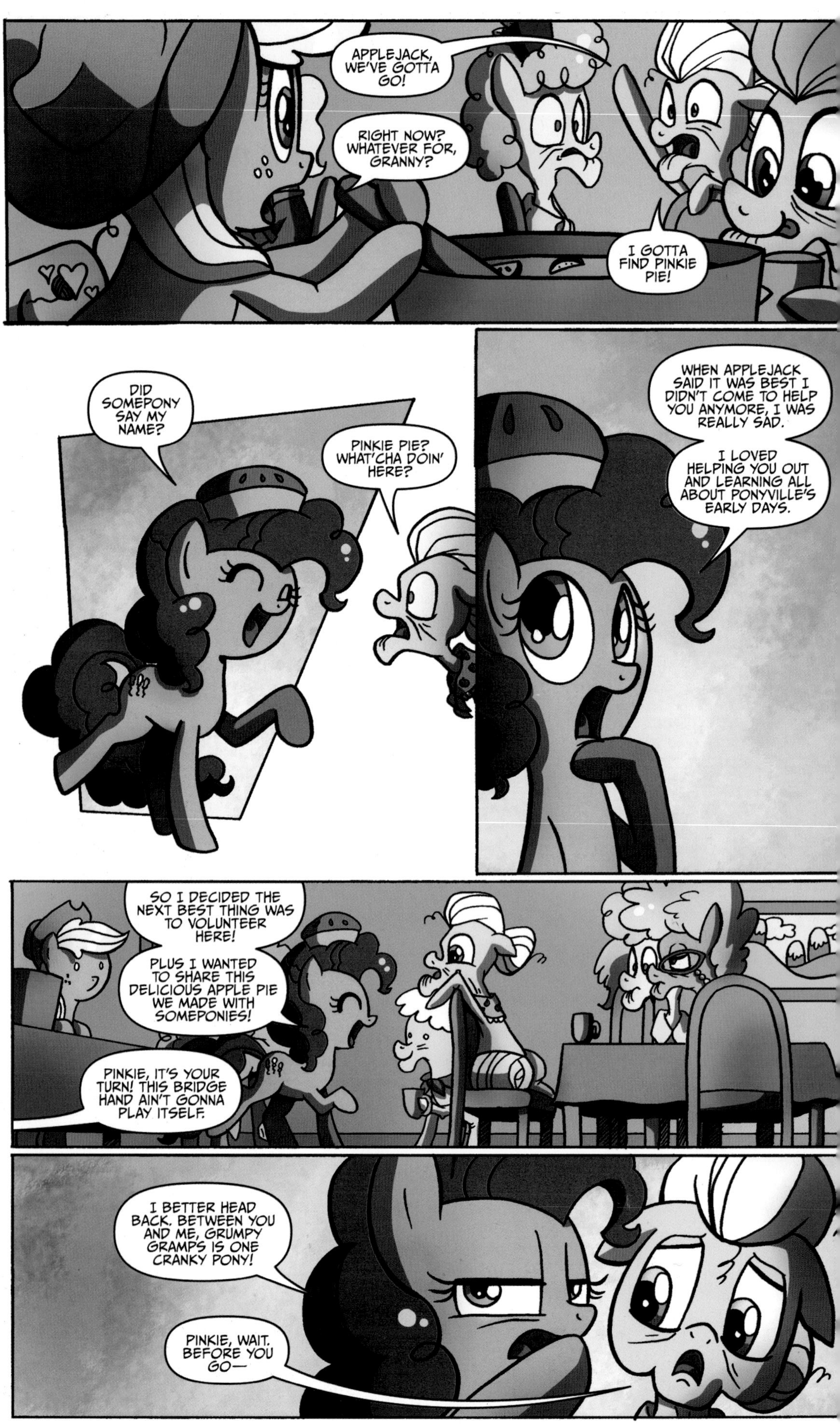
APPLEJACK, WE'VE GOTTA GO!
RIGHT NOW? WHATEVER FOR, GRANNY?
I GOTTA FIND PINKIE PIE!
DID SOMEPONY SAY MY NAME?
PINKIE PIE? WHAT'CHA DOIN' HERE?
WHEN APPLEJACK SAID IT WAS BEST I DIDN'T COME TO HELP YOU ANYMORE, I WAS REALLY SAD.
I LOVED HELPING YOU OUT AND LEARNING ALL ABOUT PONYVILLE'S EARLY DAYS.
SO I DECIDED THE NEXT BEST THING WAS TO VOLUNTEER HERE!
PLUS I WANTED TO SHARE THIS DELICIOUS APPLE PIE WE MADE WITH SOMEPONIES!
PINKIE, IT'S YOUR TURN! THIS BRIDGE HAND AIN'T GONNA PLAY ITSELF.
I BETTER HEAD BACK. BETWEEN YOU AND ME, GRUMPY GRAMPS IS ONE CRANKY PONY!
PINKIE, WAIT. BEFORE YOU GO—

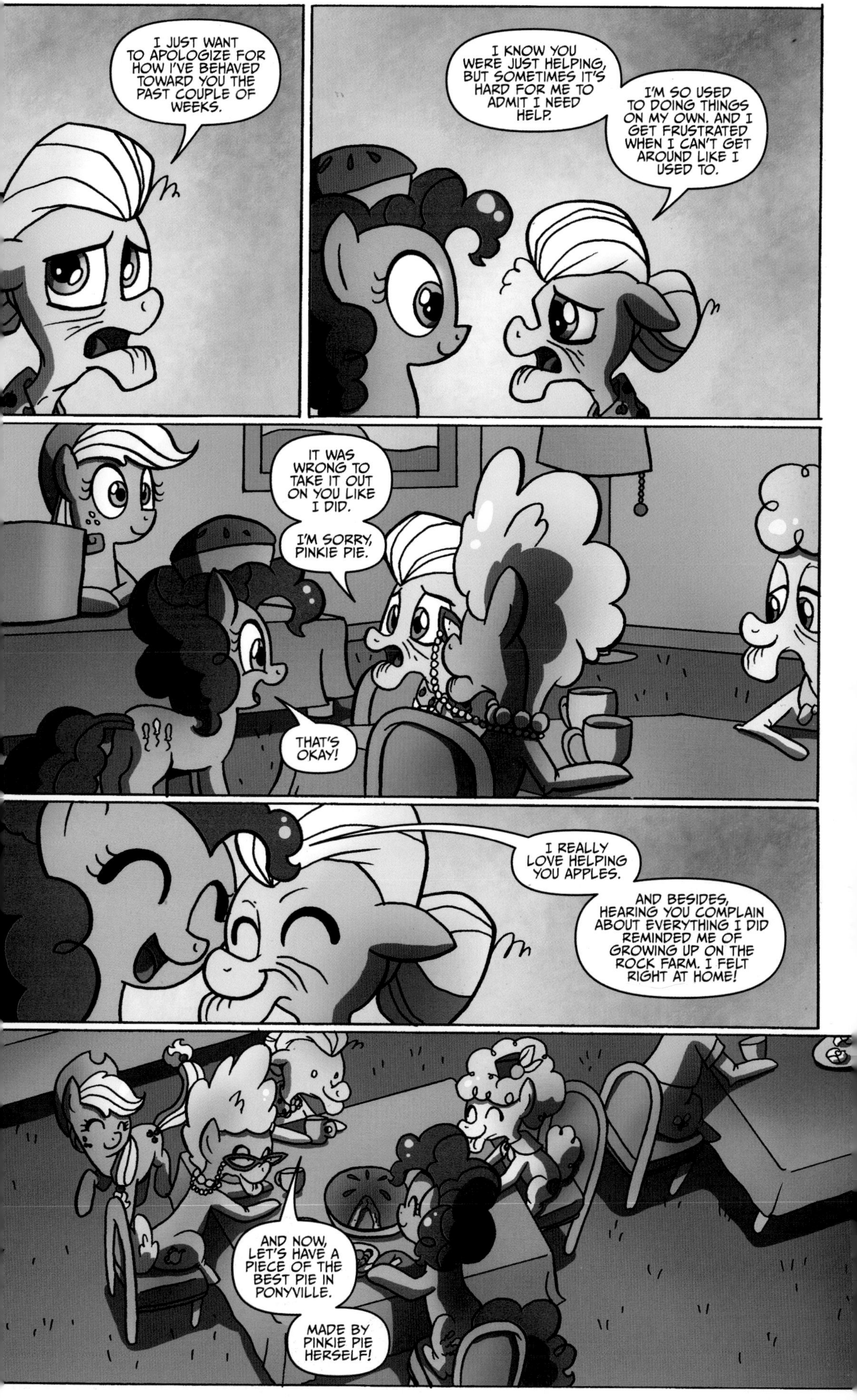
I JUST WANT TO APOLOGIZE FOR HOW I'VE BEHAVED TOWARD YOU THE PAST COUPLE OF WEEKS.
I KNOW YOU WERE JUST HELPING, BUT SOMETIMES IT'S HARD FOR ME TO ADMIT I NEED HELP.
I'M SO USED TO DOING THINGS ON MY OWN. AND I GET FRUSTRATED WHEN I CAN'T GET AROUND LIKE I USED TO.
IT WAS WRONG TO TAKE IT OUT ON YOU LIKE I DID.
I'M SORRY, PINKIE PIE.
THAT'S OKAY!
I REALLY LOVE HELPING YOU APPLES.
AND BESIDES, HEARING YOU COMPLAIN ABOUT EVERYTHING I DID REMINDED ME OF GROWING UP ON THE ROCK FARM. I FELT RIGHT AT HOME!
AND NOW, LET'S HAVE A PIECE OF THE BEST PIE IN PONYVILLE.
MADE BY PINKIE PIE HERSELF!

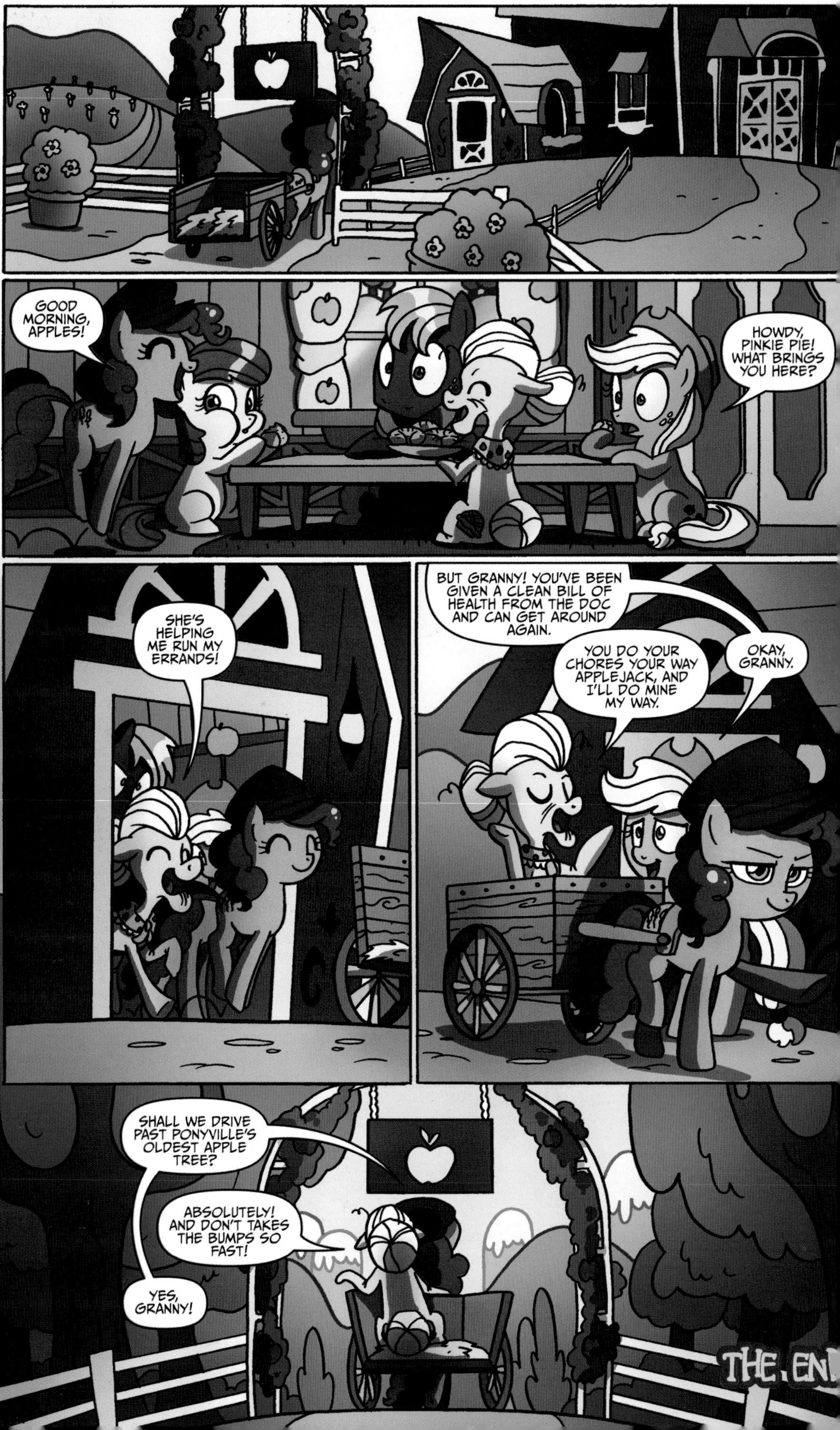
GOOD MORNING, APPLES!
HOWDY, PINKIE PIE! WHAT BRINGS YOU HERE?
SHE'S HELPING ME RUN MY ERRANDS!
BUT GRANNY! YOU'VE BEEN GIVEN A CLEAN BILL OF HEALTH FROM THE DOC AND CAN GET AROUND AGAIN.
YOU DO YOUR CHORES YOUR WAY APPLEJACK, AND I'LL DO MINE MY WAY.
OKAY, GRANNY.
SHALL WE DRIVE PAST PONYVILLE'S OLDEST APPLE TREE?
ABSOLUTELY! AND DON'T TAKES THE BUMPS SO FAST!
YES, GRANNY!
THE END

my LITTLE PONY

FRIENDS FOREVER

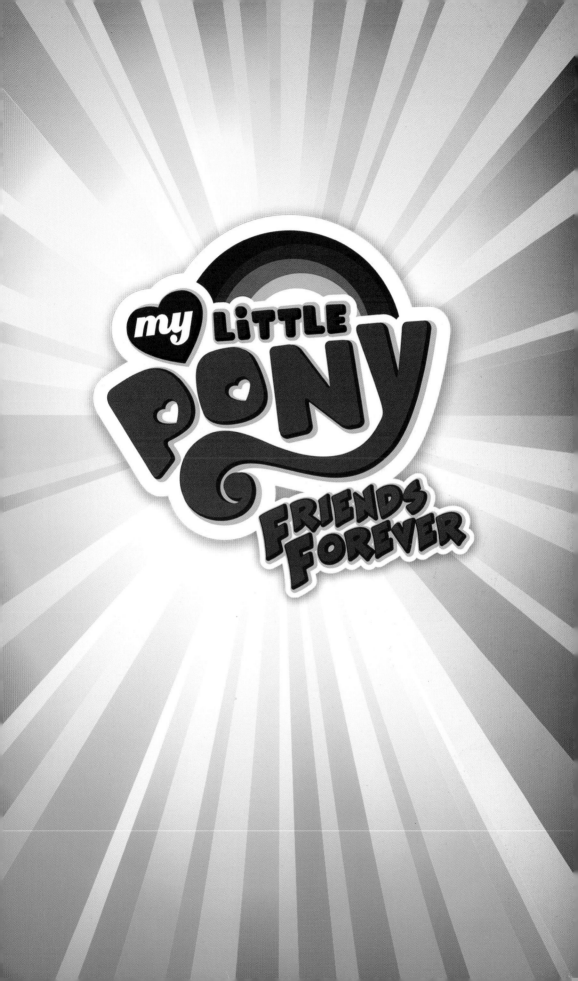

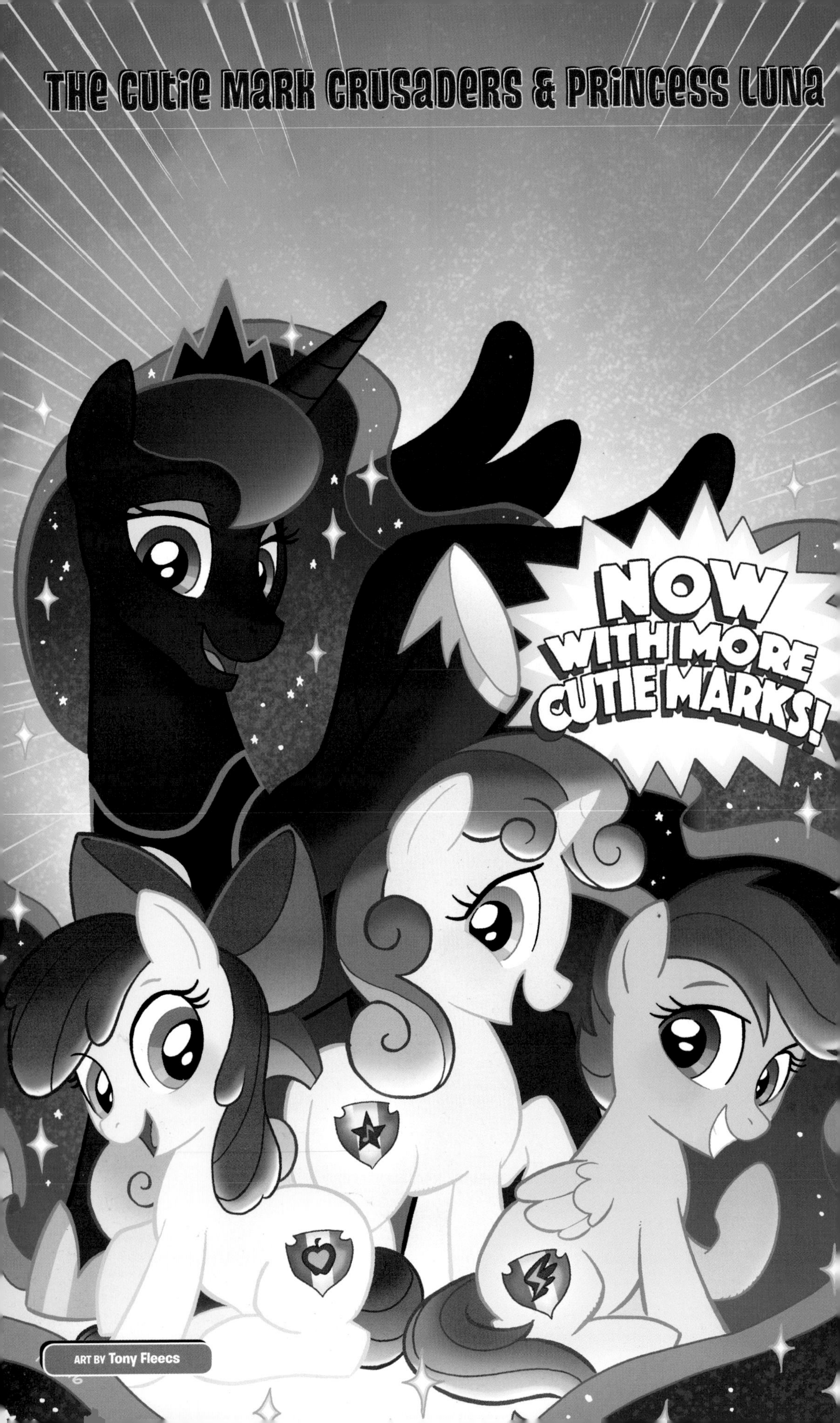
The Cutie Mark Crusaders & Princess Luna
NOW WITH MORE CUTIE MARKS!
ART BY Tony Fleecs

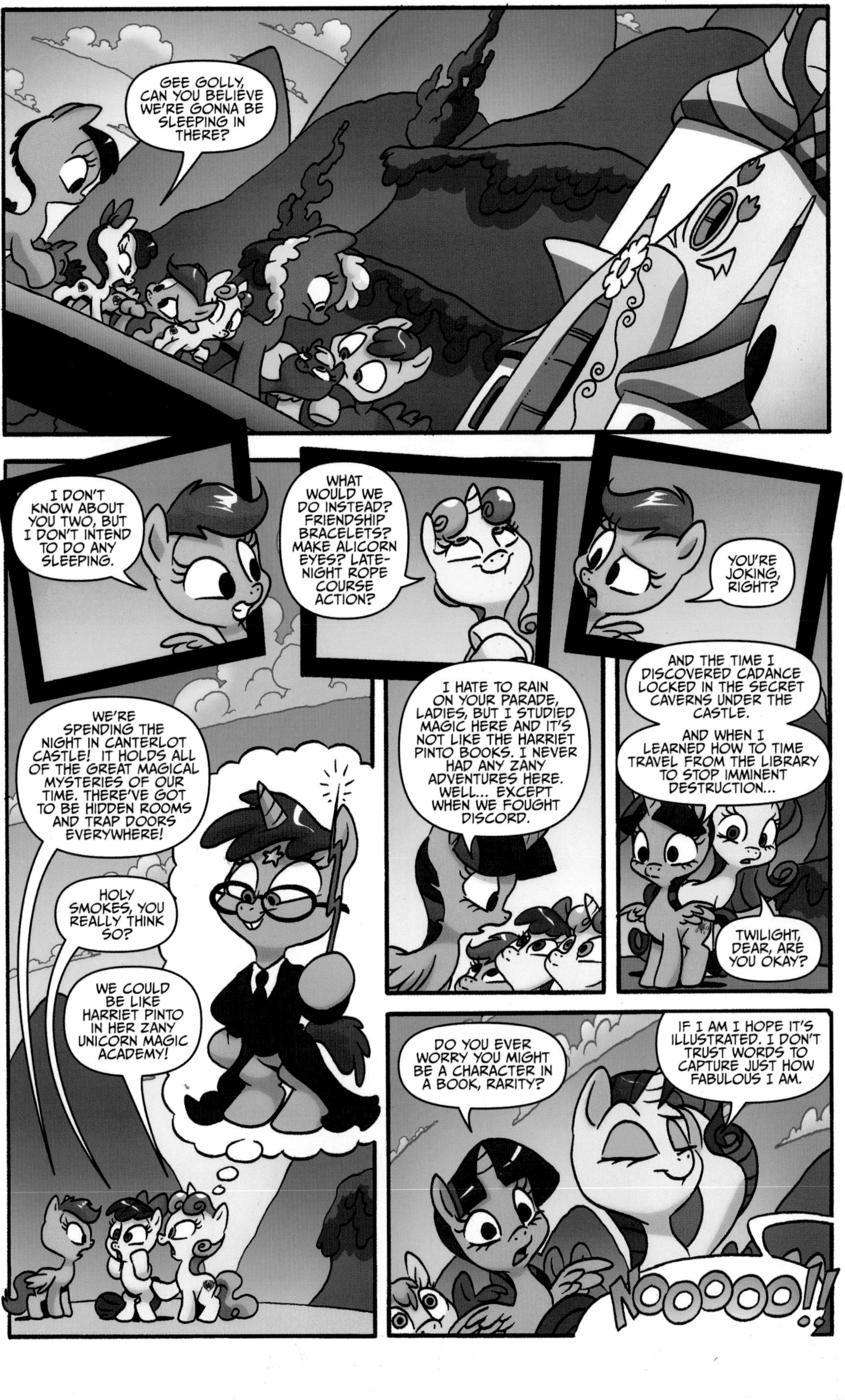
GEE GOLLY, CAN YOU BELIEVE WE'RE GONNA BE SLEEPING IN THERE?
I DON'T KNOW ABOUT YOU TWO, BUT I DON'T INTEND TO DO ANY SLEEPING.
WHAT WOULD WE DO INSTEAD? FRIENDSHIP BRACELETS? MAKE ALICORN EYES? LATE-NIGHT ROPE COURSE ACTION?
YOU'RE JOKING, RIGHT?
WE'RE SPENDING THE NIGHT IN CANTERLOT CASTLE! IT HOLDS ALL OF THE GREAT MAGICAL MYSTERIES OF OUR TIME. THERE'VE GOT TO BE HIDDEN ROOMS AND TRAP DOORS EVERYWHERE!
HOLY SMOKES, YOU REALLY THINK SO?
WE COULD BE LIKE HARRIET PINTO IN HER ZANY UNICORN MAGIC ACADEMY!
I HATE TO RAIN ON YOUR PARADE, LADIES, BUT I STUDIED MAGIC HERE AND IT'S NOT LIKE THE HARRIET PINTO BOOKS. I NEVER HAD ANY ZANY ADVENTURES HERE. WELL... EXCEPT WHEN WE FOUGHT DISCORD.
AND THE TIME I DISCOVERED CADANCE LOCKED IN THE SECRET CAVERNS UNDER THE CASTLE.
AND WHEN I LEARNED HOW TO TIME TRAVEL FROM THE LIBRARY TO STOP IMMINENT DESTRUCTION...
TWILIGHT, DEAR, ARE YOU OKAY?
DO YOU EVER WORRY YOU MIGHT BE A CHARACTER IN A BOOK, RARITY?
IF I AM I HOPE IT'S ILLUSTRATED. I DON'T TRUST WORDS TO CAPTURE JUST HOW FABULOUS I AM.
NOOOOO!!

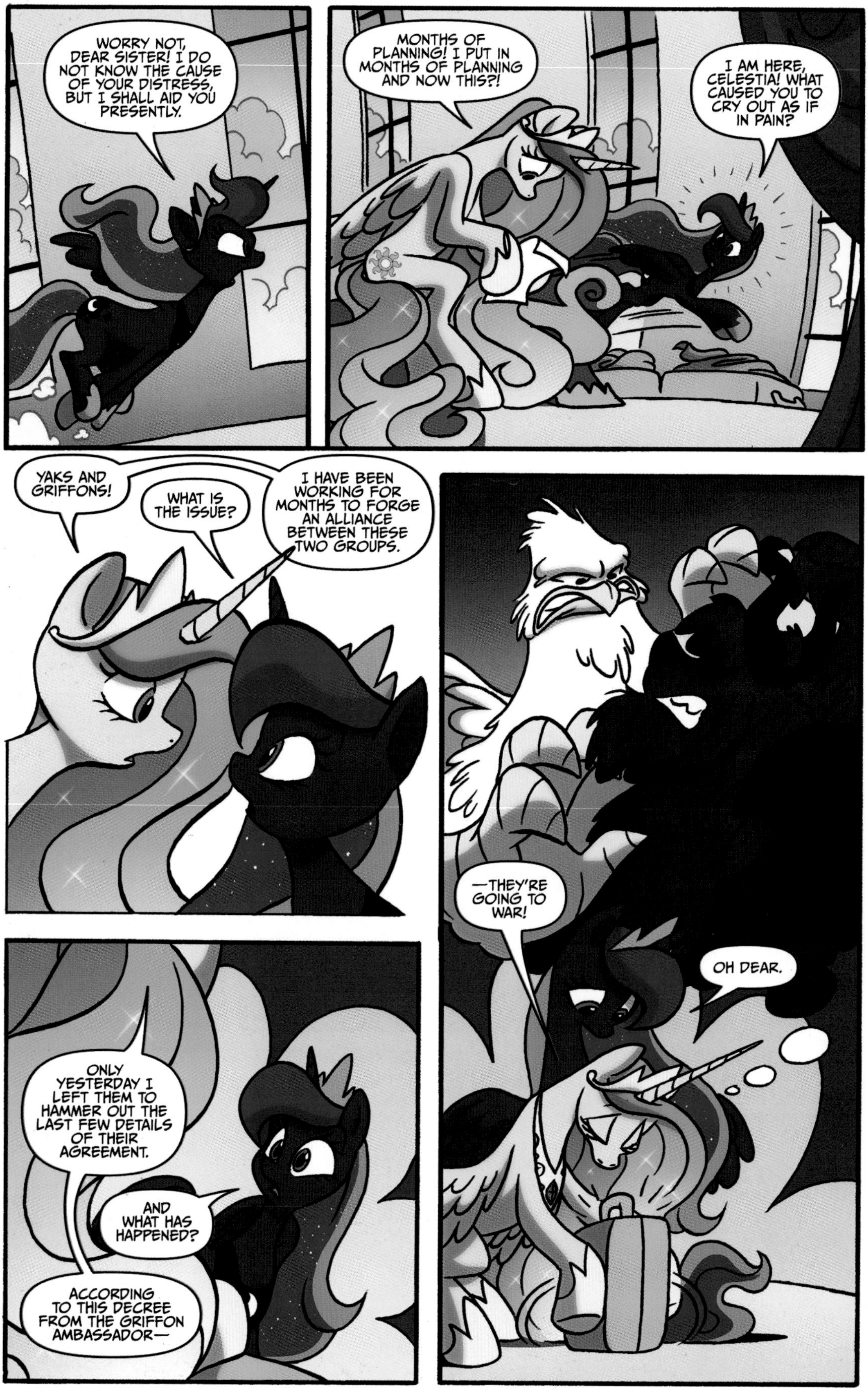
WORRY NOT, DEAR SISTER! I DO NOT KNOW THE CAUSE OF YOUR DISTRESS, BUT I SHALL AID YOU PRESENTLY.
MONTHS OF PLANNING! I PUT IN MONTHS OF PLANNING AND NOW THIS?!
I AM HERE, CELESTIA! WHAT CAUSED YOU TO CRY OUT AS IF IN PAIN?
YAKS AND GRIFFONS!
WHAT IS THE ISSUE?
I HAVE BEEN WORKING FOR MONTHS TO FORGE AN ALLIANCE BETWEEN THESE TWO GROUPS.
ONLY YESTERDAY I LEFT THEM TO HAMMER OUT THE LAST FEW DETAILS OF THEIR AGREEMENT.
AND WHAT HAS HAPPENED?
ACCORDING TO THIS DECREE FROM THE GRIFFON AMBASSADOR—
—THEY'RE GOING TO WAR!
OH DEAR.

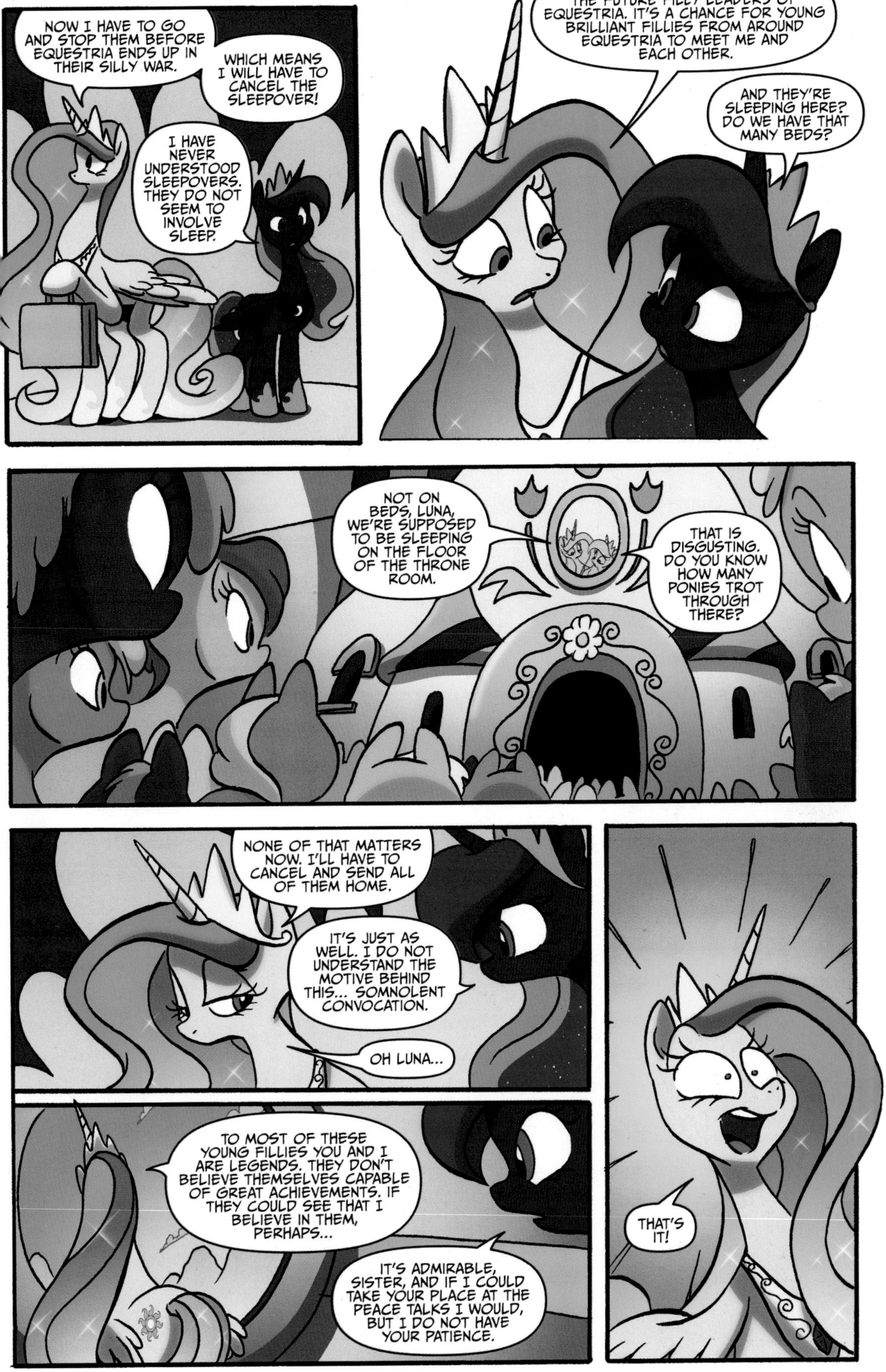
NOW I HAVE TO GO AND STOP THEM BEFORE EQUESTRIA ENDS UP IN THEIR SILLY WAR.
WHICH MEANS I WILL HAVE TO CANCEL THE SLEEPOVER!
I HAVE NEVER UNDERSTOOD SLEEPOVERS. THEY DO NOT SEEM TO INVOLVE SLEEP.
TWILIGHT ARRANGED IT FOR THE FUTURE FILLY LEADERS OF EQUESTRIA. IT'S A CHANCE FOR YOUNG BRILLIANT FILLIES FROM AROUND EQUESTRIA TO MEET ME AND EACH OTHER.
AND THEY'RE SLEEPING HERE? DO WE HAVE THAT MANY BEDS?
NOT ON BEDS, LUNA, WE'RE SUPPOSED TO BE SLEEPING ON THE FLOOR OF THE THRONE ROOM.
THAT IS DISGUSTING. DO YOU KNOW HOW MANY PONIES TROT THROUGH THERE?
NONE OF THAT MATTERS NOW. I'LL HAVE TO CANCEL AND SEND ALL OF THEM HOME.
IT'S JUST AS WELL. I DO NOT UNDERSTAND THE MOTIVE BEHIND THIS... SOMNOLENT CONVOCATION.
OH LUNA...
TO MOST OF THESE YOUNG FILLIES YOU AND I ARE LEGENDS. THEY DON'T BELIEVE THEMSELVES CAPABLE OF GREAT ACHIEVEMENTS. IF THEY COULD SEE THAT I BELIEVE IN THEM, PERHAPS...
IT'S ADMIRABLE, SISTER, AND IF I COULD TAKE YOUR PLACE AT THE PEACE TALKS I WOULD, BUT I DO NOT HAVE YOUR PATIENCE.
THAT'S IT!

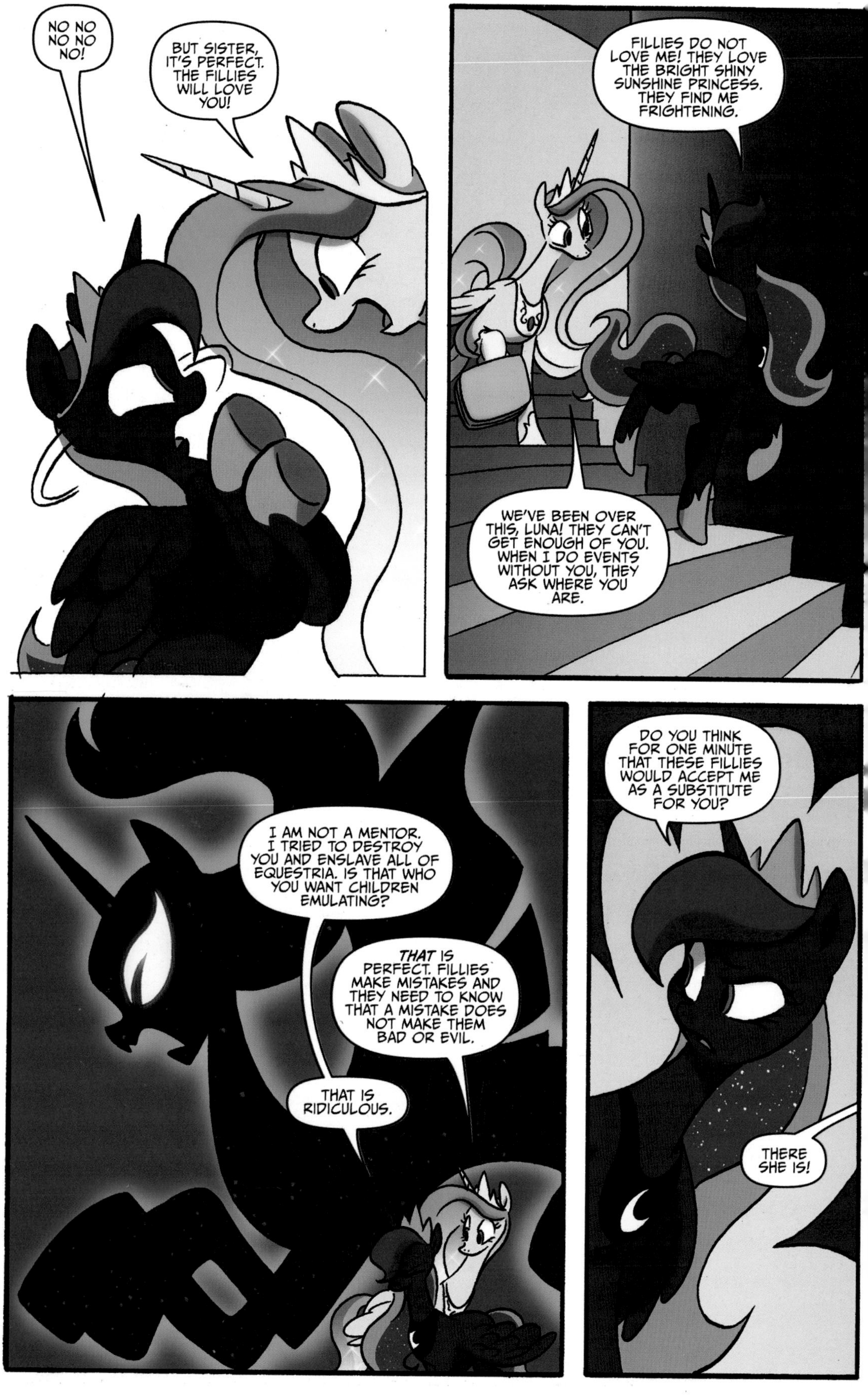
NO NO
NO NO
NO!
BUT SISTER, IT'S PERFECT. THE FILLIES WILL LOVE YOU!
FILLIES DO NOT LOVE ME! THEY LOVE THE BRIGHT SHINY SUNSHINE PRINCESS. THEY FIND ME FRIGHTENING.
WE'VE BEEN OVER THIS, LUNA! THEY CAN'T GET ENOUGH OF YOU. WHEN I DO EVENTS WITHOUT YOU, THEY ASK WHERE YOU ARE.
I AM NOT A MENTOR. I TRIED TO DESTROY YOU AND ENSLAVE ALL OF EQUESTRIA. IS THAT WHO YOU WANT CHILDREN EMULATING?
THAT IS PERFECT. FILLIES MAKE MISTAKES AND THEY NEED TO KNOW THAT A MISTAKE DOES NOT MAKE THEM BAD OR EVIL.
THAT IS RIDICULOUS.
DO YOU THINK FOR ONE MINUTE THAT THESE FILLIES WOULD ACCEPT ME AS A SUBSTITUTE FOR YOU?
THERE SHE IS!

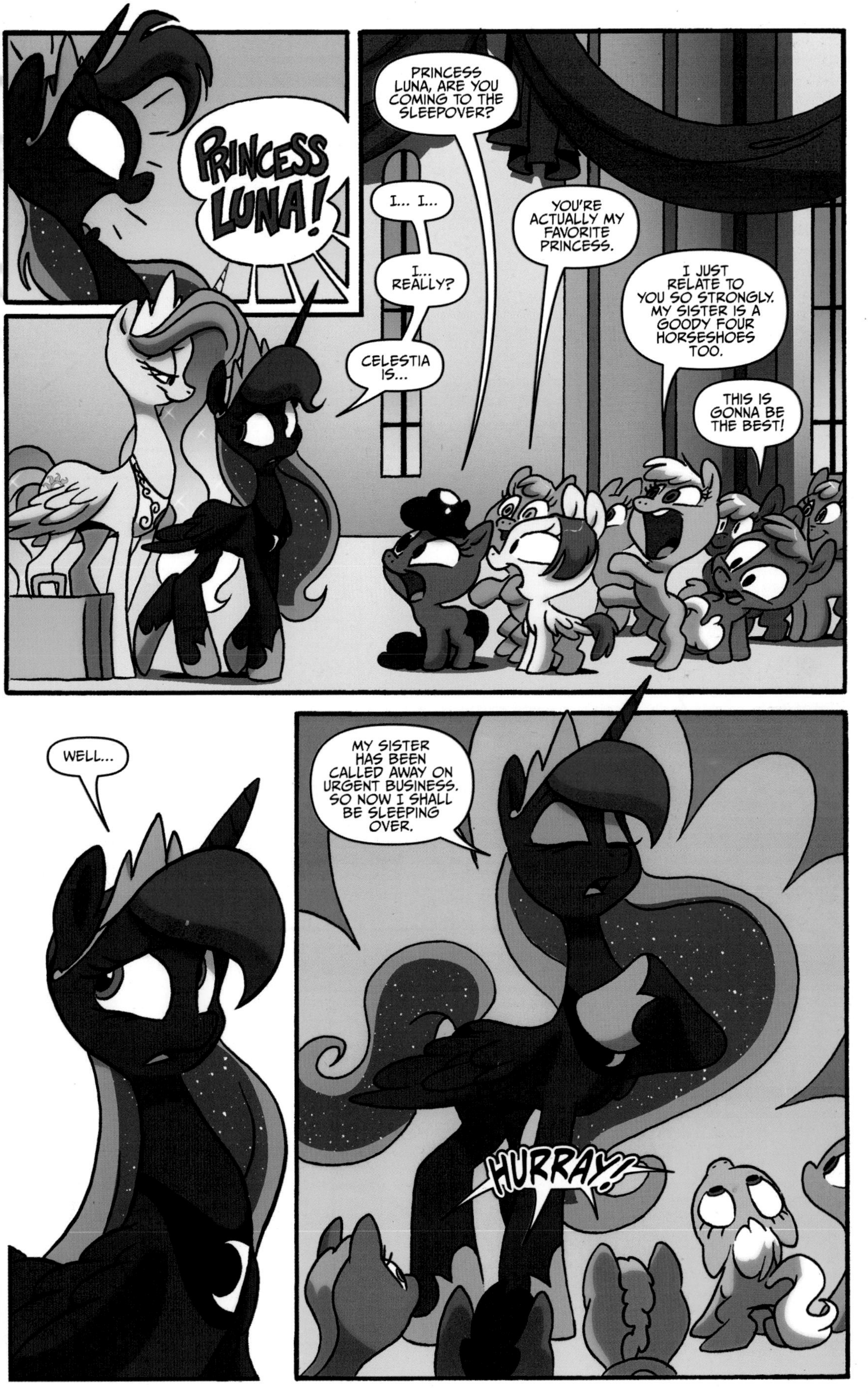
PRINCESS LUNA!
PRINCESS LUNA, ARE YOU COMING TO THE SLEEPOVER?
I... I...
I... REALLY?
CELESTIA IS...
YOU'RE ACTUALLY MY FAVORITE PRINCESS.
I JUST RELATE TO YOU SO STRONGLY. MY SISTER IS A GOODY FOUR HORSESHOES TOO.
THIS IS GONNA BE THE BEST!
WELL...
MY SISTER HAS BEEN CALLED AWAY ON URGENT BUSINESS. SO NOW I SHALL BE SLEEPING OVER.
HURRAY!

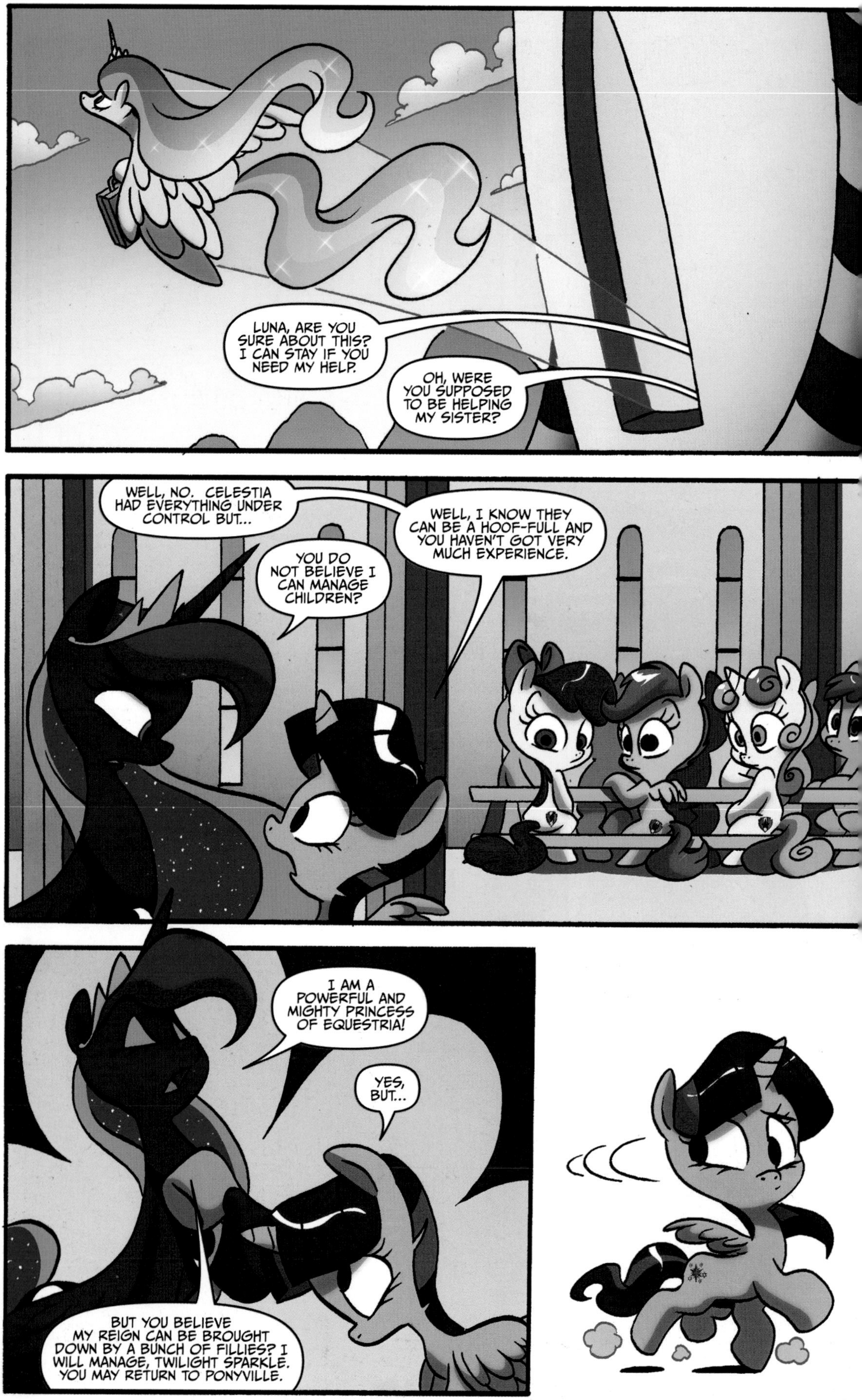
LUNA, ARE YOU SURE ABOUT THIS? I CAN STAY IF YOU NEED MY HELP.
OH, WERE YOU SUPPOSED TO BE HELPING MY SISTER?
WELL, NO. CELESTIA HAD EVERYTHING UNDER CONTROL BUT...
YOU DO NOT BELIEVE I CAN MANAGE CHILDREN?
WELL, I KNOW THEY CAN BE A HOOF-FULL AND YOU HAVEN'T GOT VERY MUCH EXPERIENCE.
I AM A POWERFUL AND MIGHTY PRINCESS OF EQUESTRIA!
YES, BUT...
BUT YOU BELIEVE MY REIGN CAN BE BROUGHT DOWN BY A BUNCH OF FILLIES? I WILL MANAGE, TWILIGHT SPARKLE. YOU MAY RETURN TO PONYVILLE.

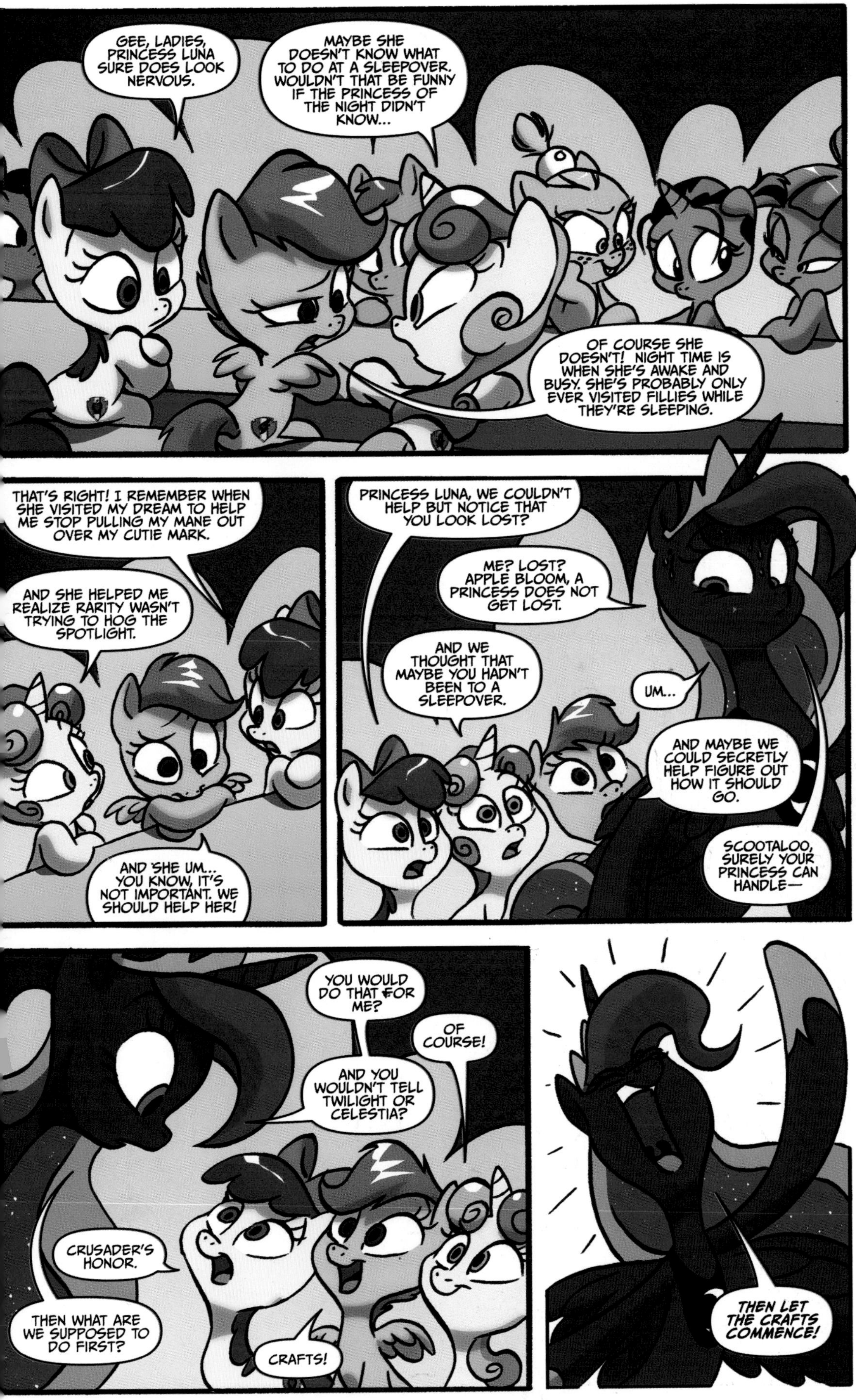
GEE, LADIES, PRINCESS LUNA SURE DOES LOOK NERVOUS.
MAYBE SHE DOESN'T KNOW WHAT TO DO AT A SLEEPOVER. WOULDN'T THAT BE FUNNY IF THE PRINCESS OF THE NIGHT DIDN'T KNOW...
OF COURSE SHE DOESN'T! NIGHT TIME IS WHEN SHE'S AWAKE AND BUSY. SHE'S PROBABLY ONLY EVER VISITED FILLIES WHILE THEY'RE SLEEPING.
THAT'S RIGHT! I REMEMBER WHEN SHE VISITED MY DREAM TO HELP ME STOP PULLING MY MANE OUT OVER MY CUTIE MARK.
AND SHE HELPED ME REALIZE RARITY WASN'T TRYING TO HOG THE SPOTLIGHT.
AND SHE UM... YOU KNOW, IT'S NOT IMPORTANT. WE SHOULD HELP HER!
PRINCESS LUNA, WE COULDN'T HELP BUT NOTICE THAT YOU LOOK LOST?
ME? LOST? APPLE BLOOM, A PRINCESS DOES NOT GET LOST.
AND WE THOUGHT THAT MAYBE YOU HADN'T BEEN TO A SLEEPOVER.
UM...
AND MAYBE WE COULD SECRETLY HELP FIGURE OUT HOW IT SHOULD GO.
SCOOTALOO, SURELY YOUR PRINCESS CAN HANDLE—
YOU WOULD DO THAT FOR ME?
OF COURSE!
AND YOU WOULDN'T TELL TWILIGHT OR CELESTIA?
CRUSADER'S HONOR.
THEN WHAT ARE WE SUPPOSED TO DO FIRST?
CRAFTS!
THEN LET THE CRAFTS COMMENCE!

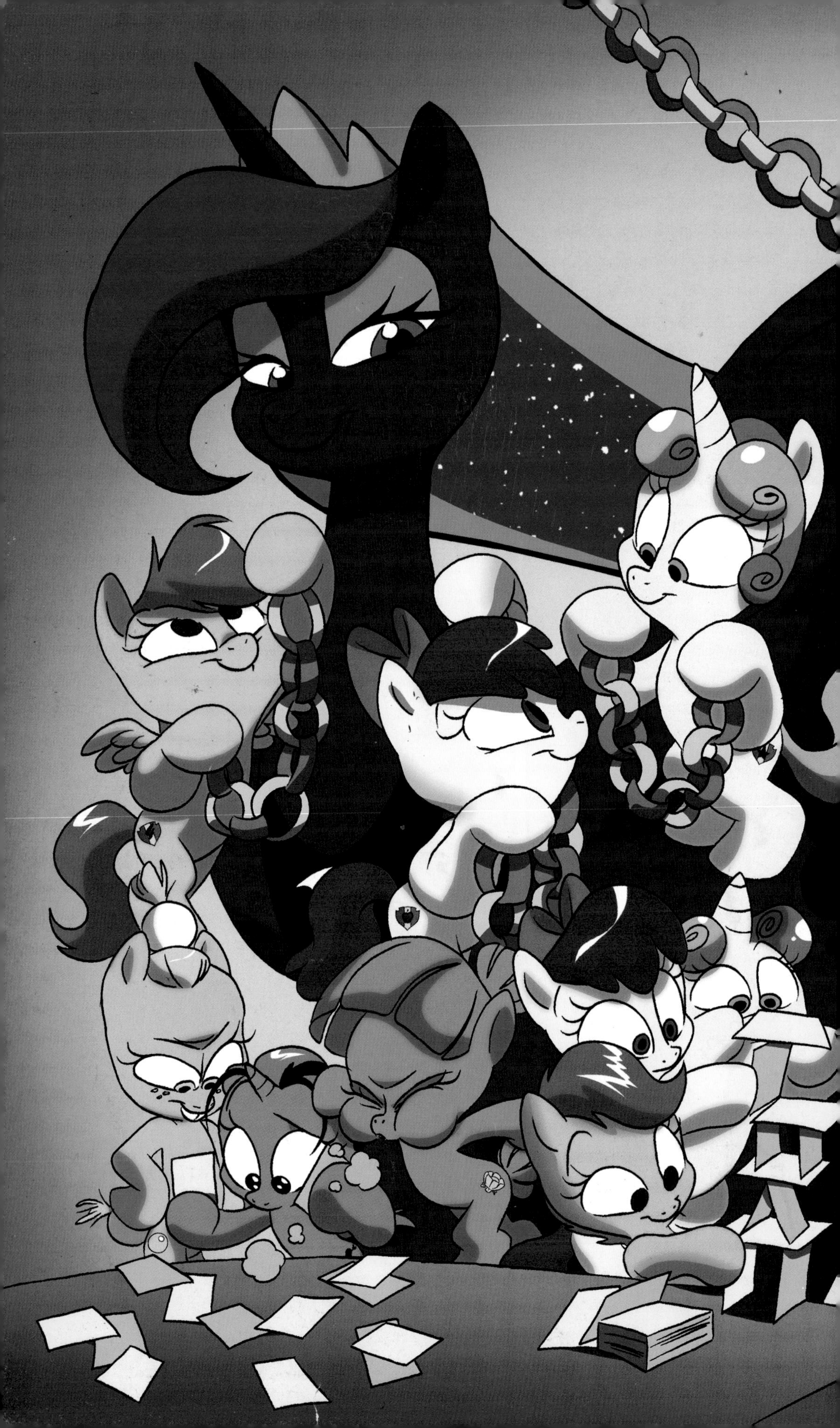

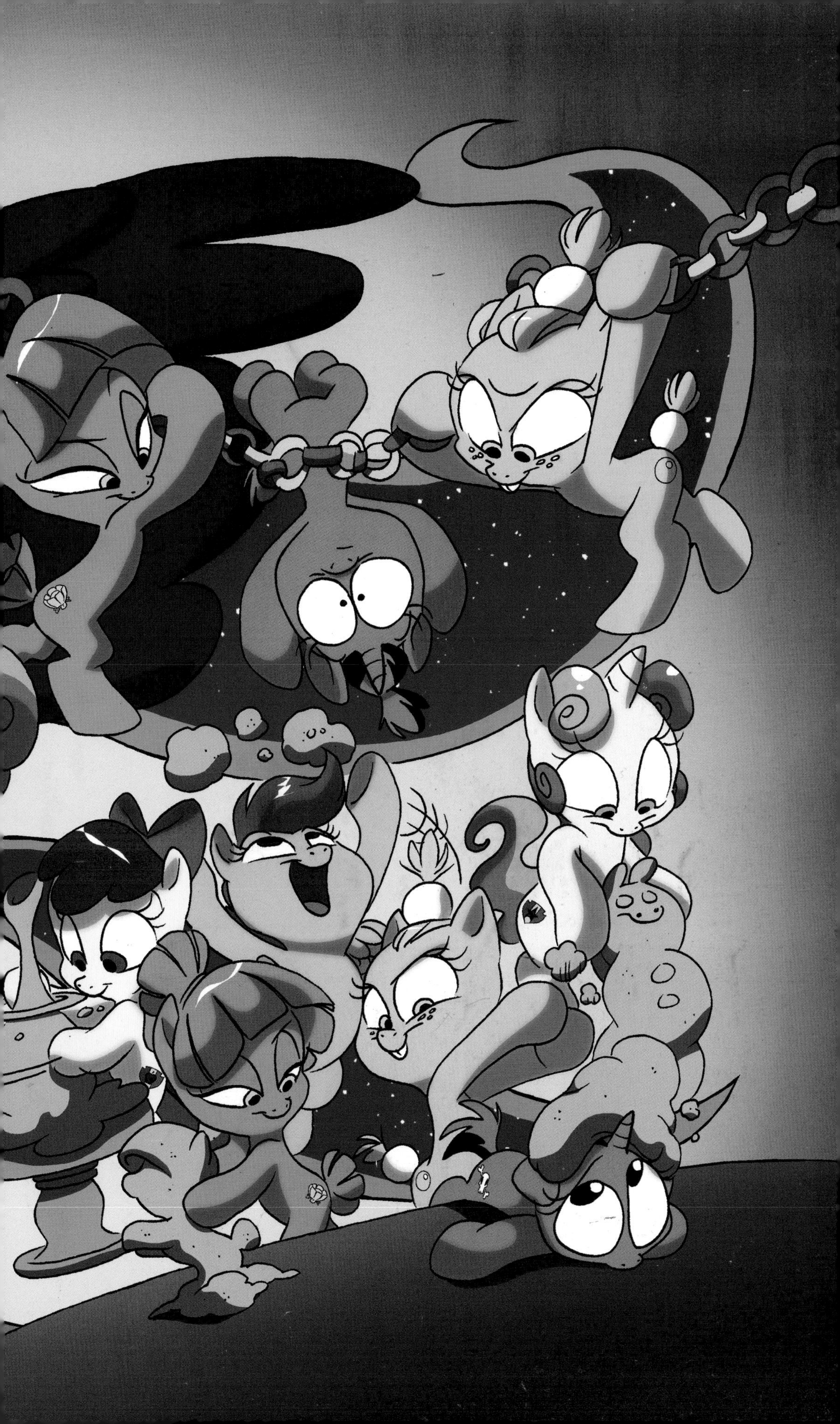

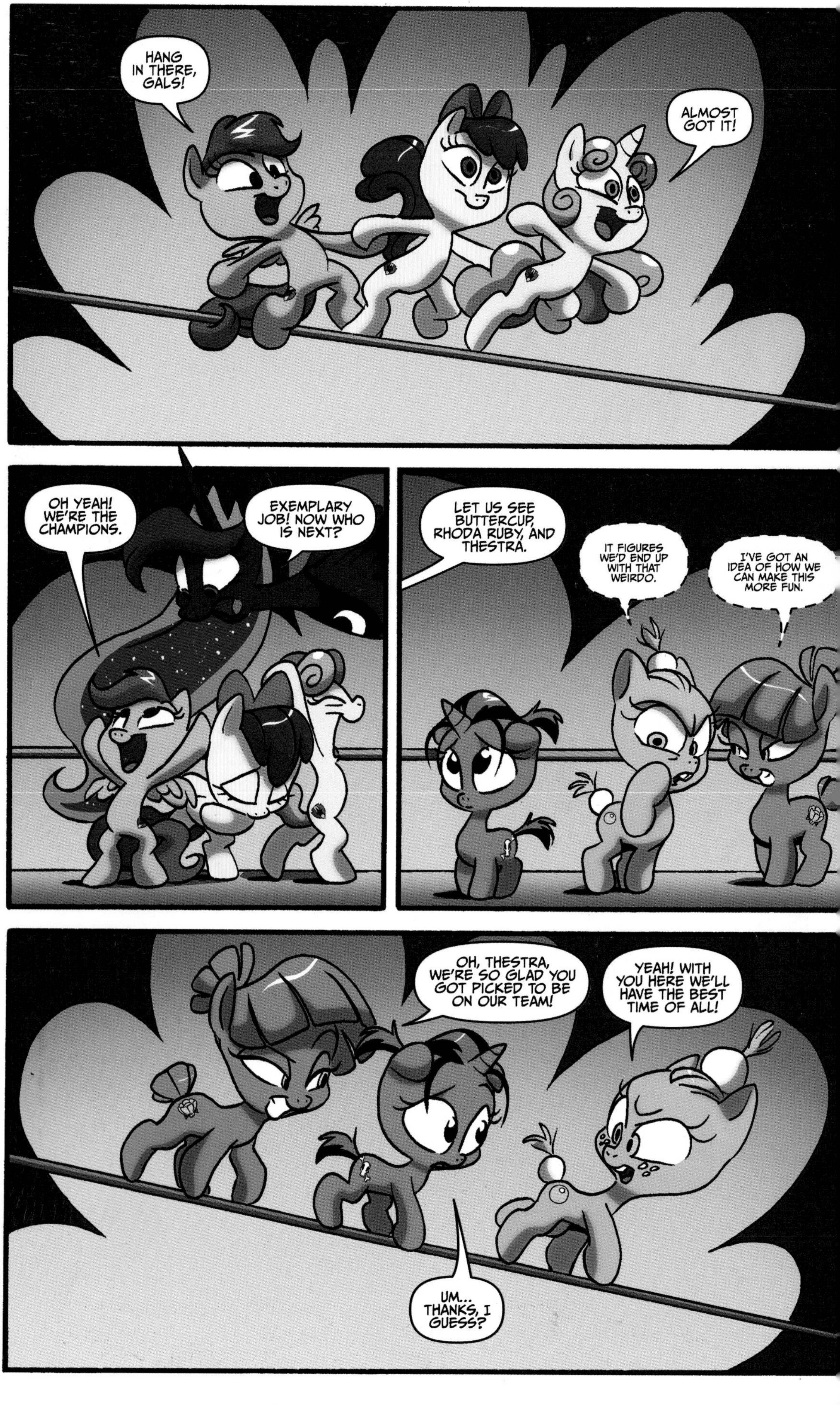
HANG IN THERE, GALS!
ALMOST GOT IT!
OH YEAH! WE'RE THE CHAMPIONS.
EXEMPLARY JOB! NOW WHO IS NEXT?
LET US SEE BUTTERCUP, RHODA RUBY, AND THESTRA.
IT FIGURES WE'D END UP WITH THAT WEIRDO.
I'VE GOT AN IDEA OF HOW WE CAN MAKE THIS MORE FUN.
OH, THESTRA, WE'RE SO GLAD YOU GOT PICKED TO BE ON OUR TEAM!
YEAH! WITH YOU HERE WE'LL HAVE THE BEST TIME OF ALL!
UM... THANKS, I GUESS?

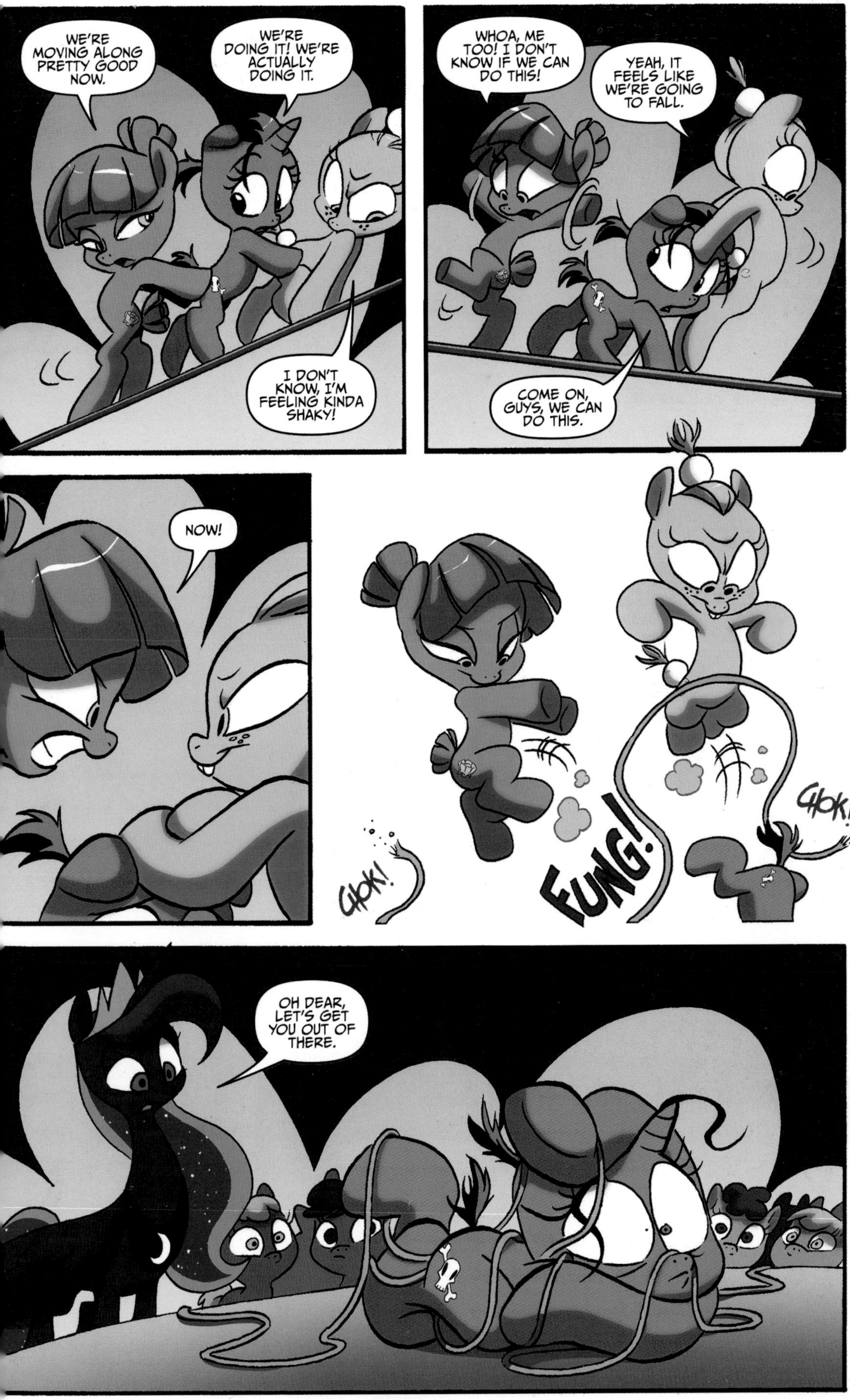

WE'RE MOVING ALONG PRETTY GOOD NOW.
WE'RE DOING IT! WE'RE ACTUALLY DOING IT.
I DON'T KNOW, I'M FEELING KINDA SHAKY!
WHOA, ME TOO! I DON'T KNOW IF WE CAN DO THIS!
YEAH, IT FEELS LIKE WE'RE GOING TO FALL.
COME ON, GUYS, WE CAN DO THIS.
NOW!
CHOK!
FUNG!
CHOK!
OH DEAR, LET'S GET YOU OUT OF THERE.

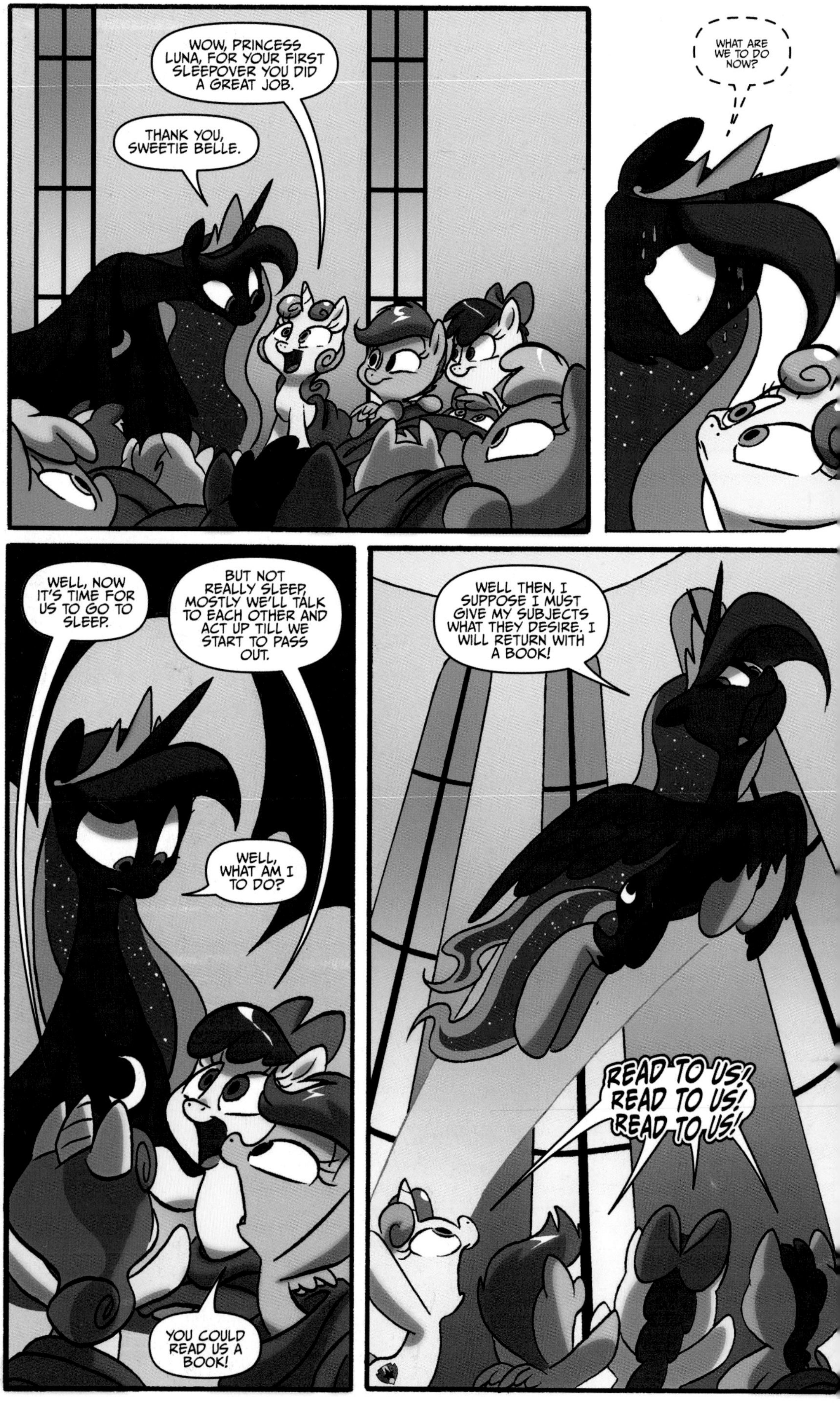
WOW, PRINCESS LUNA, FOR YOUR FIRST SLEEPOVER YOU DID A GREAT JOB.
THANK YOU, SWEETIE BELLE.
WHAT ARE WE TO DO NOW?
WELL, NOW IT'S TIME FOR US TO GO TO SLEEP.
BUT NOT REALLY SLEEP, MOSTLY WE'LL TALK TO EACH OTHER AND ACT UP TILL WE START TO PASS OUT.
WELL, WHAT AM I TO DO?
YOU COULD READ US A BOOK!
WELL THEN, I SUPPOSE I MUST GIVE MY SUBJECTS WHAT THEY DESIRE. I WILL RETURN WITH A BOOK!
READ TO US! READ TO US! READ TO US!

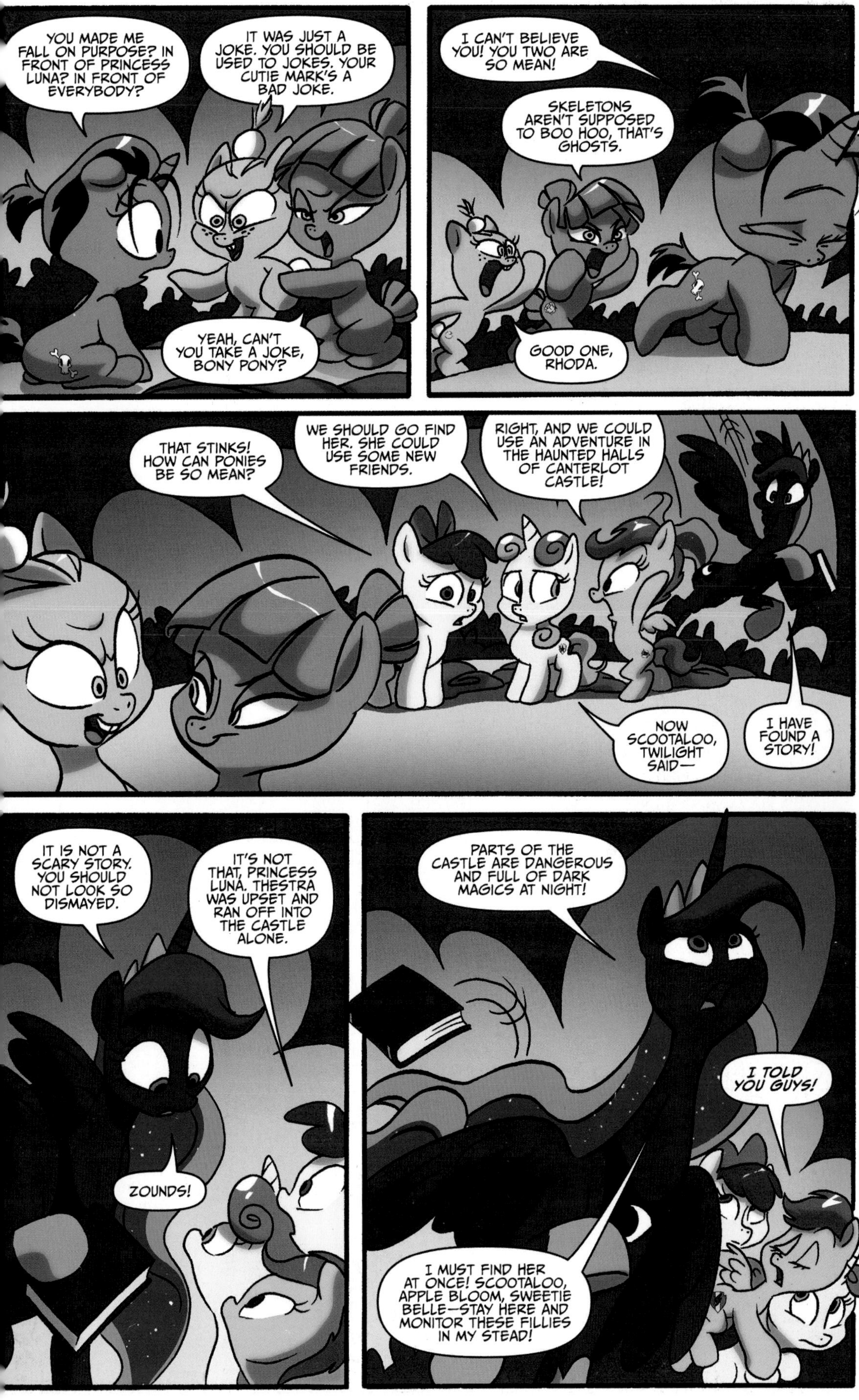
YOU MADE ME FALL ON PURPOSE? IN FRONT OF PRINCESS LUNA? IN FRONT OF EVERYBODY?
IT WAS JUST A JOKE. YOU SHOULD BE USED TO JOKES. YOUR CUTIE MARK'S A BAD JOKE.
YEAH, CAN'T YOU TAKE A JOKE, BONY PONY?
I CAN'T BELIEVE YOU! YOU TWO ARE SO MEAN!
SKELETONS AREN'T SUPPOSED TO BOO HOO, THAT'S GHOSTS.
GOOD ONE, RHODA.
THAT STINKS! HOW CAN PONIES BE SO MEAN?
WE SHOULD GO FIND HER. SHE COULD USE SOME NEW FRIENDS.
RIGHT, AND WE COULD USE AN ADVENTURE IN THE HAUNTED HALLS OF CANTERLOT CASTLE!
NOW SCOOTALOO, TWILIGHT SAID—
I HAVE FOUND A STORY!
IT IS NOT A SCARY STORY. YOU SHOULD NOT LOOK SO DISMAYED.
IT'S NOT THAT, PRINCESS LUNA. THESTRA WAS UPSET AND RAN OFF INTO THE CASTLE ALONE.
ZOUNDS!
PARTS OF THE CASTLE ARE DANGEROUS AND FULL OF DARK MAGICS AT NIGHT!
I TOLD YOU GUYS!
I MUST FIND HER AT ONCE! SCOOTALOO, APPLE BLOOM, SWEETIE BELLE—STAY HERE AND MONITOR THESE FILLIES IN MY STEAD!

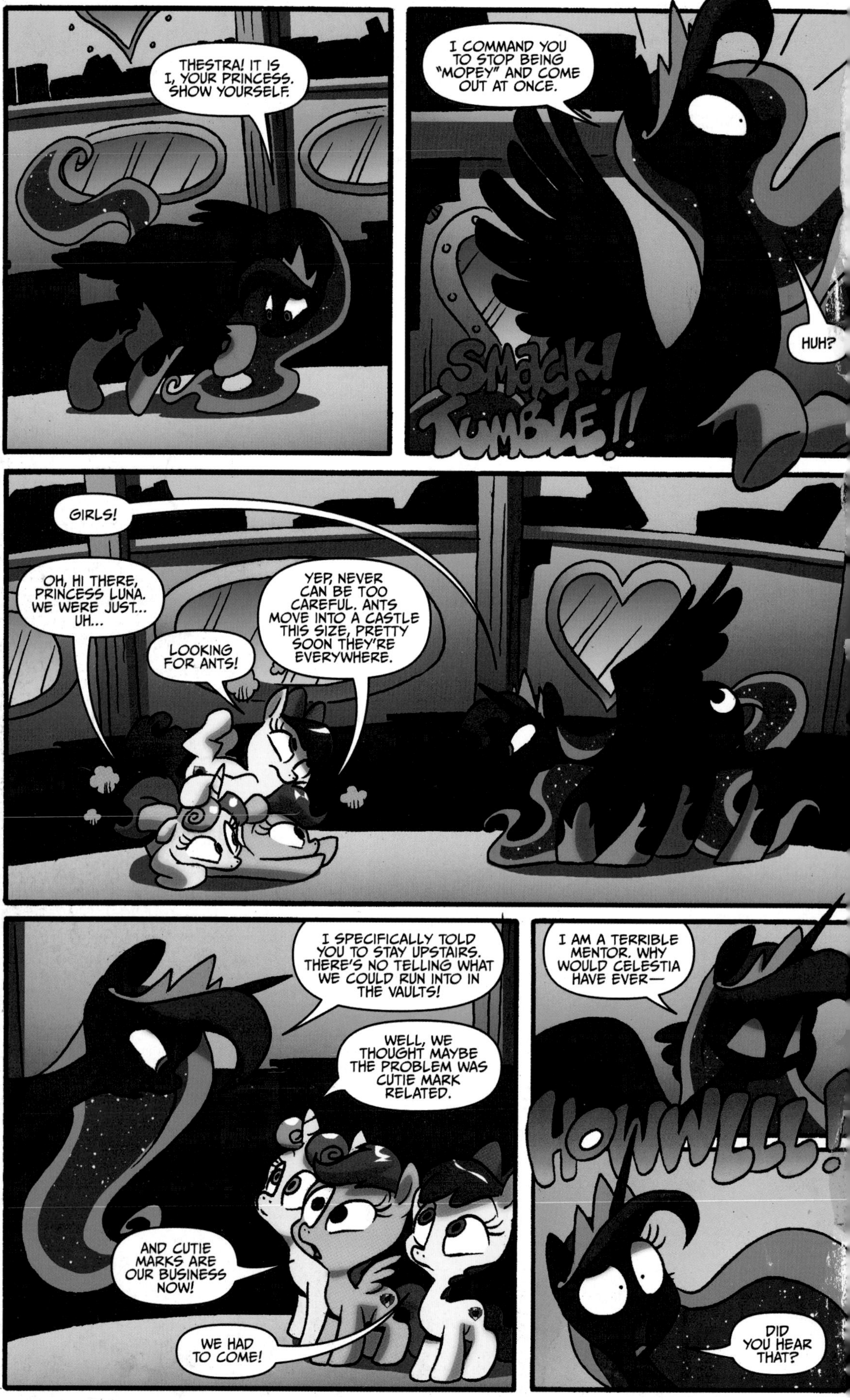

THESTRA! IT IS I, YOUR PRINCESS. SHOW YOURSELF.
I COMMAND YOU TO STOP BEING "MOPEY" AND COME OUT AT ONCE.
SMACK!
TUMBLE!!
HUH?
GIRLS!
OH, HI THERE, PRINCESS LUNA. WE WERE JUST... UH...
LOOKING FOR ANTS!
YEP, NEVER CAN BE TOO CAREFUL. ANTS MOVE INTO A CASTLE THIS SIZE, PRETTY SOON THEY'RE EVERYWHERE.
I SPECIFICALLY TOLD YOU TO STAY UPSTAIRS. THERE'S NO TELLING WHAT WE COULD RUN INTO IN THE VAULTS!
WELL, WE THOUGHT MAYBE THE PROBLEM WAS CUTIE MARK RELATED.
AND CUTIE MARKS ARE OUR BUSINESS NOW!
WE HAD TO COME!
I AM A TERRIBLE MENTOR. WHY WOULD CELESTIA HAVE EVER—
HOWWLLL!
DID YOU HEAR THAT?

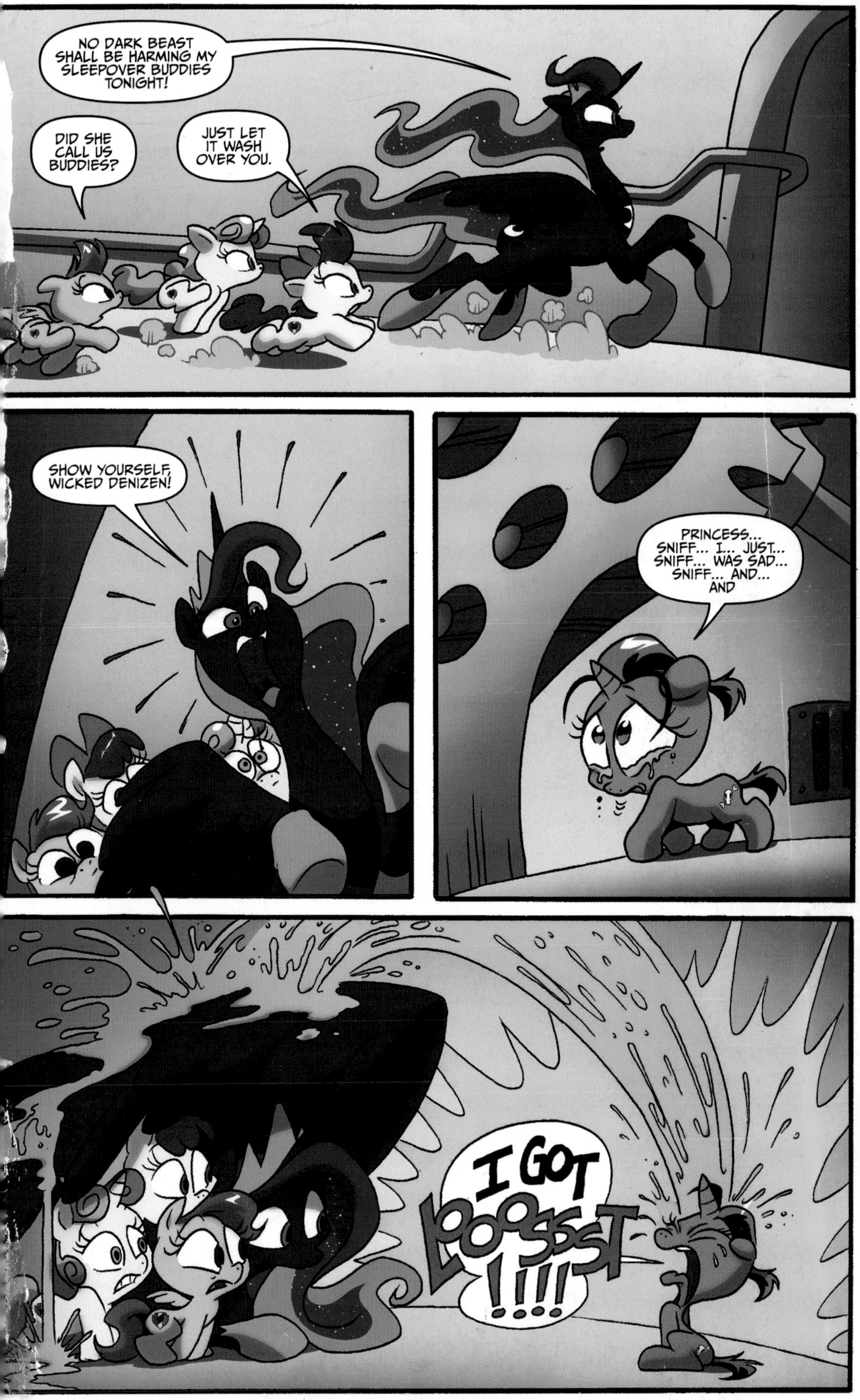
NO DARK BEAST SHALL BE HARMING MY SLEEPOVER BUDDIES TONIGHT!
DID SHE CALL US BUDDIES?
JUST LET IT WASH OVER YOU.
SHOW YOURSELF, WICKED DENIZEN!
PRINCESS... SNIFF... I... JUST... SNIFF... WAS SAD... SNIFF... AND... AND
I GOT LOOOSSST!!!!

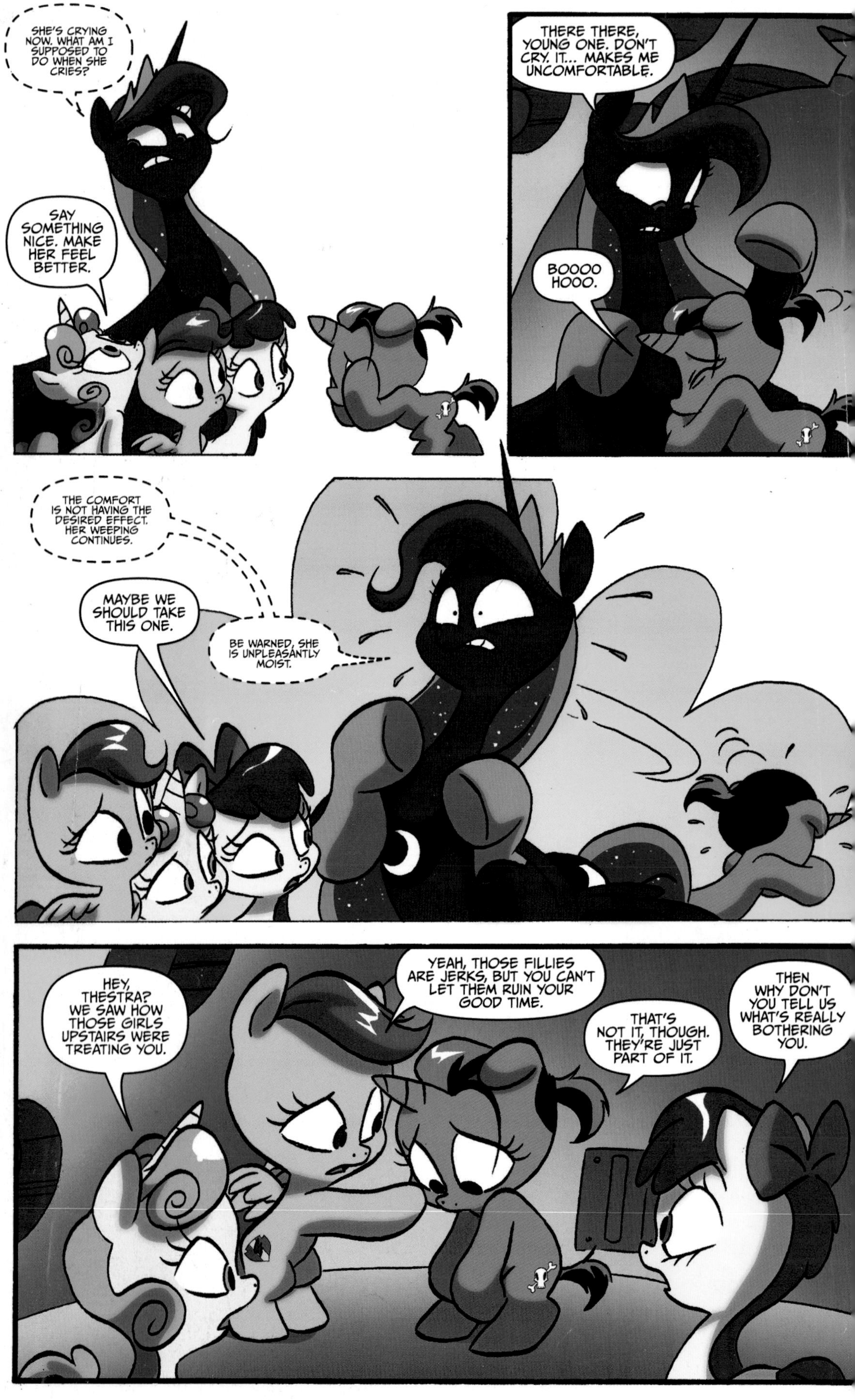
SHE'S CRYING NOW. WHAT AM I SUPPOSED TO DO WHEN SHE CRIES?
SAY SOMETHING NICE. MAKE HER FEEL BETTER.
THERE THERE, YOUNG ONE. DON'T CRY. IT... MAKES ME UNCOMFORTABLE.
BOOOO HOOO.
THE COMFORT IS NOT HAVING THE DESIRED EFFECT. HER WEEPING CONTINUES.
MAYBE WE SHOULD TAKE THIS ONE.
BE WARNED, SHE IS UNPLEASANTLY MOIST.
HEY, THESTRA? WE SAW HOW THOSE GIRLS UPSTAIRS WERE TREATING YOU.
YEAH, THOSE FILLIES ARE JERKS, BUT YOU CAN'T LET THEM RUIN YOUR GOOD TIME.
THAT'S NOT IT, THOUGH. THEY'RE JUST PART OF IT.
THEN WHY DON'T YOU TELL US WHAT'S REALLY BOTHERING YOU.

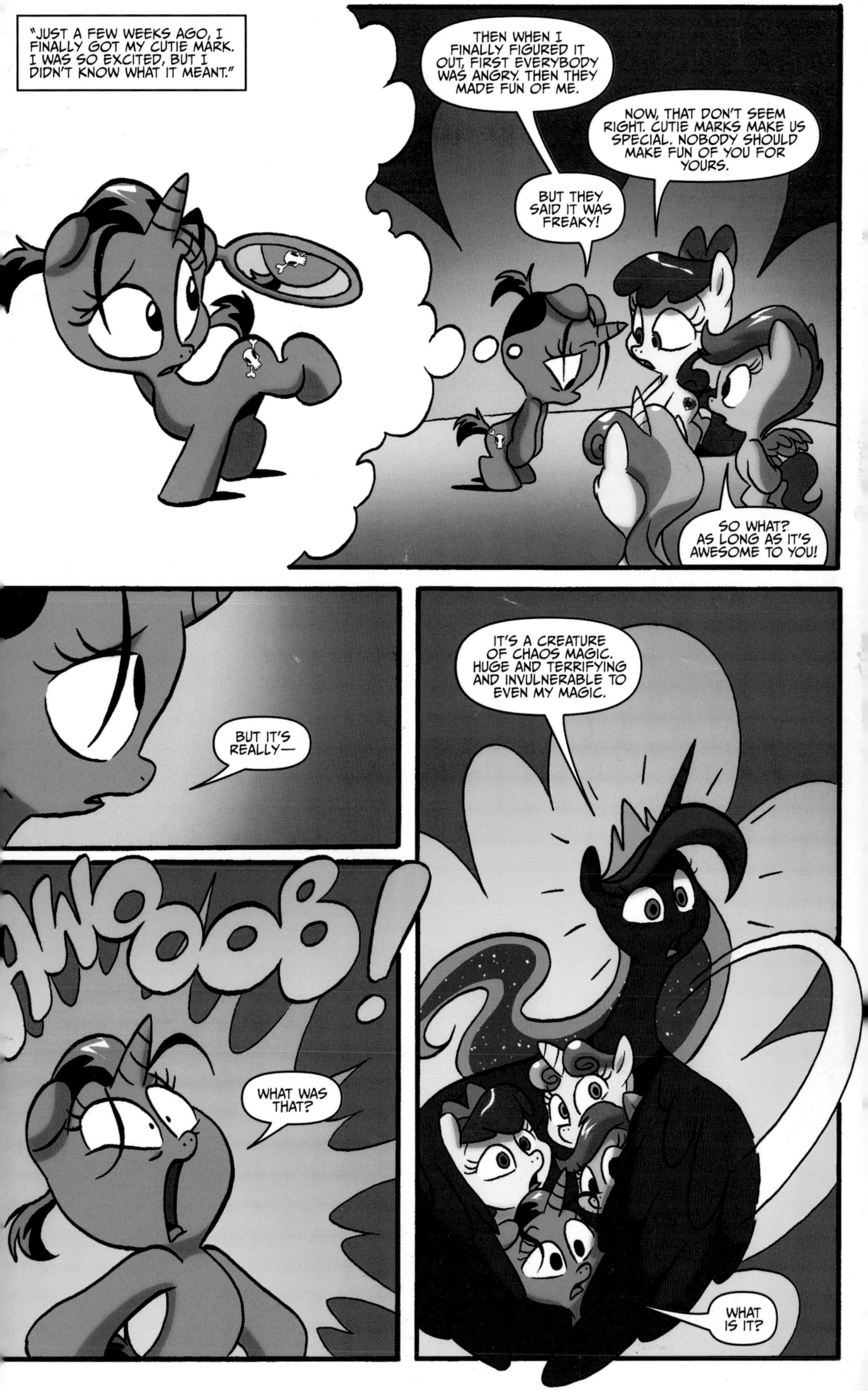
"JUST A FEW WEEKS AGO, I FINALLY GOT MY CUTIE MARK. I WAS SO EXCITED, BUT I DIDN'T KNOW WHAT IT MEANT."
THEN WHEN I FINALLY FIGURED IT OUT, FIRST EVERYBODY WAS ANGRY. THEN THEY MADE FUN OF ME.
BUT THEY SAID IT WAS FREAKY!
NOW, THAT DON'T SEEM RIGHT. CUTIE MARKS MAKE US SPECIAL. NOBODY SHOULD MAKE FUN OF YOU FOR YOURS.
SO WHAT? AS LONG AS IT'S AWESOME TO YOU!
BUT IT'S REALLY—
AWOOOB!
WHAT WAS THAT?
IT'S A CREATURE OF CHAOS MAGIC. HUGE AND TERRIFYING AND INVULNERABLE TO EVEN MY MAGIC.
WHAT IS IT?

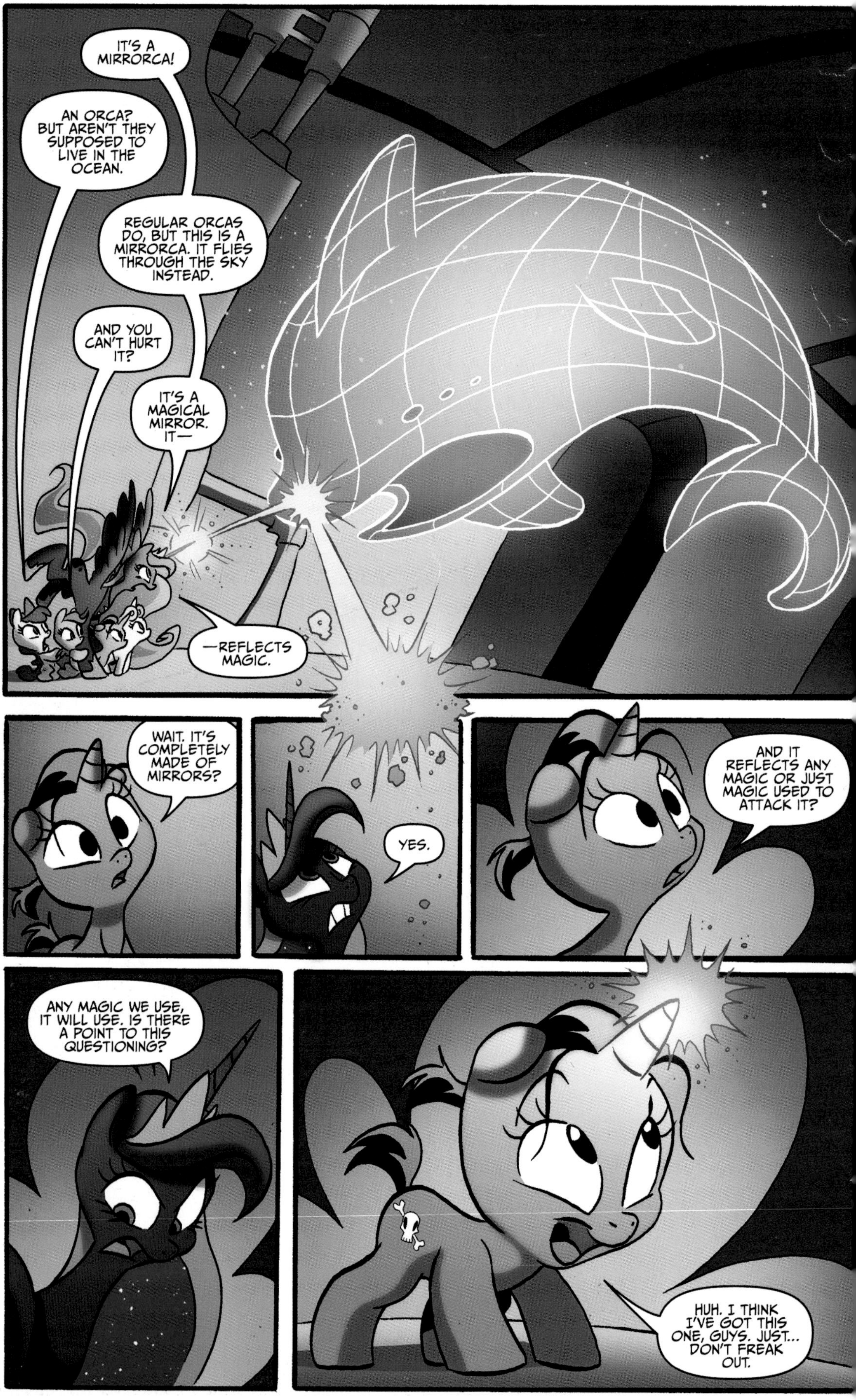
IT'S A MIRRORCA!
AN ORCA? BUT AREN'T THEY SUPPOSED TO LIVE IN THE OCEAN.
REGULAR ORCAS DO, BUT THIS IS A MIRRORCA. IT FLIES THROUGH THE SKY INSTEAD.
AND YOU CAN'T HURT IT?
IT'S A MAGICAL MIRROR. IT—
—REFLECTS MAGIC.
WAIT. IT'S COMPLETELY MADE OF MIRRORS?
YES.
AND IT REFLECTS ANY MAGIC OR JUST MAGIC USED TO ATTACK IT?
ANY MAGIC WE USE, IT WILL USE. IS THERE A POINT TO THIS QUESTIONING?
HUH. I THINK I'VE GOT THIS ONE, GUYS. JUST... DON'T FREAK OUT.

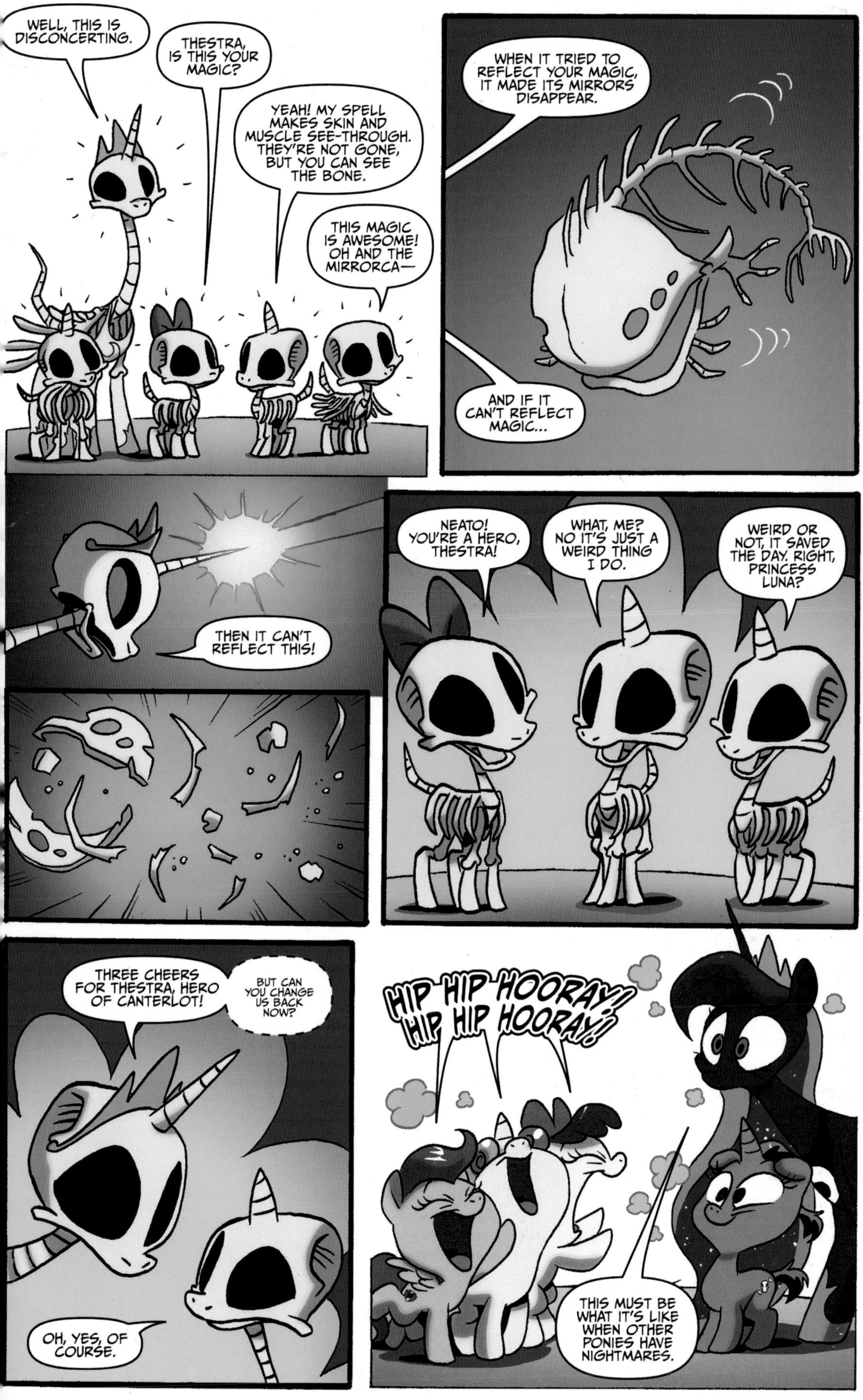
WELL, THIS IS DISCONCERTING.
THESTRA, IS THIS YOUR MAGIC?
YEAH! MY SPELL MAKES SKIN AND MUSCLE SEE-THROUGH. THEY'RE NOT GONE, BUT YOU CAN SEE THE BONE.
THIS MAGIC IS AWESOME! OH AND THE MIRRORCA—
WHEN IT TRIED TO REFLECT YOUR MAGIC, IT MADE ITS MIRRORS DISAPPEAR.
AND IF IT CAN'T REFLECT MAGIC...
THEN IT CAN'T REFLECT THIS!
NEATO! YOU'RE A HERO, THESTRA!
WHAT, ME? NO IT'S JUST A WEIRD THING I DO.
WEIRD OR NOT, IT SAVED THE DAY. RIGHT, PRINCESS LUNA?
THREE CHEERS FOR THESTRA, HERO OF CANTERLOT!
BUT CAN YOU CHANGE US BACK NOW?
OH, YES, OF COURSE.
HIP HIP HOORAY! HIP HIP HOORAY!
THIS MUST BE WHAT IT'S LIKE WHEN OTHER PONIES HAVE NIGHTMARES.

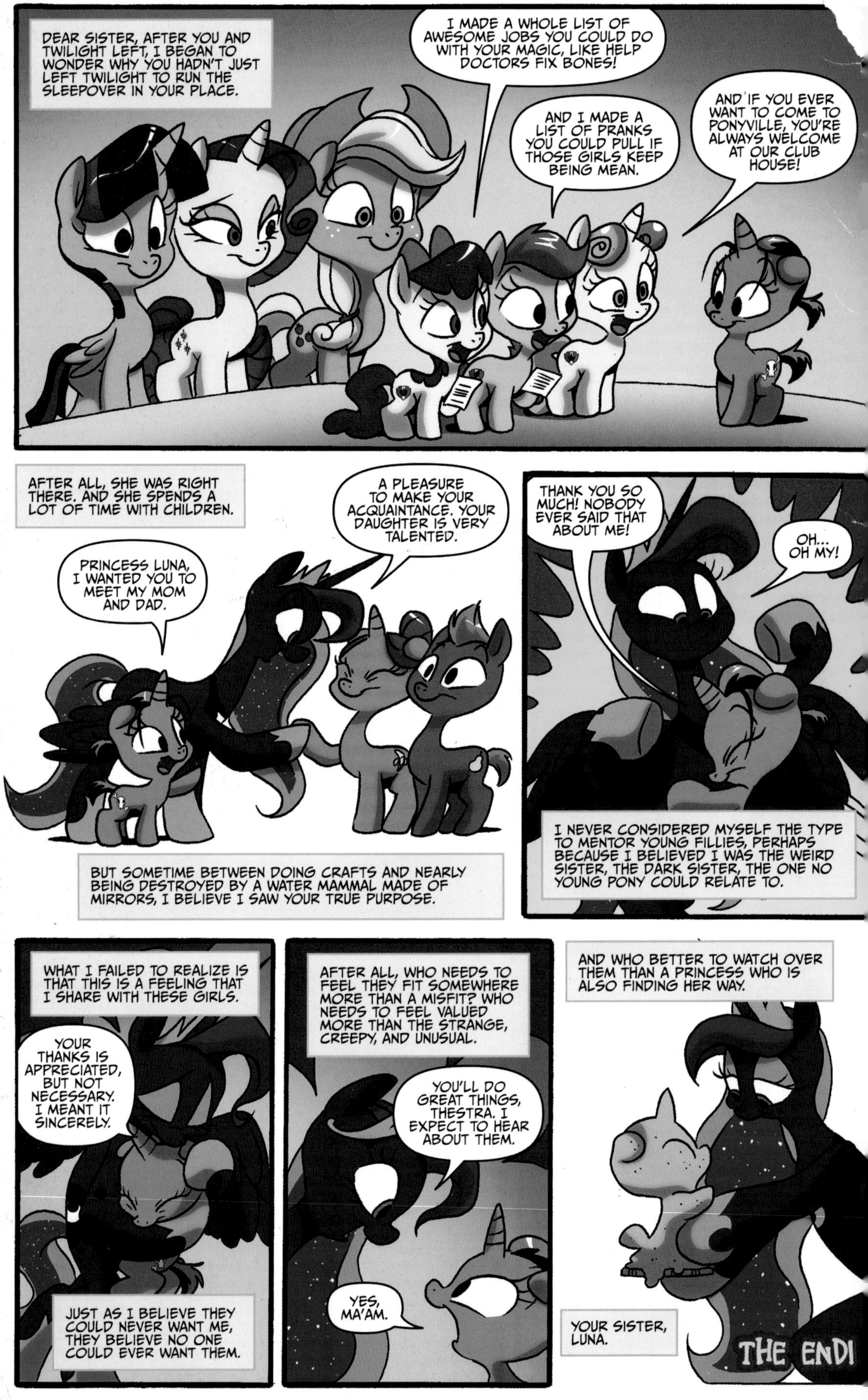

DEAR SISTER, AFTER YOU AND TWILIGHT LEFT, I BEGAN TO WONDER WHY YOU HADN'T JUST LEFT TWILIGHT TO RUN THE SLEEPOVER IN YOUR PLACE.
I MADE A WHOLE LIST OF AWESOME JOBS YOU COULD DO WITH YOUR MAGIC, LIKE HELP DOCTORS FIX BONES!
AND I MADE A LIST OF PRANKS YOU COULD PULL IF THOSE GIRLS KEEP BEING MEAN.
AND IF YOU EVER WANT TO COME TO PONYVILLE, YOU'RE ALWAYS WELCOME AT OUR CLUB HOUSE!
AFTER ALL, SHE WAS RIGHT THERE. AND SHE SPENDS A LOT OF TIME WITH CHILDREN.
PRINCESS LUNA, I WANTED YOU TO MEET MY MOM AND DAD.
A PLEASURE TO MAKE YOUR ACQUAINTANCE. YOUR DAUGHTER IS VERY TALENTED.
BUT SOMETIME BETWEEN DOING CRAFTS AND NEARLY BEING DESTROYED BY A WATER MAMMAL MADE OF MIRRORS, I BELIEVE I SAW YOUR TRUE PURPOSE.
THANK YOU SO MUCH! NOBODY EVER SAID THAT ABOUT ME!
OH... OH MY!
I NEVER CONSIDERED MYSELF THE TYPE TO MENTOR YOUNG FILLIES, PERHAPS BECAUSE I BELIEVED I WAS THE WEIRD SISTER, THE DARK SISTER, THE ONE NO YOUNG PONY COULD RELATE TO.
WHAT I FAILED TO REALIZE IS THAT THIS IS A FEELING THAT I SHARE WITH THESE GIRLS.
YOUR THANKS IS APPRECIATED, BUT NOT NECESSARY. I MEANT IT SINCERELY.
JUST AS I BELIEVE THEY COULD NEVER WANT ME, THEY BELIEVE NO ONE COULD EVER WANT THEM.
AFTER ALL, WHO NEEDS TO FEEL THEY FIT SOMEWHERE MORE THAN A MISFIT? WHO NEEDS TO FEEL VALUED MORE THAN THE STRANGE, CREEPY, AND UNUSUAL.
YOU'LL DO GREAT THINGS, THESTRA. I EXPECT TO HEAR ABOUT THEM.
YES, MA'AM.
AND WHO BETTER TO WATCH OVER THEM THAN A PRINCESS WHO IS ALSO FINDING HER WAY.
YOUR SISTER, LUNA.
THE END

my LITTLE PONY

FRIENDS FOREVER

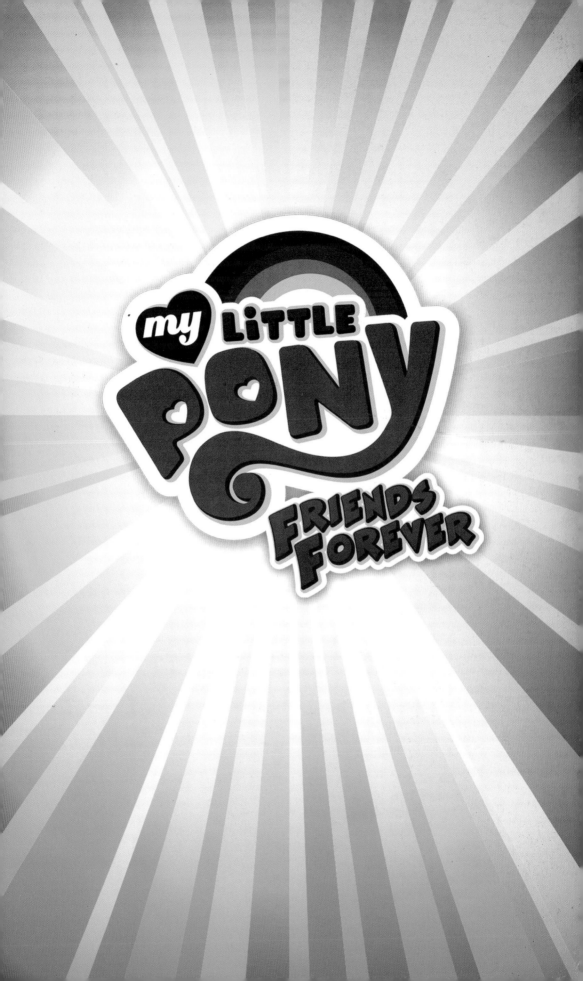

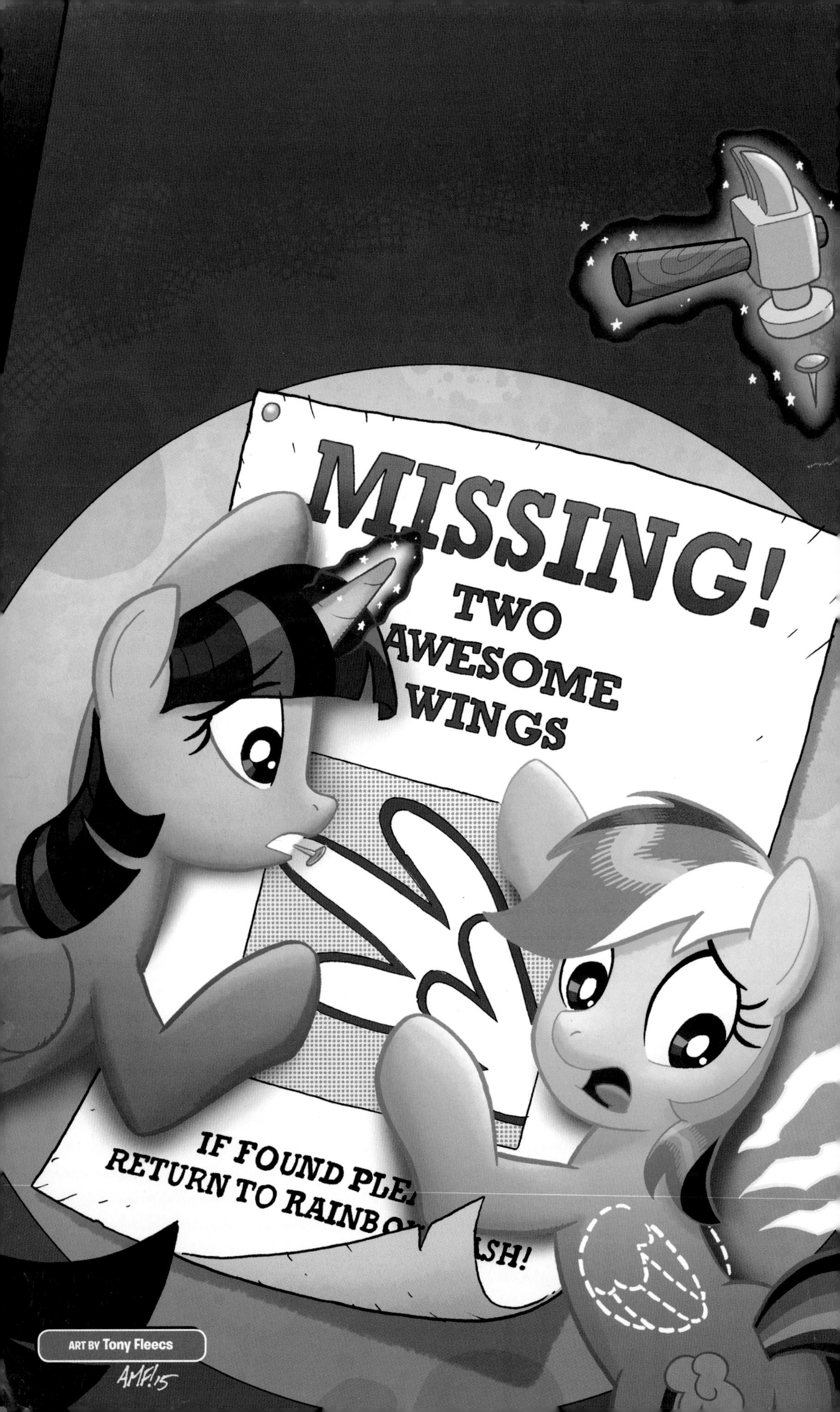
MISSING!
TWO AWESOME WINGS
IF FOUND PLE
RETURN TO RAINBO
SH!
ART BY Tony Fleecs
AMF! 15

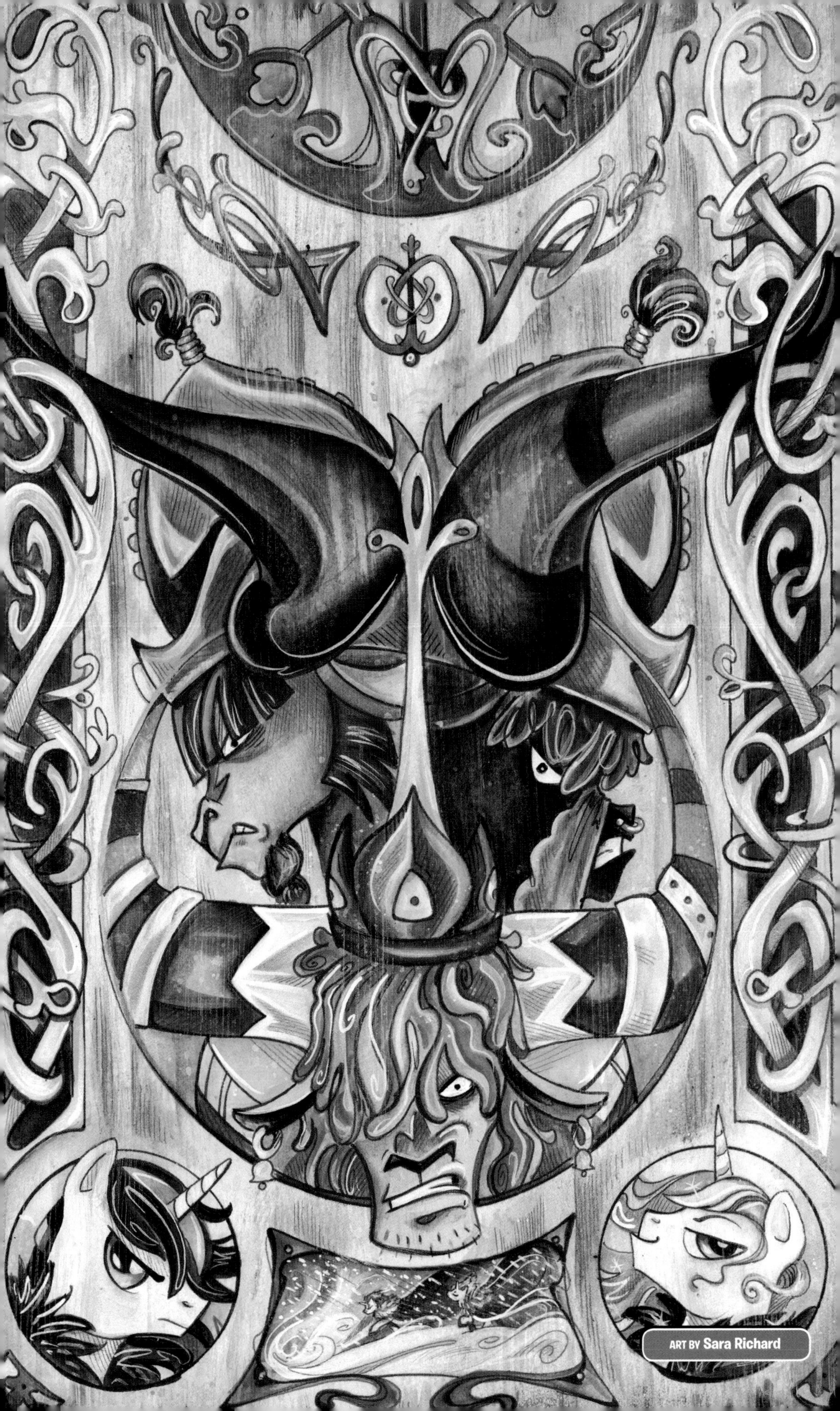
ART BY Sara Richard

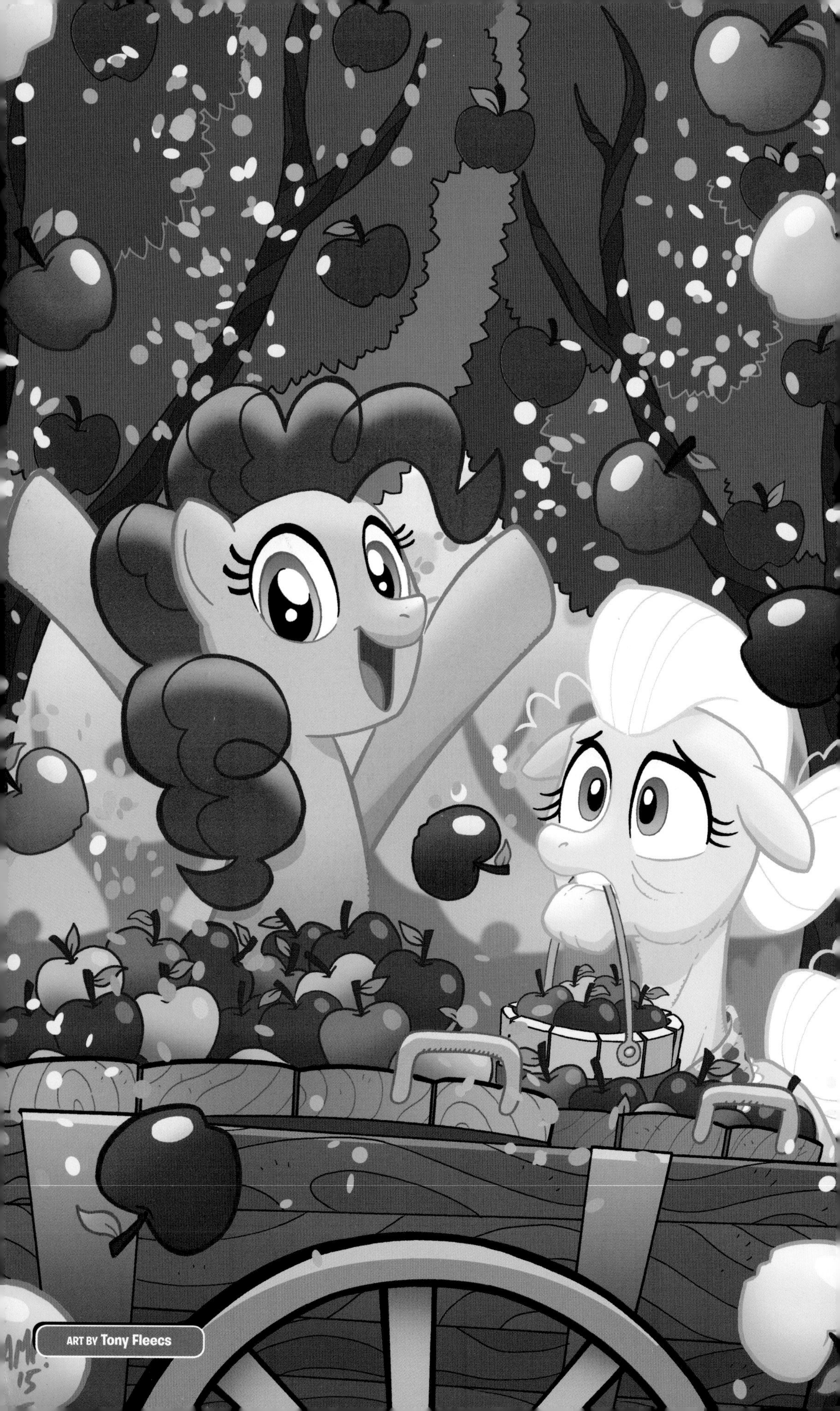

ART BY Tony Fleecs

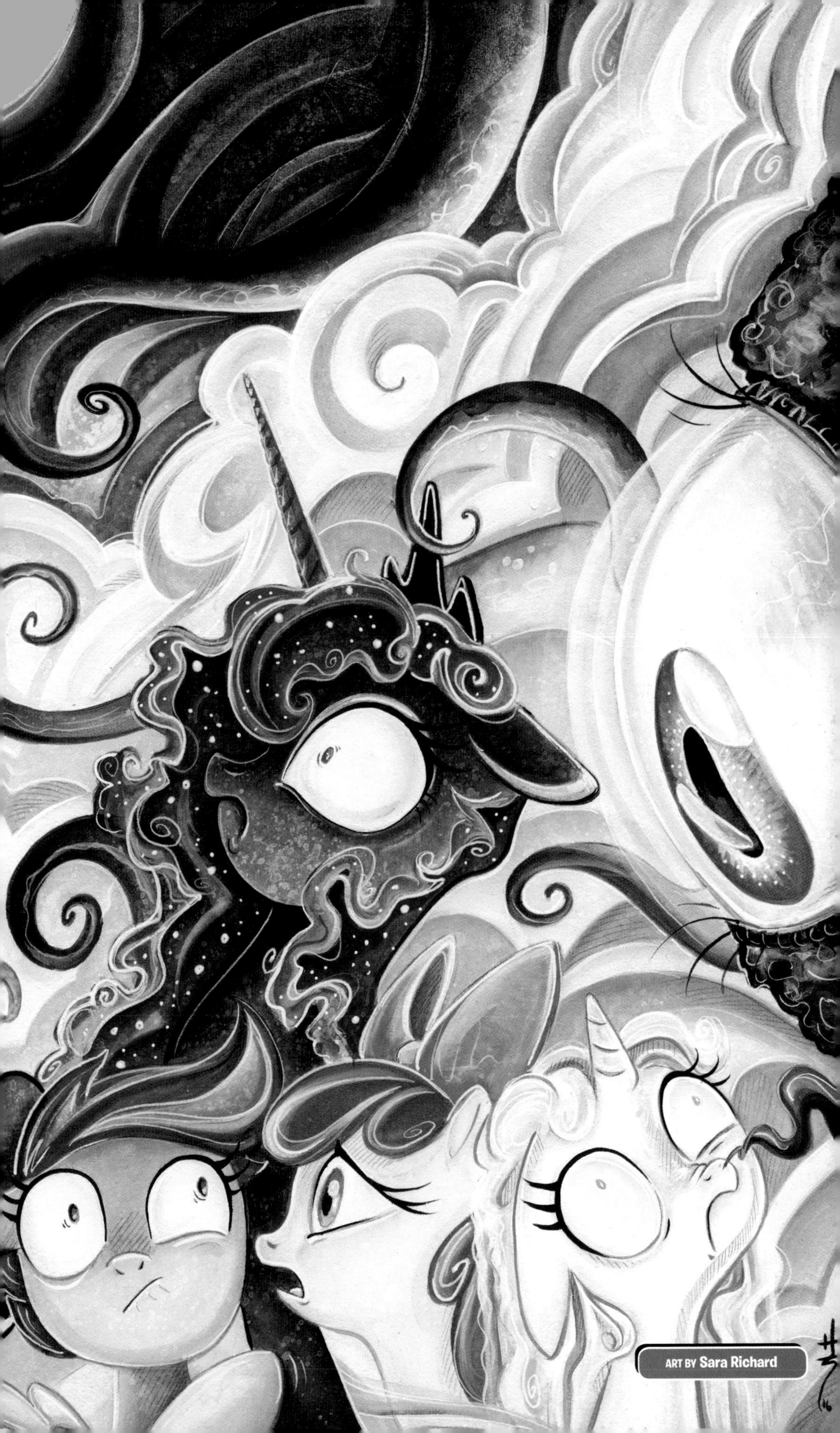

ART BY Sara Richard

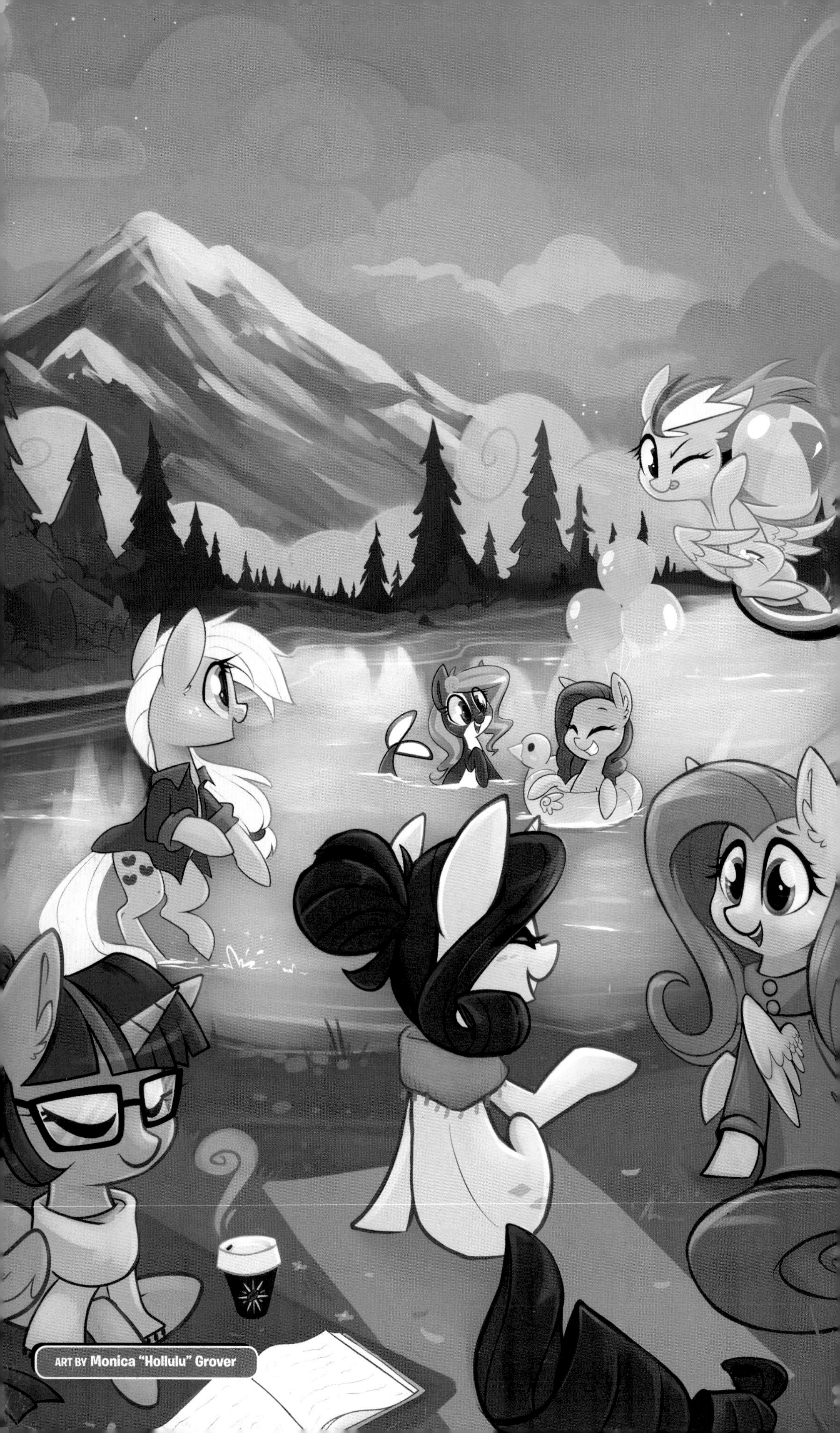
ART BY Monica "Hollulu" Grover

my LITTLE PONY
FRIENDS FOREVER

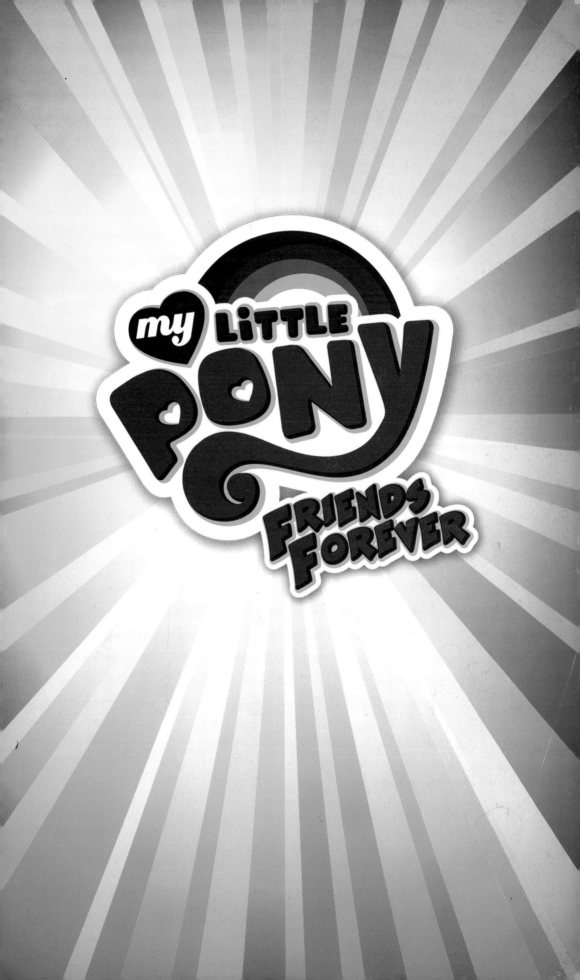

my little PONY

THE ONGOING ADVENTURES OF EVERYONE'S FAVORITE PONIES!

PONIES UNITE IN THIS TEAM-UP SERIES!

My Little Pony:
Friendship is Magic, Vol. 1
TPB • $17.99 • 978-1613776056

My Little Pony:
Friendship is Magic, Vol. 2
TPB • $17.99 • 978-1613777602

My Little Pony:
Friends Forever, Vol. 1
TPB • $17.99 • 978-1613779811

My Little Pony:
Friends Forever, Vol. 2
TPB • $17.99 • 978-1631401596

SPECIALLY SELECTED TALES TO TAKE WITH YOU ON THE GO!

GET THE WHOLE STORY WITH THE MY LITTLE PONY OMBINUS'!

My Little Pony:
Adventures in Friendship, Vol. 1
TPB • $9.99 • 978-1631401893

My Little Pony:
Adventures in Frienship, Vol. 2
TPB • $9.99 • 978-1631402258

My Little Pony:
Omnibus, Vol. 1
TPB • $24.99 • 978-1631401404

My Little Pony:
Omnibus, Vol. 2
TPB • $24.99 • 978-1631404092

IDW® WWW.IDWPUBLISHING.COM

ON SALE NOW!